# "ADDS UP TO ONE OF THE BEST BETS OF THE YEAR"
—SAN FRANCISCO CHRONICLE

*I got out the old pistol . . . I slipped into the dark jungle garden of the Lane house . . . I don't know now what I thought I would or could do . . . The window was open . . . I saw his face, just as I opened my lips to call his name, and found them frozen and sound- less. He was there, his face hideously wounded and mutilated.*

The town cried "Murder! . . . and I cried out for help —knowing I might be next on the murderer's list . . .

*"Builds up to a grand and exciting finish"*
—PHILADELPHIA RECORD

## "PLENTY OF MYSTERY"
—NEW YORK HERALD TRIBUNE

## ABOUT THE AUTHOR

LESLIE FORD has been an important and highly successful author of mystery novels since 1928. Her books have been translated into nine languages, winning a world-wide audience for her colorful characters and effective story backgrounds.

# THE TOWN CRIED MURDER

*By Leslie Ford*

**WILDSIDE PRESS**

## *The Town Cried Murder*

Published by Wildside Press LLC
www.wildsidepress.com

# 1

The first I knew that Faith Yardley was actually going to marry Mason Seymour was the afternoon her aunt Melusina Yardley stopped me going into the Powder Horn in Market Square to a meeting of the Society for the Preservation of Virginia Antiquities. I don't now recollect what we were meeting about, except that it concerned something the Restoration was doing in Williamsburg that Melusina didn't think they ought to do. And as everybody who knows Melusina Yardley knows she will some day object to the way the milk and honey flow through the streets of the heavenly Jerusalem, nobody was particularly concerned about it, except to get through in time to get to an affair they were having at the college green, at the end of the Duke of Gloucester Street.

I myself was too perturbed to do more than vote "No" automatically with everybody else when we heard Melusina vote "Yes." All I could think of was what she'd said:

"Lucy, it's still a secret, but Faith is going to marry Mason Seymour, and I want you to come over and see what we can do about her mother's wedding dress."

If the Restoration Company had proposed razing Bruton Parish Church to the ground, or paving Palace Green, I don't think I should have had the mind to worry about it just then. Maybe I'm too old-fashioned—or maybe modern, I'm sure I don't know—but I still think it's wrong to force a girl of twenty to marry a man of forty, or even more for all I know, just because the family needs money. And to all those people who instantly say, "Nonsense, you can't force modern girls to do anything," there's always the answer that there are a thousand ways of forcing people to do things without using a club or locking them up in a safe room on bread and water, the way they did our recalcitrant grandmothers. A club can be real without being made of blackthorn, and the club Melusina Yardley held over her niece young Faith was a good deal realer than one of the tomahawks of old Powhatan that we still preserve in the Powder Horn.

Because Faith Yardley adored her father, and ever since she's been old enough to want any of the things that her Aunt Melusina doesn't see any sense in her having, she's been effectively stopped at the point of rebellion by Melusina's reminding her all over again of her own sacrifice for Peyton Yardley, Faith's father who's Melusina's older brother. And Faith, who would have given her bright head for her father, had always given up. I never thought she'd have to give up her heart for him too . . . but when Melusina said she was going to marry Mason Seymour, I knew she'd done just that.

I have to go a long way back to make it clear. In Williamsburg everything goes back . . . just as each yellow and purple fall crocus you see in Virginia gardens in August and September goes back to the bulbs they brought from the Mediterranean and planted in the Palace gardens when the Royal Governors lived here in colonial days. Williamsburg itself is like the fall crocuses. It bloomed in its great heyday, the center of royal colonial society, and then it lay for long years of proud poverty and the desolation of war, stretching out a bare existence on barren ground, as the crocus bulbs buried in the stony ruins of the Palace gardens stretched out theirs. Then its fairy godparents came along and restored its old beauty and grandeur for the whole nation, as the garden clubs rescued the crocus bulbs struggling in the ruins and planted them all over Virginia. And the Yardleys are rather like Williamsburg and the crocuses, although they definitely haven't been restored and Faith is the only one who resembles a flower at all.

The Yardleys, like everybody else, were completely impoverished after the Civil War. And, like all the rest of us, they clung desperately to their houses and their land. The plantation on the James River was sold when Faith's father was sent to take his medical degree at the University. He came back to Williamsburg and practised, but he never sent bills to any one who couldn't afford to pay for his services, and so few people could that he finally gave up sending them altogether. The only ones that were ever sent after that were sent by Miss Melusina, who was born managing other people's affairs, and after her brother stopped telling her to whose houses he went in the old buggy behind Nellie the bay mare, she never knew where to send the bills, and gave up too, reluctantly and not gracefully.

Then came Melusina's Great Sacrifice—except that she didn't, at the time, know it was a sacrifice or she certainly never would have made it. The reason I happen to know is that it was my sacrifice too. I've never been able to make the use of it that Melusina has, because I've never had any one to throw it up to. And our sacrifice, if I may call him that, was a young man whose family moved to Williamsburg when we were grown girls. They owned the livery stable on Buttermilk Hill, and were, of course, definitely outside the pale. But the young man, whom we considered—and our parents certainly considered—an impertinent young upstart, managed to address Melusina Yardley . . . which is what we called proposing marriage to her. She was a handsome high-spirited creature of nineteen then, and she's supposed to have boxed his ears soundly and sent him packing. A little later—it was in the ruined tower of the old church at James-town—he did me the same honor. I was just seventeen, and while I didn't box his ears I did run back to the picnic party the color of a peony and avoided him thereafter as I would the plague. After that he left Williamsburg, and when he came back ten years later he was doing very well in the auto-mobile business. I remember how sorry we were for the pale girl he'd married, because obviously nothing would ever come of a mode of locomotion so opposed to nature and reason.

And then, just about the time the Yardleys were finally forced to sell the panelling of the old library to a Northern museum, we heard that our sacrifice had become one of the very wealthy men of the United States; and Melusina con-vinced herself that she'd recognized the seeds of genius in the poor but honest son of a livery stable, and she'd listened to the call of duty, forsaking love, and forsaking wealth, be-cause her brother needed her to take care of him. That was just before the last war. The immediate reason for this extraordinary volte-face wasn't entirely the fact that our former beau had got to be a multi-millionaire, though I expect that was part of it. It was chiefly because Melusina's brother Doctor Peyton Yardley suddenly began to act in the most amazing and inexplicable—though quite natural— fashion.

He was, or so everybody, including Miss Melusina, had assumed, a double-twisted old bachelor. He'd reached the age of forty-five, which seemed so much older then to me than it does now, without having shown the slightest interest in any woman. Melusina, who was five years younger than he, had tried for years to persuade him to marry the widow of a Chicago packer who had bought Whitehall on the James River, and who, having first married Money, was now looking out for Family. Doctor Yardley was not interested, and Melusina saw great wealth pass them by a second time. Then one evening Doctor Yardley was called out to Rosewell to see a young lady who had been thrown from her horse while taking a fence with some other young people in an impromptu hunt. He went out once a day until she seemed to everybody to be mending very nicely, then began going twice a day. Suddenly Miss Melusina smelled a rat, but it was too late. It was just at that point that her great sacrifice sprang full grown . . . like whoever it was from the forehead of Zeus. Everybody was stunned by it; but they were so much more stunned by Doctor Yardley and the girl, whose name was Faith, whose family no one had ever heard of, since they weren't Virginians, that Melusina's fiction gradually became accepted fact, and people shook their heads over her selfless devotion and the ingratitude and folly of the middle-aged male. Everybody, that is, except her brother, who went quietly along in his own unperturbed fashion and married the girl whom he adored and who adored him.

By that time my father, who was a lawyer, had died, and another man who had been at the picnic at Jamestown too, and at other picnics, had gone to the Philippines and had fallen there. And I was taking in a little sewing to help keep the house we've lived in in Francis Street since it was built in 1732, and where I still live . . . except that the restoration people have made it habitable again and painted the corner press with the Chinese Chippendale cornice and the pine panelling in the drawing room that I almost sold a dozen times to dealers down from Richmond. So I made Faith's wedding dress. It was the first one I'd made. I watched it move down the nave of Bruton Church, and I couldn't keep my eyes off the spot at the narrow waist line where I'd pricked my finger, working late one night on it, and made a tiny scarlet spot on the white satin . . . so that I always thought of part of myself standing at the chancel rail, between the canopied pew of the royal governor and the high old pulpit with its massive bell-shaped sounding board that I used to sit as a child and watch, and expect to fall like the upper millstone and grind the white-surpliced rector to grist.

Perhaps that was why Melusina, sitting in the square Royal pew that day, absolutely convinced by then that she really had sacrificed wealth and honor to a brother who was repaying her by marrying a chit of a girl as poor as a Bruton church mouse, seemed unusually vinegary lipped to me. And perhaps that's why I always liked Peyton Yardley's young wife, and why, when she died of the flu during the war years, little Faith, who was just three, became almost like a child I might have had if there'd never been malaria in the rice fields of the Philippines.

Doctor Yardley made no more calls after that, and mixed no more powders in the old stone mortar that his grandmother's slaves had used to grind spices in . . . which was supposed to be why his medicines had a far-off taste of Samarcand, and cured things more quickly than powders do today, or the other doctors' powders did then. He retired to his panelled study that overlooks the long alleys of old box and the garden with those hundred-petalled roses that they make attar of roses out of. Sometimes he walked in the garden with its carpet of periwinkle and violets, and its white sand paths bordered with spice pinks and yellow pansies and great pink poppies and lemon lilies, down past the hundred-and-fifty-year-old crape myrtles shrouded in pink rambler, to the white picket fence covered with woodbine and honeysuckle, beyond the lily and mosquito pond, where the line of hackberry and chinaberry and mulberry and locusts is, up the ravine beyond the old spring house. Otherwise he never went out, except once a year to Commencement at William and Mary College, and once a year to the Phi Beta Kappa dinner—until they began having it in the Apollo Room of the restored Raleigh Tavern, and then he stopped that. His own life was like Williamsburg and the fall crocuses from the Palace gardens: it flowered briefly and beautifully, and stopped.

Then Melusina took it over. She moved Marshall Yardley, a cousin's child eight years or so older than little Faith, into Yardley Hall, and lavished on him all the adoration that the automobile manufacturer and an ungrateful brother had forfeited. She sold the Peale portrait of Washington that used to hang in the drawing room to send him to the University. Some people thought Doctor Yardley never knew it was gone, or knew for that matter when young Marshall came, or went, or came back again. He paid the scantiest possible attention to little Faith, and I don't think anybody who knew them ever called her by her name in front of him . . . not consciously, but out of a kind of respect, I suppose, or maybe awe, even, at what the other Faith had meant to him. It always seemed to me he'd never really seen his daughter, not with any vision deeper than the barest surface of his retina at any event. I know now that I was right, for I was in the room the moment he really saw her for the first time.

Faith, however, worshipped her father. The idea that she had a right to a more intimate relationship with him never for an instant occurred to her. I've seen her tiptoe past the library where he sat as a nun would go past a shrine. I've seen her little nose flattened against the window pane as she watched him pace slowly back and forth in the garden, his head bent forward, his hands behind his back, and seen her watch him from a stool in the corner the way a spaniel puppy watches his master. He was like a being far removed from her life, yet a hallowed and precious part of it.

When the Restoration came, and started buying up the properties that make up the so-called restoration area, and Williamsburg became the Cinderella town of America, Faith came to see me one day. She was little more than a child. I don't know who'd explained the situation to her. I can see her now, standing in my door that was pretty dingy then, not at all the way you'd see it now. She was a homely child, with a funny freckled nose and enormous tranquil grey eyes in a pointed, almost comically earnest little face. Her hair was an odd gold color, and pulled back in such tight little plaits that it always seemed to me her head must hurt. She had on a pink check sunbonnet and high buttoned shoes —that was the way Melusina had dressed when she was

Faith's age. She stood in the door, those big-calm grey eyes raised to mine.

"It'll be a very fine thing for us, Cousin Lucy," she said soberly. "Because you know we're very poor, and they'll let Father and Aunt Melusina go on living there as long as they keep on living, without costing them anything. They'll even put on a new roof, and pay the insurance that costs so much, and then Aunt Melusina won't have to sell any more of the pictures—because pretty soon Father will notice they're gone, and she can't keep on telling him they're in Richmond being repaired. Then, you see, if Father doesn't have to pay the taxes or anything, he can use the money he's got to buy books, and Aunt Melusina can have the fur coat she saw in Richmond."

I was surprised, of course, because just the day before at the meeting of the Guild in the Parish House, which was the old Wythe House on Palace Green, Melusina had delivered herself on the subject at a right considerable length.

"Has your father decided to sell?"

Her big eyes widened.

"I thought everybody had, except . . ." She named several of the important recalcitrants of the town . . . not knowing, the lamb, that her Aunt Melusina would have been the chief recalcitrant in Paradise.

But the next afternoon when she paid her daily call on me, she sat very primly for a moment with her ridiculous shoes crossed—I never could feel they had any relation to the little feet in them—and her hands, grubby in spite of Melusina, folded in her lap.

"I shouldn't have said what I did yesterday, Cousin Lucy. We're very proud, even if we are poor. We think the idea of being tenants in our own house is very impertinent."

I knew she was blinking her long lashes to keep back the tears, though all I could see at the moment was the tight stretched part on the top of her head.

"So we aren't going to have Yardley Hall painted new white like the Tucker House."

She stopped for a moment, and I couldn't think of a single thing to say.

Then she looked up at me. "—But it would have been right nice, wouldn't it, Cousin Lucy?"

I nodded.

# 2

That wasn't, of course, the last I heard about the Yardleys not selling out to the Yankees, but—in effect—it was the whole thing in a nutshell. It had the indubitably authentic ring of Melusina in it. I could hear her thin bitter voice as Faith Yardley was repeating her ultimatum, almost by rote.

Then a little later Faith went to stay with some cousins in Richmond so she could go to a church school there. I watched the growing bewilderment in her wide-set grey eyes as she came back for occasional school holidays and saw the face of Williamsburg change into what was its old self for us, but for her generation was something entirely new. Some five hundred of the buildings she'd known came down, fully grown trees, box and crape myrtle a hundred years old were planted, old grey tumble-down ghosts of houses were straightened and painted a gleaming white again. Service stations were moved out beyond Woodpecker Street, a royal palace reappeared on a refuse lot this side of the railroad tracks, behind two schoolhouses that had desecrated Palace Green. The schoolhouses were torn down and a fine new schoolhouse built on what we used to call Peacock Hill. The Capitol at the end of Duke of Gloucester Street rose in what had been an empty lot with a few foundations marked with bronze plates by the Society for the Preservation of Virginia Antiquities. White fences with woodbine and honeysuckle and trumpet vine and wisteria trailing on them appeared, and jonquils along the roadsides were so thick that the children forgot to pick them. Very soon we who lived

there forgot what the town had come to look like in
the years during and following the last war, the way one
forgets a bad dream or a severe pain, and began to think
we'd always lived surrounded by gardens . . . or would
have, if it weren't for the hundreds of cars bearing licenses
from every state in the Union and Canada that came and
went up and down Duke of Gloucester Street. The time the
service stations were on it seemed as remote as the year they
had a railroad running down the center of it to carry
soldiers to the Yorktown Centennial.

Then Faith Yardley came home to stay. She'd changed
almost as much as Williamsburg. She'd grown up to those
wonderful eyes she'd had as a child. Her freckles were gone,
her hair, released from Melusina's iron hand, had darkened
until it was a burnished gold. She'd cropped it, to Melusina's
horror, and she'd also taken to using lipstick, and powder on
her nose, and although Melusina didn't like that either, with
the example of the girls at William and Mary always before
her she subsided eventually, and was even thought by some
of her contemporaries to use a touch now and then herself.
The Yardleys still hadn't sold the Hall, and with the rest of
Williamsburg so spruce and clean and grand it looked pretty
seedy and run down. Faith never mentioned selling it again
to me, but when somebody suggested that she be one of the
hostesses in their paniered colonial gowns and frilled caps
who show visitors around the Palace and the Raleigh and the
Capitol, she shook her head.

"I'd love to," she said wistfully one morning, as we
watched the blue coach with its liveried coachman and footman driving up to the Palace gate and saw Hallie Taswell
in sprigged muslin with a yellow petticoat flutter down, as
grand if she hadn't probably covered up the breakfast dishes
and left them in the kitchen sink to gather flies.

"Some other people who haven't sold work for the Restoration," I said casually.

She gave me a sideways impish glance and raised her eyebrows, black and thick and unplucked.

"We Yardleys are as proud as Lucifer."

"Yes, I remember," I said.

She laughed. "And rather silly, if you ask me—but don't
tell Aunt Melusina."

It was just about then that Mason Seymour came to Williamsburg.

He came with a white man servant, and an open car that looked very expensive to me, and took the Davis house in Scotland Street, and presented letters to everybody in town, and was accepted by everybody, because his mother was from Fauquier County—which means a lot in Virginia. Mason Seymour was, I believe, what is known as God's gift to women. And since Williamsburg has been essentially a woman's town as long as I've known it—the fire of the signers burns more ardently in the feminine bosom, it seems, and furthermore every man between sixteen and sixty marched out of Williamsburg in 1861 and few came back, and each generation that's come up since has gone out into the world—I suppose Mason Seymour was also God's gift to Williamsburg. He had nothing to do with the Restoration, except that he was a sort of restoration in himself. For the first time since old Colonel Dandridge lay down with his forefathers in Bruton Churchyard, the ladies of Williamsburg had a gentleman of means and leisure who had nothing to do but make himself agreeable. I don't mean there weren't other men in the town who were charming and agreeable, and even gallant upon occasion, with sufficient provocation or a mint julep or two, but they never made a life work of it. They hadn't time, for one thing, and most of them were married. Even the students at the college had work to do, from time to time, and in any case their interest was bounded by the ripe age of eighteen, or possibly twenty.

Mason Seymour was subject to no such limitation. He could be—and was—as agreeable to Miss Melusina, who was sixty, as he was to Ruth Napier who was twenty-eight; and each of them, it appeared to me, was as susceptible to his particular charm as Hallie Taswell was, and Hallie was forty-six on Christmas Day last in spite of anything she says to the contrary. I know it because my mother went over to her mother's to help out, and ruined a day I'd looked forward to for weeks, because we were to have gone in the buggy to York to spend the day with some cousins, and couldn't go on account of Hallie, who had to be kept wrapped up in warm flannel cloths saturated with sweet oil.—I dare say that's why I've always been prejudiced against Hallie. Certainly I've never blamed the Restoration for her, the way Melusina does. Although I do think that if you put the average woman who has never been much to look at even when she was young in the sprigged muslin paniers of a colonial dame, which is the most flattering costume in the world, with its crisp white tissue berthas and velvet ribbons and white frilled beribboned cap, and put her in a room filled with priceless beautiful things, you've done all that is humanly possible to make her lovely to look at, and the least she can do is to act as charming as she looks.

And Hallie Taswell is the only one of all the Williamsburg ladies I know who, when she took off her mustard-colored homemade knit dress and put on fancy dress, let it go to her head. Because, to give the devil his due, I don't think Mason Seymour, when he whispered into the ever so faintly rouged lobe of Hallie's ear, in the state dining room of the Royal Palace, that she was as lovely as the chelsea figure on the carved mantel, had the faintest notion that he meant anything further than that. I expect, as a matter of fact, that he was merely keeping his hand in . . . or it may have been habit too strong to break. But he didn't know Hallie. He didn't know that she had at one time nursed an ambition to go on the stage—a thing no nice girl did, especially if she had no talent—as well as a hundred other romantic impossible ambitions that marriage to Hugh Taswell could only be the most pedestrian substitute for.

The little old Williamsburg lady who kept a dame's school and never married—or so she said—because she read *Paradise Lost* and fell in love with Satan came nearer her heart's desire, I expect. Because Hugh Taswell is pleasant, but he's not romantic. His life is bounded by his insurance business, his lawn, his roses that he's continually spraying with one noxious thing after another, his dinner, his pipe, a rubber of bridge and his bed. They say a gypsy once at Capitol Landing told Hallie she was cut out for a glamorous life. Whoever it was who put her, one day when there were two thousand tourists in town, in a colonial costume with frilled cap, and let her ride down the Palace Green and up Duke of Gloucester Street to the Capitol in a blue coach with a liveried coachman in the peach broadcloth draped box and a liveried footman up behind, certainly finished the gypsy's job.

But Hallie Taswell would have been a silly woman anywhere. It just happened that she was born in Williamsburg, and that Mason Seymour happened, at a psychological moment, to tell her she was as lovely as a chelsea figure on a palace mantelpiece. It might have been John W. Smith in the waiting room of the Grand Central Station in New York. It was just unfortunate that it happened at precisely the moment Melusina Yardley decided that Mason Seymour would make an excellent match for Faith. Because when Melusina decides anything, there's not much she'll stop at to go through with it. I didn't know at the time, and I doubt if any one else did, that it wasn't only that Mason Seymour was agreeably well-to-do, but also—and I'm not sure that it wasn't quite as important—that Marshall Yardley was in love with that strange girl Ruth Napier, who had come since the Restoration to live in the Aspinwall house in South England Street.

The connection between Faith and Mason Seymour and Marshall Yardley and Ruth Napier isn't very obvious unless you happen to know what has been fairly common gossip for some time, that Ruth was very much interested in Mason Seymour, and not the least interested, apparently, in the young lawyer who commuted daily from Yardley Hall to Norfolk so he could see her.

I thought, as I went up the Palace Green and turned right into Scotland Street by the old vine-covered Brush house with its little turreted brick office and old box gardens, and turned again on Palace Long Wall Street into the elm-shaded carriage drive that leads to Yardley's pillared doorway, that it seemed odd Melusina should have forgotten that the chief argument she advanced against her brother's marrying Faith's mother was that he was forty-seven and she was only twenty-two. Mason Seymour was forty-five, Faith was twenty. But I suppose the fact that Melusina was sixty instead of forty made the difference . . . or part of it, anyway.

I went in the dim old panelled hall with its faded turkey carpet and old mahogany, and the faint scent of potpourri mingling with the clouds of yellow roses that grew jungle-thick over the front of the old house, and up the carved stairway with its inset of hollywood, like the stairs at the Palace.

Old Abraham, the white-haired darkey who's been with the Yardleys as long as any one can remember, came out of the pantry and greeted me.

"Go right up, Mis' Lucy. Mis' Faith's in Mis' Mel'ciny's room."

They were there, the two of them, and also old Miss Alicia, a cousin of Melusina's so old and fragile that if it hadn't been for her black cloth dress, I thought, you could have seen the chair through her. She didn't look at me when I came into the room. I saw it was because her eyes were fixed on the thick folds of old white satin that Melusina had taken from the mahogany press in the hall and laid on her high fourposter bed while she took the old tissue paper from the folds. A faint odor of orris root and musk came from it, and from the delicate cobweb folds of the lace veil that lay beside it.

Miss Alicia bent forward and picked up a piece of yellowed tissue that Melusina had let fall, and unwrapped brown pressed petals of orange blossom, and let them lie in her frail hand a moment.

Faith, who stood by watching all this with a detachment almost as objective as Melusina's own, was suddenly still. I've never known her attitude toward her long dead mother. I don't suppose Melusina had had much to say about her, and I hadn't supposed, some way, that Faith had ever associated her father's retirement from the world with any very definite cause, though she certainly must have heard it spoken of. But young people today are practical, and I rather think Faith had regarded the business of wearing her mother's wedding gown as something one did, just as she'd wear the old lace veil that the Yardley women and the women the Yardleys married had worn since Lafayette brought it to one Anne Yardley on his last visit to Williamsburg in 1824.

But the pressed orange blossoms in Miss Alicia's delicate transparent hand seemed suddenly to move her. The three of us, old Miss Alicia, Faith and I, stood silently looking at it.

Melusina turned and saw it.

"Oh, that's just some old rubbish," she said practically. "Here, Faith—let's see if you can get into this."

Faith stiffened, and I saw her eyes darken almost black. I put my hand on her arm. She relaxed, and looked away quickly. Then she slipped off the brown linen sport frock she had on, and stood while Melusina put her mother's wedding gown on her. I smiled at the brown throat and the brown hands. Her mother's skin had been like buttermilk.

"Of course it's got to be let out everywhere," Melusina said brusquely. "Here are the scissors, Lucy. After all, you made it, and you ought to know what to do with it now."

"Did you make it, Cousin Lucy?" Faith asked.

I nodded.

"And here's the spot of my life's blood I left on it, hurrying to get it done that Tuesday night."

I pointed to the tiny faint brown spot on the belt.

"That's why I've always felt you belonged partly to me," I said.

She bent down quickly and kissed the top of my head, her eyes suddenly wet with tears.

"I'd like to take it off!" she whispered. "Oh, please—take it off!"

Melusina put her hands on her hips and pressed her lips to a thin colorless line.

"Faith Yardley!" she exclaimed angrily. "Are we going to be favored with another fit of temperament?"

"Oh, no, but I can't wear it, Aunt Melusina—I can't, really!"

"Your father wants you to wear it, Faith. And anyway, we can't possibly afford to buy you a gown, with all the other expense we're being put to. I should think you're old enough to understand a little of our position."

She picked up the heavy white satin folds.

"Of course, it isn't very well made, but it's sufficiently traditional, and the stuff's fine enough, to overlook that."

Faith's fingers pressed lightly on my shoulder.

"I think it's beautifully made. It isn't that. It's . . ."

"Well, what is it, then?" Melusina demanded sharply.

"Oh, nothing.—Nothing that you'd understand," she added, so softly that for an instant I thought I was the only one who heard—Melusina being a little deaf actually, as well as totally deaf and totally blind when she wants to be, though I don't think she's ever been dumb, in the sense of being mute.

I snipped the seams at the waist. If Faith had been corseted as her mother was, the dress would have been too loose. Her slim ungirdled body was as graceful and delicate as her mother's had been. They were the same height—the only difference was that Faith's shoulders were a little sturdier and she was as straight as a young sapling.

I took the dress off her.

"You'll do it here, won't you, Lucy?" Melusina asked.

I nodded. "I'll do it tomorrow."

"I've given the announcement to the papers," Melusina said.

Faith was staring at her, the blood drained completely from her face. She put her hand out and steadied herself against the reeded post of the old bed. Melusina, folding up the dress, didn't even glance at her.

"We couldn't go on putting it off forever," she said curtly. She put an old linen sheet around it and laid it on the satin-wood chest between the windows.

"But . . . Aunt Melusina! You promised not to, until I told——"

"Do you think Mason Seymour wants to be kept dangling all spring like a college boy?" her aunt asked calmly.

"But you *promised*——"

"Don't be absurd, Faith. If you're going around with him all the time things have got to be put on a proper and re-spectable basis. I don't want people talking about you the way . . ."

She stopped abruptly.

"The way they are about Ruth Napier!"

That was old Miss Alicia's voice, high and reedy and sharp as a needle.

Melusina was conveniently deaf, and Faith's waxen face flushed.

"Precisely, Miss Alicia!"

There was a sob in her voice that she tried desperately to choke back.

"This is all perfectly ridiculous," Melusina said. She folded the lace veil, put it in a pillow slip and put it in the drawer of the Chippendale highboy at the end of the room. Faith put her dress back on, her eyes almost black again, her red lips as vivid against her pale face as blood against snow.

# 3

Marshall Yardley was just coming in the house when I went downstairs.

"Hello, Miss Lucy," he said. He tossed his brief case on the inlaid sunburst Sheraton table under the old print of Cornwallis' surrender at Yorktown. "It's hot today."

He wiped his forehead with his handkerchief. I looked at him, thinking how much he was like the portrait of Doctor Yardley's father that hangs in the Blue Room at the College, with his prominent jaw and the Yardley nose that is more serviceable than beautiful. He has the Yardleys' dark, almost somber and rather deep-sèt eyes and thin flexible mouth.

He took the folded paper out of his pocket and handed it to me. He didn't look very happy.

"Seems funny to think of Faith getting married," he said.

I read the announcement.

"Daughter of Doctor Peyton Yardley to Wed New Yorker," was the heading of a column on the front page of *The Evening Journal*. Then followed the long line of the Yardley ancestors, beginning with Sir Robert Yardley, who came with the Jamestown Expedition of 1607, and including a thumbnail sketch of their careers in Revolution and Civil War and public life, and ending with an account of Doctor Yardley's life. In a sentence at the end it said, "Mr. Mason Seymour's mother was Miss Frances Mason of Parkersburg, Fauquier County." The date of the wedding was to be announced later.

"I didn't know it was all set," Marshall said.

"Neither did Faith, apparently," I heard myself saying before I realized what I was doing.

He looked at me, the Yardley jaw tightening. I thought he was going to say something, but he evidently thought better of it. Instead he glanced at the smoked panel of the library door, and bit his lower lip, as if for a moment he'd had the extraordinary idea of barging in on his uncle. Then —and I don't suppose he actually planned it that way—his dark brilliant eyes moved up to the cracked discolored plaster of the ceiling, and an odd defeated look came in them. A mirthless and rather hopeless smile twisted his thin flexible mouth for an instant.

"It was always going to be me who retrieved the family fortunes, not Faith," he said bitterly. "And it's all I can do to pay office rent."

"It's something to do that, these days," I said. I didn't mean it to sound as banal and sententious as it must have done.

"But not enough."

I looked around at the dingy cracked walls and the old panelling that hadn't been painted for twenty years. There was a certain sardonic humor in my even noticing that its grandeur was so shabby. I never had done, in all the years my own panelling needed paint, and grandfather's old tin footbath sat under the leak in the bedroom dormer and often had to be emptied two or three times a day in a heavy downpour. But now that my panelling was rubbed down to the satin-smooth old pine, and a stone roof looking like slate shingles that the Restoration people put on kept me snug, I found myself looking patronizingly at the sagging place above the old eight-panelled door that showed that my cousin Yardley's hall needed a good deal of jacking up. It wasn't that I'd ever envied them Yardley, or all the things in it. My mother had sold all the things that came to her out of it, through her mother.

I turned back to Marshall.

"Do you want to sell the Hall, to the Restoration?"

He opened and shut his long hands—all the Yardleys have long narrow sensitive hands—and shook his head, as if he was trying to shake the cobwebs out of it.

"I'd hate to—. If we could keep it up . . ."

He shrugged.

"I suppose Faith will inherit it," I said. I hadn't meant to be cruel. But he turned away abruptly.

"Or Mason Seymour."

He said it so bitterly that I was stunned.

"Why, Marshall!" I gasped. "—Don't you want her to marry him?"

"Oh, how could I, Cousin Lucy?"

He spoke almost passionately.

"He's old enough to be her father, in the first place. He's the worst sort of philanderer . . . the kind that makes all sorts of a fool out of a woman without ever getting his own fingers burned."

I knew he was thinking of Ruth Napier. I didn't look at him directly, because I knew he was suffering considerably more than any Yardley would care for any one to know they could suffer. What he'd said about retrieving the family fortunes wasn't only on account of repairing the cracked plaster and the sag in the carved stairway.

"Why don't you tell your aunt and uncle that?" I said.

"I've told Aunt Mel. She's such an innocent on the one hand, and such a damned realist on the other. And Mason Seymour's got her just as fooled as he has Hallie Taswell, and . . . all the rest."

"And Ruth Napier," I said.

"And Ruth Napier," he repeated evenly.

"But what about Faith's father?"

Marshall raised his hands in the sort of despairing gesture that it seems to me I've seen people make whenever they speak of Peyton Yardley as long as ever I can remember.

"He wouldn't know what I was talking about," he groaned. "I don't think he knows who I am. Or who Faith is, for that matter. Well, why not? If you can escape everything you don't like by just shutting yourself up, you might as well do it. Miss Alicia says the only time he ever came to life was the few years Faith's mother was here.—What was she like, Cousin Lucy? I mean, according to Miss Alicia she was a feather from an angel's wing, and according to Aunt Mel she was whatever they'd have called a gold digger twenty-five years ago."

"She was just like Faith," I said. "Except that her childhood must have been—well, freer. Or had more open affection in it. Because certainly Melusina, with all her very ster-

ling virtues, hasn't been what you'd call an indulgent mother
to Faith."

He grunted, and picked up the paper. I saw him staring
at that announcement again.

"Maybe she won't marry him," I said. "There's many a
slip 'twixt the cup and the lip, you know."

He shook his head.

"It's a matter of honor, now. No Yardley lady jilts
a lover—not since the little lady Anne."

He nodded through the open door to the picture hanging over the Hepplewhite table beside the window over-
looking the grape arbor, parallel with Scotland Street. It was
a portrait of a dark-haired girl in a low-cut white gown
with a chaplet of pearls on her head. Where her hands
should have been was a large jagged hole. It was Anne Yardley, the first daughter of Yardley Hall, born at Jamestown
in 1701. In her hands there had been a letter, a love letter
supposedly, because she was a lovely capricious creature
with as many beaux as there were gentlemen in the colony
—one of whom she agreed to marry, and then jilted without rime or reason. And one evening he came to Yardley
Hall—it was in 1718—in the bitter winter weather, strode
through the hall, drew his saber and slashed the letter out of
her hands, tossed it into the fire, went out and across to the
canal in the Palace grounds; and there they found him the
next morning, with a lock of dark hair and a note that still
lie in the little chest under the portrait on the table there
where we were looking. The note says something to the
effect that the ice was warm compared with Lady Anne's
cold heart and death was kind where she was cruel.

"Well, I can't imagine Mason Seymour jumping into the
Canal, with the bullfrog and the goldfish and the ducks," I
said. "And anyway, it's summer now."

"I know," Marshall said. "You didn't, fortunately, grow
up under the portrait of Lady Anne. Faith did."

He picked up his brief case and opened the great door
with its enormous brass lock polished so that its surface was
brighter than any of the old mirrors in the house. You
looked grey and ill in the mirrors and hard and jaundiced in
the lock, so it was best just never to look at all. We always
thought that was why Melusina, when she finally took to using what she called a soupçon of paint on her face, looked

more like one of the Indians who massacred her great-great-great-great-grandfather at Jamestown than the blush of a rose, which I dare say she thought she looked like. Yet she always thought Faith, who never used rouge at all, looked unnatural because she used lipstick.

I was thinking that as I went along the Palace Green and out across Court House Green, stopped a moment to speak to the old gentleman who pastures his two pleasant cows on its broad velvet lawn, and across behind the Powder Horn —or the Magazine, as they call it now—up Francis Street to my white clapboard house with the silver moon rose twined with wisteria and woodbine at the door. And there I stopped abruptly.

If only one's guardian angel could pluck at one's sleeve—and if one could feel it when he did pluck—when the threshold of a momentous event is reached, it would be extraordinarily convenient. Because as it was, I hadn't the remotest notion, now, that the young man sitting on my door step was going to mean anything in my life, beyond the possible four dollars a day I might—if he was properly introduced —charge him for the privilege of being my guest . . . if, of course, he was a tourist, and the license plate on his rather undistinguished open car indicated that he was and that he came from Massachusetts.

He scrambled to his feet as I came up. He was very tall, and if he hadn't had blue eyes and crisp tow-colored hair I might have thought he was an Indian, he was burned so black. He grinned at me in the most infectious and irresistible fashion.

"I was hoping you'd be wearing a hoop skirt and a cap with lavender ribbons, Miss Lucy," he said, with rather engaging impudence. In fact it was so engaging that it really wasn't in the least impudent.

"You don't mind if I call you Miss Lucy, do you, because you're going to see an awful lot of me. My name's Bill Haines—William Quincy Adams Haines, no less, and furthermore I've got a card."

He fished about in I never saw so many pockets full of ill-assorted trash, produced a dog-eared card, and handed it to me. And I started—for it was a long time since I'd seen the name of Melusina's and my own Great Sacrifice. Not since he'd got to be a very wealthy man, certainly.

"My dear Lucy," it read. "As a favor to an old friend will

you take in this young man? Feed him batter bread and pecan pie, tell him about our livery stable on Buttermilk Hill, and how you ran away from me when I proposed to you in the ruined tower at Jamestown. He wants to be an architect."

It ended, "Affectionately—if you will allow me—Summers Baldwin."

I don't know why everything seemed awfully misty all of a sudden, because I certainly never entertained the least romantic notion about Summers Baldwin, and heaven knows there was no reason I should blush, except for the ridiculous solemn expression on the face of that young man, who apparently had got the amazing idea into his head that he was gazing on the ashes of a beautiful romance, and that I was the forlorn but reconciled little woman that the great man had left behind him.

I opened my mouth to snap—I suppose—that I hadn't any room for him, and then, seeing him look so sympathetic and long-eared and lugubrious and comical, I laughed and said, "My office is empty, if you'd like that."

He looked a little puzzled. I suppose he had a vision of a desk and a typewriter and a finished business basket. So I opened the door of the gleaming white little house that stands at the side of my own, that had been my father's law office, and my grandfather's, and so on back, even before that ancestor of ours who in the House of Burgesses listened to Patrick Henry's speech in the Capitol at the head of Duke of Gloucester Street and met with Washington and Jefferson and the rebellious patriots in the Apollo Room at the Raleigh. It still had their ink-stained table in it, and my great-grandfather's arm chair. The bed was an old sleigh back that my mother had given to old Aunt Sally our darkey cook and I'd bought back from her for fifty cents. The old fire irons were made from the iron band around the wheels of my grandfather's buggy at the old forge in Nicholson Street.

"Gosh, this is swell!" Bill Haines exclaimed.

"You'll have to use the bathroom in the house," I said. "And I'll have your breakfast sent over."

Bill Haines could not have been more pleased, apparently, if he had been put up in the State Bedroom in the Palace. He stood in the middle of the floor, making the room seem astonishingly small, grinning and rubbing his hands together like one of the lunatics farther down the street.

"I'm going to like this," he said.

"Just use one of the ashtrays for cigarettes, is all I ask," I said—almost as waspishly as Miss Melusina, I suppose. But I felt something was owing to the provincial character of the town. Not that it dampened Mr. William Quincy Adams Haines in the slightest degree.

"Okay, Miss Lucy," he grinned.

"And supper's at half-past six," I said. "And if you want anything between half-past two and half-past five, you'll have to get it yourself, because in Williamsburg the house servants are off then."

"Yes, ma'am," he said, so meekly that we both laughed. I went back to the house.

It's strange how sometimes memories suddenly start crowding in on one. I know I had a number of things to do that evening—afternoon, I believe Mr. Haines would have called it, but we call it evening below the Mason and Dixon's line—but I didn't seem to do any of them. If it hadn't been for that noisy young man next door, banging his luggage about and putting books in Grandfather's shelves, and whistling until every mocking-bird in the garden seemed to me to have learned "There's an old spinning-wheel" and whistled it with him, I'd have been out of the present, back in the remote past entirely. At least I should have until I heard the Bruton chimes strike five, and the door opened and Faith Yardley walked in.

Even then it wasn't much of a wrench with the past. For a moment I almost thought it was the other Faith I was seeing—she was so lovely in an odd pinkish-grey dress that made her eyes a deeper grey behind her long black lashes, and her hair above her warm sunbrowned forehead brighter gold.

She came quickly across the room and sat down on the little needle-point stool at my feet, and put her hand on my knee.

"Cousin Lucy—you didn't think I meant the wedding dress wasn't made well enough for me, did you?" she asked.

I shook my head. "Of course I didn't, you precious lamb."

"Aunt Melusina said besides being undutiful and ungrateful I was rude and hurt your feelings."

I laughed. I really couldn't help it. I'd only sewed to help hold things together because it was the only thing I could do at all. I'd always hated it, really. The Restoration that had taken the needle forever out of my somewhat rheumatic fingers had been a godsend. And after all, it was Melusina who said the gown wasn't very well made, not Faith.

"Because that wasn't it at all," Faith said. "It was just that —oh, I don't know . . . But, all of a sudden, seeing it, and those pressed orange blossoms, and . . . and that speck where you'd pricked your finger, before I was born, everything became . . . clear. I mean, Father shutting himself up from everybody, after she died, and . . . —He must have loved her terribly much, Cousin Lucy?"

"He did," I said.

"So that's why . . . I mean, I don't mind marrying Mason Seymour if it will . . . save the Hall for him—so he can just have her there, all his life. But I—oh, Cousin Lucy!"

She buried her head in my lap, and I could just hear her.

"It doesn't seem right to marry anybody I don't love, or who doesn't love me! I mean the way she and Father loved each other when she . . . wore that dress and pressed those flowers!"

"Then don't do it, Faith," I said quietly. "Don't marry him. The Restoration will buy the Hall. He can live there just as he is, as long as he lives."

"But he won't sell it," she said.

"You mean your Aunt Melusina won't," I said sharply. "I doubt if your father knows a thing about it. Have you told him why you're marrying Mason Seymour?"

She looked up at me with wide-eyed horror.

"Oh, of course not!"

"Because he'd never allow this," I said. "And your aunt certainly has no right to ask any such sacrifice. . . ."

"Except that she sacrificed *her* life for Father."

"Rubbish!" I said.

It was the first time I'd ever said it, out loud, about Melusina's sacrifice, and I was shocked hearing myself. That card Mr. Bill Haines had brought looked up at me from the table against the wall.

Faith was too much involved in her own thoughts.

"You see, Cousin Lucy, I'd really just as leave marry Mason. I wish he wasn't quite so old, but he's attractive, even apart from . . . saving the Hall. Maybe if I were in love with anybody else, it would be different, but I'm not. And Aunt Melusina says most women don't really love their husbands until after they're married to them. And anyway—

love's never been a very happy thing for the Yardleys. Look at Father, and look at Aunt Melusina. And Miss Alicia—lots of times I see her looking at an old daguerreotype."

"That was a cousin of my grandfather," I said. "People used to say there were reasons why they never married. No one ever said what they were. He died an old man right here in Williamsburg. They used to sit in opposite pews at Bruton Church, when the nave and Lord Dunmore's gallery were closed off and we just used the transepts. I remember them when I was a child. They'd bow very ceremoniously, but they never spoke."

"Oh, it seems horrible, doesn't it—so many thwarted lives!" Faith cried.

"But you're letting your aunt thwart yours, my sweet," I said.

She got up quickly.

"You mustn't say that, Cousin Lucy. I'd do anything for Father, and for Yardley. And I'm really very fond of Mason. He couldn't be sweeter to me, really. Anyway, it's all settled now."

She turned away a little.

"I couldn't go back on my word—now that it's out."

"As that devil Melusina knew very well," I said to myself. To Faith I said, "I hope you'll be happy."

# 4

Suddenly from outside came the blast of a motor horn. Williamsburg is so quiet that any noise sounds a thousand times louder than it is. I looked out the window. It was Mason Seymour's big open car, and it was Mason Seymour at the wheel, wearing that kind of cap they tell me Breton sailors wear.

He got out, slammed the door and came jauntily through the gate, stopped to pick a red rambler rose growing in a scarlet carpet on my whitewashed fence—the Restoration planted it too, even if it does look as if it had been there since the beginning of time; stuck it in the lapel of his light grey flannel jacket, came up the path and pushed open the door without the formality of using the brass knocker.

"Hello, Miss Lucy!" he called. "Faith here?"

He came on into the drawing room.

"Oh, there you are, my dear."

He came over to her. "You didn't tell me you were going to announce the happy event today."

He bent his head and kissed her lightly—too lightly, I thought, if he had to kiss her at all—on the lips. I felt, rather than saw, her slim back stiffen. And he must have felt it too, for he put his arm around her shoulders and pulled her playfully to him. A faint flush had come to her cheeks, her eyes had darkened almost the color of coals, but she managed to smile and disengage herself. And in a swift intuitive instant I saw what I'd never in the world have guessed. Faith Yardley was afraid of the man. She was frightened and repelled,

as I in my simple spinster way was always brought up to
believe that innocence was always frightened and repelled
by too apparent worldliness and sophistication.

I don't know why it was that Mason Seymour, who certainly was known to be a most accomplished man of the
world, hadn't sense enough then to see she was alarmed and
let her alone. Whether he was acutely piqued, or perhaps had
had a cocktail too many, or whether simply what my grandmother would have called his lower nature had got the best
of him, I don't know. But his hand clasped on hers and he
drew her toward him and pressed his mouth to hers.

It was just then that I looked around and saw, standing in
the hall doorway, my new boarder, Mr. Bill Haines. And I
don't know whether it was the shocked and horrified look
on my own face, or the terrified girl trying to release herself, without making a scene, from Mason Seymour's arms;
but I do know that the surprising young man stepped
promptly into the room and up to Seymour, calmly and with
apparently very little effort tore his arms from Faith's body
and gave him an apparently polite little shove that sent him
back about two yards.

"I beg your pardon," Mr. Bill Haines said affably. "But
where I come from, gentlemen don't kiss ladies unless they
have first found out if it's perfectly all right."

Faith shrank against the table, her face the color of a
peony, her eyes black with anger and mortification.

Mason Seymour was the color of dirty putty. But not, I
must say, the consistency of it. He caught his balance and
straightened himself in the best Virginia manner. "I *beg* your
pardon, sir," he said.

Mr. Haines stood, his hands thrust loosely in his jacket
pockets, a pleasant smile on his face, a dangerous look in his
eyes.

It is a tradition in Virginia that a lady is never visibly surprised at anything. I had certainly lapsed disgracefully, but
at this point I was able to collect myself.

I said, "Miss Yardley, this is Mr. Haines.—And Mr.
Haines, this is Mr. Seymour . . . Miss Yardley's fiancé . . ."

If it hadn't been so very awful, I should have been irre-
sistibly amused at the sudden horrible look of utter consternation on Bill Haines's face. I don't know how to describe
the color he turned. If a Peel boot could turn the color of a
brick, it would about approach it.

"I . . . I beg your pardon," he said. "I'm dreadfully sorry!"

He didn't so much as look at Faith, although it was to her he spoke as much as Mason Seymour.

"I . . . guess the romantic setting's getting me down. I'm really frightfully sorry."

"I'm sure Miss Yardley understands," Mason Seymour said stiffly. He bowed. "If you're ready, Faith. Good evening, Miss Lucy."

They closed the door and we heard the motor purr. Bill Haines sank down on the ottoman in front of the fire and mopped his dripping forehead.

"Well, my God!" he groaned. "What would you think of that?"

"You were quite right," I said.

He looked up, his face blanker than ever.

"What do you mean, quite right?" he demanded.

"I mean, she hated having him kiss her, like that. It was brutal and vulgar of him."

He gave me a sidelong look out of one eye. I could see he thought it was because I didn't know the so-called facts of life, and no doubt I would think any man kissing any woman was vulgar and brutal. It is, of course, what most young people think about old ones, so I don't know why I should have minded his thinking it. But I did, some way. We sat there, each engaged in his own thoughts.

He looked up abruptly. "What's a girl like that marrying him for?"

I hated just to say "Money," so I said, "To keep from selling Yardley Hall."

He frowned. I don't think he believed that either. It must have seemed awfully nineteenth century, I'll admit.

"It's quite true," I said.

"Is that the big place across from the Palace Wall?"

I nodded.

"The Royal Governors had the fence set in the wall there, so the Yardleys could have the Palace garden vista. You can see straight through across the garden from Yardley Hall's front door."

"Why don't they sell to the Restoration?"

"It's a long story," I said. "And I think you'd have to have lived in Virginia to understand it."

"Is it Doctor Yardley?"

I nodded.

"Mr. Baldwin told me about him. Was that his daughter?"

I nodded again. And I suppose it's because I'm a woman that I asked, "Did he tell you about Miss Yardley, Miss Melusina—Doctor Yardley's sister?"

"No," he said.

I'm afraid I winced in spite of myself. I'd never heard Melusina dismissed before with so short a "No." For the first time it occurred to me that I might have been wrong about Melusina's Sacrifice. If Summers Baldwin hadn't mentioned her, when he had mentioned all the rest of us, it was probably because she lay deeper in his secret heart than I had known.

"How is Summers Baldwin?" I heard myself asking then.

He shook his head.

"Not so well, since his wife died."

"Is she dead?"

"Two months ago. She was an awful snob. I think that's why the old boy keeps looking back here, where things were simple and you don't devote two servants to the care, feeding, and bathing of one lousy pomeranian."

"Melusina was a snob, of course," I said, "but she never had a pomeranian."

"What did you say?"

"Nothing," I said.

He'd got up and was pacing back and forth between the door and the corner fireplace like a caged circus tiger. He spent the rest of the evening doing it, it seemed to me—at least, he was still there, and still moving about, when supper was served, and although he ate prodigiously I doubt if he could have told half an hour later what he'd eaten. Finally he went back to the office, and I drew a deep breath and sat down to my work. But he was back again almost immediately.

"Say—will she come here again?"

"Who?"

"Miss Yardley."

"Her name's Faith," I said. "And I don't reckon she'll have the courage to chance meeting you here again."

"I was afraid of that," Bill Haines said, very seriously. "Look. You tell her I've left on the night train, will you?"

I know I looked surprised, because he grinned suddenly.

"You're just to *tell* her that," he said. He grinned again, and was gone. I heard him come in very late. The old hinge on the office door groans even now. My father used to say it was haunted by the ghost of one of his clients whose case he'd lost.

And next morning he brought his breakfast tray over to the house.

"This guy Seymour, now, Miss Lucy," he said, rather quietly, pouring himself a cup of coffee. "—I saw him last night out at Jamestown."

"Everybody in Williamsburg drives out there to get the air," I said, no doubt rather primly.

"Yeh. But he wasn't getting it, he was trying to give it— to a gal with black hair in a sort of page boy bob. And boy, was that baby telling him something.—What's the matter?"

"Nothing," I said.

I couldn't tell him that that was Ruth Napier he'd seen, or that Faith's cousin Marshall was in love with her, and that she was in love with Mason Seymour.

"Well, all I mean is, if he's going to marry Faith Yardley, what's he doing with the black-haired gal? Or do I just come from the more conventional North?"

He looked at me with that funny puzzled sort of pucker between his eyes, set down his tray, reached over and took my hand. "I'm sorry—what have I done now?"

"Oh, nothing," I said. "It's just that Faith is very dear to me, and I . . . well, I just . . ."

"I know," he said.

He gave my hand a warm hard squeeze. Then he picked up his tray and finished his breakfast in silence. I didn't see him any more that morning. He didn't come in to dinner. It was about two, I imagine, that I went over to Yardley Hall to fix Faith's wedding dress.

I'd hoped all night that the scene in my parlor would be enough to make her break with Mason Seymour, and yet I'd had no word not to come. And the scene with Ruth Napier at Jamestown must have meant, of course, that he had succeeded in apologizing to Faith, and that the Yardley pride was still to be reckoned with. I thought as I went along Palace Green, crowded with tourists oh-ing and ah-ing at a dead past, how surprised they would be if they knew what the living present was behind our quaint other-world charm. But they wouldn't have been any more surprised than I was as I walked down under the old elm-bordered path, opened the door at Yardley, stopped, and stood there blinking more, I'm afraid, than a lady should.

What I heard was the unmistakable cheerful voice of my new boarder, and it was saying:

"And this cornice, Miss Yardley? Was that in the original house?"

And it wasn't Melusina who answered, it was Faith. She was saying, "Yes, Mr. Haines. The entire room is original."

And Mr. Haines said:

"But it isn't original at all, Miss Yardley, to marry somebody you aren't in love with, just to pay off the old family mortgage. That was done in all the old melodramas."

I heard Faith gasp, as well she might.

"I'm sorry . . . but I'm not sorry about yesterday. I couldn't stand seeing that fellow kiss you, even if I didn't know who you were. I mean——"

"Mr. Haines—will you kindly leave this house?"

"No," said Mr. Haines. "Your father said you were to show me around, and you've got to do it."

"I certainly do not."

"You certainly do. Or I'll steal the silver, and the linen, and the portrait of your grandmother.—And this mantel, Miss Yardley, is *it* original?"

I don't know what Faith said. My head was swimming quite a bit anyway, with just plain incredulity and amazement at all this. But I heard Mr. Bill Haines then.

"You know this table is like one we've got at home, Miss Yardley. Except that written right across the center of ours there's a motto. It says, 'Who ever loved that loved not at first sight?' Now don't you think that's interesting?"

"If true," Faith said coolly.

"Oh, it's true. I can vouch for it myself. May I tell you about an experience I had yesterday?"

"You certainly may not, Mr. Haines."

His voice was suddenly very quiet, then, and very gentle.

"Look," he said; "you won't believe it—not right away, maybe—but it's true. I know it sounds crazy. You think I'm a fool or a boor, or both. But I'm not. Something just happened to me, yesterday. I've known you all my life. I knew the minute I saw you nothing would ever be the way it was again.—Listen: don't marry this fellow . . . not just yet, anyway. Give me a chance . . . Faith."

She didn't even see me as she flew out of the room and

up the stairs, and I slipped behind the door as old Abraham came out and saw Bill Haines looking very intently at a most uninteresting oil painting of the well house before they put the new roof on it.

"Miss Yardley was called away," he said calmly. "Will you tell her, please, that I'll let her know how things develop?"

"Yas, suh. Ah'll cert'nly tell her, suh. Good evenin', suh."

Abraham bowed the brash young man out, and retired to the pantry, and I slipped up the stairs.

# 5

Melusina was in her room with the wedding dress out and ripped and ready.

"I don't know what on earth has come over Faith," Melusina said. Did anything happen at your house?"

She fixed me with an eye that has always terrified me.

"No," I said.

"I'll call her. If she's through showing that young man you sent here around . . ."

I gulped a little.

"I'm sure I don't understand your sending him to Peyton, Lucy—of all things. You *know* he's never disturbed in the afternoon. What on earth was there so urgent about it?"

I filled my mouth with pins—which I almost swallowed—to keep from having to answer her.

"And Peyton must have lost his mind. He had Abraham hunting all over the place for a bottle of sherry, and had the young man to lunch when he knew I was going out."

She went to the door and called Faith, and Faith came. I was almost afraid to look at her, and when I did finally my heart sank. Her lips were set, a faint flush burned in her cheeks, her eyes were almost coal black. She took off her blue linen dress and stood perfectly still while Melusina slipped the white satin wedding dress over her head. I heard Melusina draw a faint breath of relief. I think she'd expected another difficult session. But Faith was perfectly resigned, even determined, it seemed to me. It was only when Melusina, interested now, I think, in the showmanship of the

36

thing, picked up the old lace veil and put it on her head, and then reached over and picked up the mock orange sprig that I saw Faith close her eyes a moment.

Melusina stood back.

"There. You really look lovely, Faith—if you weren't so brown. Some buttermilk and cucumber paste will help that. Doesn't she look sweet, Lucy?"

I looked at her, and she looked at me. I don't know how a lump as big as the one in my throat could be there without choking a body.

And then, quite suddenly, I saw Melusina staring beyond me as if she'd seen a ghost, and I turned.

Doctor Yardley was standing in the door, looking at his daughter. I had never realized he was so old, or . . . or human, or so beautiful, indeed, as he was then. He just stood looking at her, his lips moving so you could almost see the word they breathed:

"Faith, Faith!"

And then in the utter silence of the room—the mockingbirds in the garden were still, even Melusina was speechless—he came forward and stood in front of his daughter, looking at her face as if he'd never seen her in this world before.

She stood perfectly motionless in front of him. He raised his hand and touched her sleeve and her veil, and then her face, and her forehead, and her bright gold hair under the mock orange blossoms. Then he took her face in both his hands and looked down into it a long long time before he bent his head and kissed her star-clear eyes and her forehead, and folded her to him.

"My little Faith," he whispered. "Forgive me, Faith."

I looked at Melusina. For once in her life her hands hung limp and nerveless in front of her. I think I felt sorry for her, too, for the first time in all my life.

Doctor Yardley stood there, looking at her, a slow puzzled cloud settling on his face.

"Are you unhappy, Faith?" he asked gently.

"Oh, no, no, Father!" she cried eagerly. "I've never been so happy!"

He looked at her intently.

"You're the very picture of her," he said.

We watched him retracing his slow steps to the door. He didn't look back. I think he didn't trust himself. When he had closed the door, Faith stood, her lips parted, her face radiantly lovely. I felt my throat contract sharply. She really was, just then, the image of the girl who had stood at the chancel at Bruton Church in that dress and veil, with real orange blossoms, twenty-two years before.

Even Melusina's face paled a little. But she shook the vision from her and said, even more brusquely than usual, "I hope you see now what this means to your father."

"Oh, I'd do anything, anything, for him!"

The girl almost sang the words.

I was so annoyed I could hardly take the pins out of my mouth. At the same time I was trying desperately to think whatever could have happened to bring Peyton Yardley out of his seclusion.

I said, more sharply than I would have otherwise, "If you can't stand still, Faith, I can't do a thing with this dress."

I could hardly do anything anyway, but I finally finished —I don't know how—and escaped. Doctor Yardley, I thought, must have been told she wasn't happy, and then, asking her himself, he would see that she was almost radiantly happy . . . and it would never occur to him that it was because he had at last come out of his fastness, and spoken to the child who had worshipped him for years. And he might have stopped all this if he had known. . . .

I hurried down the stairs, and halted abruptly at the bottom. Doctor Yardley was coming out of the library, coming toward me. He was even looking at me.

"Thank you, Lucy, for sending that young Haines over. I'm not sure I could help him very much, but I gave him a little information.—He has helped me a great deal."

"I . . . I'm so glad," I stammered. If I had only known what story the young rascal had told, to tread roughshod where angels had feared even to knock!

Doctor Yardley turned away. Then he turned back again, and looked at me.

"You've stood the years remarkably well, Lucy. You weren't very pretty as a girl, as I remember, but you are now."

I started backing away. This was altogether too much, and I even wondered if he was losing his mind. But he held me back—or at least his manner did, and then what he was saying.

"This marriage, Lucy . . . of my daughter.—Seymour

seems a charming fellow. The difference in age isn't important."

I remembered that his own difference of age had been the same.

"And his mother is a Mason from Fauquier County. But —she didn't look as happy as . . . Well, no matter."

I screwed up my courage.

"It's a lot of matter," I said flatly. "It's Melusina's match, pure and simple. The child isn't in love with him—she's doing it entirely for you."

He stood there for an instant, looking at me, his bent shoulders gradually straightening, his grave eyes probing, and so terribly troubled.

"For . . . *me?*" he said at last, very quietly and gently.

I heard the door upstairs slam, and I turned and fled, scuttling out and away as fast as I could go, my heart beating wildly. And I didn't stop running till I'd got to Long Wall Street.

There, sitting very calmly in his open car, and grinning at me like an ape, was Mr. William Quincy Adams Haines.

"What . . . what did you do?" I cried, when I'd got my breath.

"I just told the old gentleman you'd commissioned me to write the life and letters of your father and your grandfather, and of course I badly needed any recollections he had.—*And* put in a few home truths about Brother Seymour."

"Look, young man," I said. "You're heading for trouble."

His face sobered instantly. In fact, as he leaned forward, it was quite grim.

"No trouble that connects with Mr. Mason Seymour is too much for me," he said evenly. "I hate that guy's guts. —Begging your pardon, Miss Lucy," he added with a grin.

"But—you can't hate anybody's . . . anybody you don't even know," I said, rather helplessly.

"It just happens I do know him," Bill Haines said. "And I don't like him, or anything about him."

"I'm beginning to see that," I said.

He opened the car door.

"Get in," he said peremptorily. "I'll take you home."

I hadn't intended going home, but I got in. He started the car. "Where does Seymour live?" he asked, almost civilly.

"Up the street."

I indicated the turn, and when we passed England Street I pointed out the old Ball house, set back in a screen of mimosa and poplars covered with great pale green and orange tulips.

"He rents it," I said. "That's his servant."

He looked at the white man in a bowler hat and black sack suit just getting out of the Ford coupé there, and scowled. I glanced at him quickly, hoping he had not also seen the figure of a woman in a flowered print dress who slipped just then through the hedge and into the empty Israel Lane garden. I don't think he had; he was too much occupied in scowling, for no reason that I know, at Mason Seymour's valet Luton. But I had seen her. I never should have, if we hadn't been just in front of the gate. And I was sorry. In a small town it's better not to see too much.

Bill Haines speeded the car up, and we went along, just as Hallie Taswell came out of the Lane gate and hurried past us down toward Palace Green. Her face was streaked where the powder she'd hastily daubed on had touched tear streaks; it was as ravaged as a garden after a storm had gone over it.

I saw Bill glance at her, and I knew he'd seen her creep through the hedge. His lips twisted ever so faintly.

"You're a . . . an intolerant young man, aren't you?" I said.

He looked straight ahead.

"I . . . guess so," he said briefly.

"You haven't lived very long, yet," I said. "The only thing I'm afraid of is that you won't, unless you mend your ways. Summers Baldwin said you wanted to be an architect. You'd better stick to bricks and mortar and let people's lives alone. Especially down here. People are awfully chary about strangers interfering in their private business."

He flushed a little. "This is different. That fellow's a louse."

"I dare say," I said. "Possibly Faith might have done something about it until you blundered in. Now she'll marry him or bust, just to show you you can't do . . . all this sort of thing."

He'd drawn up on the cobblestone siding in front of my house and sat slumped down behind the wheel, his battered hat pulled down over his eyes, utterly and almost comically dejected. I started toward the house.

"Say, Miss Lucy," he called suddenly. I turned back. "I mean, people do fall in love at first sight, don't they? Or am I just nuts in the May moon?"

"Both propositions are self-evident, Mr. Haines," I said.

He grinned ruefully and slumped still farther down behind his wheel.

I opened the door and bent down to pick up a card that had been slipped under it. It was Mason Seymour's, and on it was written, "Requests the pleasure of your company at supper Saturday evening at half-past seven o'clock."

I tore it in two and threw it in the fireplace. I didn't want Bill to see it. There was something too final and rather smug about it.

That day was the first day in her life, except when she had measles and mumps and was away at school, that Faith Yardley didn't come to see me. When she was a child it had been twice a day she'd trudged across the Court House Green and into Francis Street. But today she didn't come, and I regarded Mr. Bill Haines, lurched in front of the fireplace on the needlepoint ottoman, without favor. He never stayed in the office. It was like having a sick Newfoundland puppy at my heels.

And then, all of a sudden, he got up and picked up his hat. I glanced up from the sock I was knitting for the Alaska mission, a sudden feeling of alarm contracting my heart. I could hear the church clock striking ten as I said, "Where are you going, Bill?"

"I'm going to see Seymour."

I got to my feet instantly.

"*Please* don't!"

There was something in his face that frightened me.

"You'll just be sorry you didn't keep out of this——"

He'd gone. I heard the hinge of the office door creak, and his heavy steps on the wood floor, and the hinge creak again, and then the engine of his car start.

I sat there actually trembling. How ever had I got so mixed up, I thought, with this absurd young man . . . and all in less than thirty-six hours! But I had. He'd barged into my placid life just as he had into Doctor Yardley's . . . and Faith's. He'd probably restore us, like Williamsburg, if he didn't first send us all to Bruton Churchyard from nervous prostration.

I don't know how long I sat there. I know that the church

clock had struck the half-hour, and the hour, and he hadn't come back. I suddenly realized that I was pacing the floor as I hadn't paced it since that day in 1927 when the Restoration came to Williamsburg and I knew I'd always have a roof over my head and never have to depend on the bitter charity of kinfolk, even if I lived to be as old as Methuselah.

Then I heard Bill's car stop quietly, and waited, my heart in my mouth, for his step in the hall. But it didn't come, and after a while I got up and slipped out into the bright moonlight over to the office. He was sitting on the doorstep, his head bent forward on his two hands, his elbows on his knees.

He looked up, his face as pale as death in the moonlight.

"You were right, Miss Lucy," he said. "You said I'd be sorry—and I am."

He got up, bent forward suddenly and kissed my cheek. "Good night, Miss Lucy."

If anybody ever in all the world had told me that I'd do what I did that night, I would have been utterly horrified, as well, of course, as utterly incredulous. If it hadn't been that I saw it all in the papers, over and again, for weeks afterwards, I wouldn't have believed I actually did it, even after I did. I don't even know what I had in mind. I only know that I suddenly realized that my own life would never have meant anything without Faith Yardley, and now this young man had given it another kind of meaning, and it was all a sort of destiny, my life and theirs.

And I had to do something.

I went back into the house—I know it sounds terrible and quite unbelievable, but it's quite true, it was in the New York papers—and got the old pistol that my father had always kept in the linen press and that I'd kept after I lived alone and the locks on the doors and windows were rusty and dilapidated. I put it in the old reticule that I keep bits of calico for patchwork quilts in, and turned out the lights. Then I crept out and through Miss Mary Seaman's back garden to Duke of Gloucester Street, and zigzagged to Botetourt Street and to Nicholson Street.

It was quite light, almost as light as day, in the moon, and the honeysuckle and roses along the way were almost overpowering, they were so fragrant. I slipped into the dark jungle garden of the Lane house and around in back, past the old brick kitchen and the smoke house, and through the fence down by the spring house into Mason Seymour's garden.

The great clumps of box were black where they cast their shadow, and pale grey-green where the moon touched them. The grass was wet with heavy dew, and my soles were thin. I slipped through the box at a place I knew—had known since I played there forty years and more ago—and into that secluded secret garden that helped make Mason Seymour as fascinating and dangerous as he was. Then I tiptoed across the brick path and the terrace with its elaborate summer furniture, by the pool with its yellow marble basin, and up to the lighted window of the garden room . . . library, I suppose he called it, because it does have some books, and the writing table with a marble top like the one in the upstairs hall of the Palace.

I don't know now what I thought I would or could do . . . just as I expect the old duck in the Palace Canal doesn't know very clearly what she hopes to accomplish when she sets up such a racket and clatter, drawing visitors away from the nest snuggled down in the myrtle and creeper at the foot of the chinaberry tree.

I know I crept forward very quietly. I could see him, sitting at the table in the soft shaded glow of the lamp. The window was open. As I came closer, across the elaborate planting myrtle and rhododendron and roses and bay I saw his face, just as I opened my lips to call his name, and found them frozen and soundless. Mason Seymour was there, but he was motionless and quite dead, his face hideously wounded and mutilated.

# 6

It seemed an eternity that I stood there, staring at the silent
awful figure of Mason Seymour. And when later the Commonwealth Attorney kept saying, "What did you think,
Miss Lucy?—You must have thought something!" I could
only say over and over that I hadn't. I hadn't thought anything. The slumped figure at the table blotted everything
else from my brain. It was like gazing into a brilliant incan-
descent light and turning away, the image of the filament
still burning on the retina, blinding one for the moment to
every other image. Even when I turned and groped my way
back the zigzag path I'd come by, it was all I could see, in
the glistening pool, against the moonlit box—that terrible
silent figure.

I've never understood people's doing things and not remembering they've done them. Even under the influence of
strong drink or strong emotion. I suppose it's because I was
never under the influence of anything, either drink or emotion, that was very powerful, until that night. Because I do
understand it now. I know it's possible to complete a whole
extraordinary pattern of events and have no memory of the
individual steps that composed it. All I know now is that I
reached the hedge and started back through it, and that all
of a sudden my knees turned to water and my heart gave a
nauseating lurch as something reached out, catching at me.
The soft warm leaves of the box closed in around my face,
suffocating me, so that I struggled like a drowning person,
my breath strangling in my throat. It was so silent and hor-

rible! I wrenched and fought my way through and out into
the air, staggered through the tall wet grass behind the old
spring house, through the overgrown garden, past the deserted tumble-down house into Scotland Street, too terrified to look back.

And when they asked me if there'd been any one else in
the garden, I had to admit there might have been a whole
race of giants there and I'd never have seen one of them. All
I could see was that image of Mason Seymour burned on my
brain, all I could feel was the box suffocating me with its
warm leaves and that thing pulling me back.

Then I was at the garden gate of Yardley Hall. That's
why I can believe now that people can do things and not
know they do them . . . for I didn't know I'd fled down
Scotland Street across the old mill bridge and past the hanging tree, across England Street, until I reached the white
picket gate with the cannonball weight, and stopped dead,
held by a new fear greater even than the one I'd left behind.
I think God must take care of foolish people. I don't know
any other reason there could be than that, for me to halt
abruptly as I did, suddenly aware of where I was, my hand
on the iron latch, almost as if a warning voice had spoken at
my side.

Because the sound of the chain on the old wheel in the
tiny well house was too thin and cautious to have pierced
my numbed senses by itself, and the shadowy hand moving
to draw the dripping oak bucket to the whitewashed ledge
too dark and stealthy for me to have seen without knowing
that I must look just there.

The pale unearthly light that fell on the peaked roof of
the well house cast its shadow across the figure beside it, so
that I couldn't see it, even after I heard a splash and dabble
and the thin sound of the chain again. The frogs in the little brook in the ravine down by the spring house waked,
and croaked a time or two, a catbird stirred and was still,
and after that the only sound I could hear was my own
heart pounding in my ears.

Behind me, across Scotland Street, were the dark gardens
of the old Audrey house, and the Tucker mound, and the
dark clipped cedars like ominous sentinels. In front, at the
end of the brick path, was Yardley Hall, visible only
because I knew it was there, beyond the great old elms,
through the screen of crape myrtle and mimosa and the rose

gardens. And between me and it was some one hidden in the shadows.

I've never pretended to be very brave, and I'm not really ashamed to admit that a panic such as I didn't know my mind had room for seized me. I turned and ran—certainly faster than you'd believe I could run, looking at me. I'd never known the streets of Williamsburg were so dark and silent and deserted before, or that the gnarled tumorous trunks of the old paper mulberries could be so liquid and full of terrifying movement. I fled along England Street, across the Court House green, past the Powder Horn and into Francis Street, my footsteps echoing so that it seemed to me the whole town must wake out of its sleep. I know my heart almost burst with relief as I came in sight of Bill Haines's car parked by the white hitching rail in front of my house, and the garden gate closing softly behind me brought sharp tears to my eyes.

I steadied myself against it for an instant, drew a long breath . . . and then stopped short as I happened to look down, staring with utter—oh, I don't know what to call it: horror isn't the word, for that's what I'd felt gazing in at Mason Seymour, and terror isn't it, for that was what the shadow by the well house had brought; consternation, I suppose, or deadly panic again—at the old silk cord of my reticule still clutched tightly in my frozen grasp. The reticule was gone. Only the frayed cords were there.

For one dreadful instant I stood there, then my hand felt for the latch. I had to go back! Somewhere on that journey home I had dropped my bag—with my father's pistol in it —and I had to find it.

And then I heard the hinge on the office creak and groan, and silhouetted against the white clapboard was the tall dark figure of my boarder. I tried to move, but my feet had turned to lead. My own door, with the brass knocker shaped like a lute gleaming in the moonlight, was as far away as ancient Troy. And as Bill Haines's towering figure loomed closer and closer, I felt my knees give way altogether. Melusina says it's silly to faint, and I suppose it is; but I know there was something extraordinarily restoring in feeling myself being lifted up as if my legs were feathers, not solid lead, and finding myself the next instant on the sofa in my own parlor.

Or there would have been if Bill Haines hadn't been gaz-

ing so strangely at the frayed black cords still wound
around my wrist and clutched in my fingers.

I tried to close my eyes again, but he'd seen me open
them. He reached out his big bronzed hand and smoothed
the hair back from my forehead, looking at me the way a
doctor looks at a feverish child.

"Where have you been, Miss Lucy?" he asked quietly.
"And what's this?"

He picked up the old cord.

I shook my head. "It's nothing, really." But that wasn't
true. I had to go back and find that bag. I tried to struggle
upright. He saw, I suppose, the panic in my face, because his
eyes sharpened. Then his grasp on my wrist tightened so
abruptly that I sank back, suddenly rather frightened of Mr.
Bill Haines.

Yet I know now that nothing in the world could have
held me there if I'd known that across the Green, like the
dotted lines they use in restoration drawings to connect a
missing foundation with parts they've unearthed still standing, there stretched a line, invisible but oh so horribly inex-
orable, connecting those broken ends of the cord of my reticule . . . connecting my house at the one end with Mason
Seymour's at the other. Or not Mason Seymour's house but
—murder . . . and not my house, and—oddly enough—not
me, but the young man sitting there beside me, with the old
frayed cord in his troubled hands.

I know it sounds all too dreadful. No one ever believes
that murder, or the suspicion of murder, can actually fall on
oneself, or the people one knows—being in some way reserved for persons who live in a vague limbo that people of
our sort never touch from the cradle to the grave. Ten
thousand shall fall at thy right hand and ten thousand shall
fall at thy left, but it shall not come nigh thee. Believing
that, I suppose, about all catastrophe is what makes people
go on doing dangerous, or even quite ordinary things, like
crossing streets. And, of course, the comforting thing about
it is that it's perfectly true. The surprising thing is when one
finds one is suddenly and inexplicably mixed up in the ten
thousand on his right hand.

And if anybody had told me, the morning I bought that
black cord at Miss Mullins's old store that ran back and
back like a train of toy box cars from the Duke of Gloucester Steet where the Parish house is now, and where the

hopes and fears and joys and sorrows of Williamsburg used to meet each day, that I would use it some day as a noose to tie around the neck of people who meant more than anything in all the world to me, I should have thought they had taken leave of their senses. Even while I lay there on the sofa, every muscle in my body painfully protesting against the violent and unbelievable exertion it had been put to, I didn't realize how much that cord was to mean. If I had, I should never have taken it out of Bill Haines's hands and tossed it into the fireplace.—Not without instantly getting up and setting a match to it, at any rate. And I should certainly never have left it there for the City Sergeant to unearth from under the rolls of coagulated dust and lint out of the carpet sweeper that Community, my colored maid, still deposits there and that I've long since given up the futile business of protesting against.

I suppose it's equally futile to say that if I hadn't lived all my life in a small town, and learned, not without bad blood and bitter tears, that the least said soonest mended and that saying nothing is the best of all defenses, I wouldn't then have kept on saying, "It's nothing, really it isn't!" For if, instead of saying that, I'd come out with the whole awful thing, it wouldn't have looked to everybody—including Bill himself—that I thought he'd done it, and that was why I hadn't spoken. Whether I actually thought—I've tried so many times since then to make up my mind about it—that it was all too fantastic, and like most horrible things would vanish with the light of day, or—and if this is true I hope I'll be forgiven it—whether actually, deep in my secret heart I did think Bill had done it, I don't really know. When they kept saying "Why didn't you call the police?" I couldn't think of any reasonable answer, and when Bill said, "For God's sake, Miss Lucy, why didn't you tell me?" it sounded too utterly stupid to say I wanted to deny it as long as I could. It may be I was just too exhausted for my brain to function. I know my extremities wouldn't, and for the first time in years, when I'd sent Bill back to the office, I crept up into the fourposter in the chamber behind the parlor, where my father and mother had slept and where I was born and where my father had been born, instead of climbing upstairs to my own dormered room.

That was why I didn't hear the hinge of the office door creak during the night, or hear Sergeant Priddy come the next morning. Although I'm not sure I would have, even if I'd been upstairs, because it was already eight o'clock when I woke up. Through the last remnants of sleep I heard the silver bell in Bruton Church tower, and lay there, my eyes still closed, trying to tell myself all the vague horror in the threshold of my mind was something I'd dreamed, that it had never happened, couldn't have happened—not in Williamsburg.

Then I opened my eyes. Community's black kinky head was thrust between the apricot pink of the door and the frame, her eyes the size of coconuts, her face the color of chocolate that has been exposed to the summer heat.

"If you was done gone, an' the young gennaman was done gone, Miss Lucy, Ah wasn't know *what* to think."

She drew a deep collapsible breath and licked her thick lips.

"Isn't Mr. Haines here, Munity?" I asked sharply.

"No'm. They done got him in jail, leas' that's what they tell me. John say he sawr Sergeant Priddy takin' him off fust thing this mawnin'."

She put my early coffee on the round Sheffield waiter on the table—it was my mother's that I bought back from a cousin after the Restoration came—and poured me out a cup.

"Then it's all true," I thought desperately. "Mason Seymour *is* dead. I didn't dream it."

That black hunched figure through the window swam behind my closed eyelids.

"They tell me who it war shot Mr. Seymour used an ol' shotgun lak you hunt possum with," Community said. She pushed the shutters open so that the sun streamed across the threadbare roses and lilies in the brussels carpet.

I sat up abruptly and reached for my coffee, but my hand trembled too violently. Community, who isn't as stupid as she looks, came back to the bed, emptied the saucer into the water pitcher on the washstand, and handed me the cup not quite so full.

"They say Mr. Luton—that's the valley, they call him— he foun' him stark daid this mo'nin' when he come down stairs. Say he call the po-lice. Say he runnin' roun' lak a chicken with his haid off."

I put the coffee cup down, trying desperately to keep it from rattling against the silver waiter. Community—she's the fifth generation of the family that's worked for mine; even her name, before she married a perfectly trifling worthless nigger, was the same as mine—stood looking at me for an instant. Then she bent down and picked up my white shoes. The heavy dew had drenched them so that where they'd dried, a brown stain was left like a wave above the thin soles. She scraped off a blade of grass that had stuck and dried to the glazed kidskin. Then she reached down again, picked up my damp stockings, and went out the side door onto the piazza. When I got up I saw my shoes on the rail, freshly cleaned. On the steps, drying in the sun, was the pair of brown-and-white oxfords that Bill Haines had had on the night before. They too had been freshly cleaned, and the faint line of demarcation where they'd been wet and had dried was visible where the cleaner hadn't dried yet.

I looked from one pair of them to the other, and my heart stopped very quietly for a moment. If Community hadn't known what to think when she'd first come that morning, she knew now, and was acting accordingly. The position of the two pair of shoes, Bill's and mine, almost ostentatiously having no relation to each other, was proof of that. For an instant I had an almost irresistible impulse to hurry down the narrow brick path to the kitchen and tell her that Bill Haines and I hadn't gone out, hand in hand, through the dew and put an end to Mason Seymour, but I stopped just over the threshold of the chamber and went slowly back, not at all knowing what to do. If I went out in back, Community would be eyeing me, and if I went out in front I'd probably run smack into a great many things I'd prefer to avoid permanently.

Not that I could, of course. Already every time I looked through the window I saw the glass curtain of my neighbor across the street fall hastily back into place. The phone had rung four times while I was trying to find some laces for my last summer's shoes. I had the panicky unhappy feeling a caged animal must have, sensing a strange new world closing in about him. The phone rang again as I got one shoe on, and for a moment I thought of not answering it again, and then I knew I didn't dare not, because Faith Yardley might be calling me.

But I didn't answer it. I just sat there like the child in the nursery rhyme, one shoe off and one shoe on, perfectly appalled at myself. For that was the first time it had actually and literally occurred to my odd mind that if Mason Seymour was dead, then Faith Yardley couldn't possibly marry him. I suppose that sounds like the rankest kind of nonsense, but it's true, nevertheless. And if you'd lived in Williamsburg, where there's not been a murder of any sort for years and years, and not one among the better classes since Judge Wythe's nephew—or so they say—poisoned him for his money, you'd understand it readily enough. Even that happened in Richmond, but because the Judge's ghost still haunts the house in Palace Green we tend to think of it as our own. And it happened well over a hundred years ago. And since nothing startling except the Restoration has happened that I can recall since the Armistice in 1918, you can see it isn't as surprising as it might be that the mere fact of stumbling upon a murder at a moment when I had a sort of remote degree of murder in my own heart, and a weapon in my own hand, so to speak, should have for the moment driven out everything but the murder itself.

But now, as I sat there in my grandmother's slipper chair, one shoe hanging limply in my hand, the telephone ringing, ringing, ringing in my ears, the implications of Mason Seymour's death crowded and swarmed in my brain, like a million termites, overwhelming me.

Then I could hear, plodding up the stairs, like Merimée's black Venus, Community's heavy tread. She put her head in at the door—her face is always expressionless as an ebony mask, so there's never any use of looking at her to see what to expect—and said, "Miss Lucy . . . Abraham he phone' to say Mis' Melusina feelin' po'ly this mawnin', an' would you come ovah, if it's convenient, jus' as quick as yo' can git there. Ah tol' him yes."

She paused. "An' heah's yo' shoes. They's near about dry."

She put my shoes that weren't in the least dry and still had that unhealthy grey look that shoes have before they do dry, in my lap, took the old one out of my hand, reached down and slipped the other off my foot. She set them both in the press and wiped off the door with her dust rag. I had the uneasy feeling that she was wiping off the fingerprints as they do in motion pictures, but I may have been wrong, of course. I do know, however, that never in the thirty years she's waited on me, through very lean years and some not quite so lean, has she ever so much as allowed me to carry a damp pocket handkerchief. Some one she'd

heard about had died of galloping consumption for wearing
a freshly-laundered petticoat to a ball at the College.

I put on the shoes without a word, however, feeling the
way I expect a person who thinks he's perfectly sane feels
around some one he knows thinks he's not. Community's
heavy steps plodding back down the stairs took my heart
with them, down and down. That had the effect, however,
of making me hurry. Melusina Yardley never felt poorly
without considerable justification—no ordinary vapors had
strength enough to overcome her. And whether it was just
the fact that Mason Seymour was gone, and with him the
prospect of the perpetual endowment of Yardley Hall, or
whether there was something deeper behind it, I must admit
I was almost vulgarly curious to find out. If I hadn't, in fact,
been quite so curious, I would have found out sooner. Instead of going down Francis Street, through the Travis
House gardens and through Palace Green, which would
have taken me a little longer but would have avoided the
scene of the late unpleasantness, I was in too great a hurry.
I rushed straight through Botetourt Street and into Scotland
Street, and that's as far as I got.

A car coming along pulled up at the curb. I saw with dismay that it had "Police Williamsburg Va." on the door. And
at the wheel was Sergeant Priddy, and beside him was the
Commonwealth Attorney, John Carter Crabtree.

# 7

To say that I couldn't have picked two people out of the entire universe that I'd have preferred less to see is the most definite kind of an understatement. It happens that I've known both of them since they were little more than tadpoles. John Crabtree had been a mischievous freckle-faced imp in my Sunday school class. Sergeant Priddy had been there too, but was much better behaved. It seemed almost too ironical that the two of them now filled me with as much dismay as I dare say I filled them with Sunday after Sunday in the back room of the old Wythe house, where they turned up with telltale mud from the creek on their boots and no idea of what king ate grass in the fields of Babylon.

John Crabtree ran down the window on his side and leaned out. He was definitely troubled.

"Miss Lucy, what all do you know about that young fellow that's staying with you—William Haines?" he asked.

"Nothing at all," I said. "Except that he's considerate and right well behaved."

I hesitated. If I said Summers Baldwin sent him to me it would be all over town in five minutes. I've never known about walls, but I do know that in Williamsburg the grass and trees have ears; and I didn't know just how far Summers Baldwin would care to extend his sponsorhsip of the young man. He might, I thought, quite reasonably draw the line at murder, for instance.

So I said, "A friend gave him my address. He's studying architecture."

John Crabtree grunted.

"Is it true you put him in jail?" I asked.

He shook his head. It was obvious he was puzzled about just what to do with Mr. William Quincy Adams Haines. Sergeant Priddy muttered something to him and his face brightened.

"I wonder if you'd mind steppin' over there a few minutes, Miss Lucy?" he said.

No one in all the world will ever know how very much I minded just that very thing. But with both of them—and they constituted, between them, the entire force and majesty of the local law of the Commonwealth of Virginia, in spite of the fact that they once put a frog in the font when some very important Northern baby whose parents had bought a plantation on the James River was to be baptised —craning their necks out of the police car at me, all I could do was say, "Not at all."

That's how it happened that I found myself in Mason Seymour's house instead of in Yardley Hall just then. And I wasn't alone. When Sergeant Priddy opened the door into the drawing room—it always astonishes me how professional interior decorators can make all rooms look alike and all look like museums—I saw my lodger. He was slumped down on the small of his back in a canary-yellow leather fireside chair, his chin resting on his collarbone, his jaw set, looking as if he didn't want any part of it and the sooner they took it all away the better he'd like it. I had the idea that that applied especially to the other two men in the room.

I didn't know one of them, except that I could see from his sleek dark hair and small dark mustache, and the way he closed his white even teeth and smiled so that an astonishing number of them showed, and his brown checked coat and yellow pullover sweater, that he was kin to Mason Seymour in temperament as well as in blood. I was surprised, because I hadn't known that any of Mason's relatives were in Williamsburg. The other man was Luton, the valet. He was really more than that. He was a sort of confidence man, although I think that means something I don't mean. I mean he didn't go about selling public bridges and gold bricks, which I believe is what the word implies. But he had Mason Seymour's complete confidence—managed his household affairs and the colored servants, arranged his parties and that sort of thing, and I suppose knew more about Mason Seymour's business than Mason knew himself. In fact, if he hadn't had that discreet black-coated air and worn a derby hat I don't think any one would ever have taken him for a servant. He stood by the closed door off the library. He'd been talking to the other man, stopped when I stepped in, and bowed.

"This is Mr. Talbot Seymour, Miss Lucy," Sergeant Priddy said, and as frequently happens in Williamsburg, it was just naturally assumed that outlanders know who we are. I heard Luton whisper, "Miss Randolph, sir." Mr. Talbot Seymour bowed politely.

Bill Haines had got to his feet. He favored me with a wry grin, and devoted his attention thereafter to a studied examination of an embroidered map of the counties of England framed in bird's-eye maple over a satinwood table that had a lovely old wine-cooler on it, filled with pale peonies the color of home-made strawberry ice-cream and smelling like an undertaker's parlor. In fact the room had that general air, and there was something almost professional too about the way John Crabtree pulled up a chair and told us all to sit down.

I gathered he'd only arrived on the scene a moment or so before. He glanced at Sergeant Priddy, who nodded almost reassuringly it seemed to me, and cleared his throat. But before he could begin there was a tap at the door and Marshall Yardley, of all people under the sun, walked in. He glanced around, nodded to Talbot Seymour, gave me a sort of puzzled frown as if it wasn't clear just what I was doing there, and stepped over to John Crabtree. There ensued a brief whispered conference. I heard one bit of it, and it was sufficient to explain everything.

"Aunt Mel thinks the family ought to be represented. I think we ought to stay out of it, but you know Aunt Mel."

John Crabtree nodded sympathetically, and Marshall Yardley came over and sat down on the gold brocatelle upholstered sofa between the windows, beside me. He crossed his legs and folded his arms, his jaw set very like Bill Haines's.

Life as Melusina's favorite certainly had its corduroy stretches, I thought. Then I wondered, all of a sudden, looking at Marshall with oddly new eyes, if it had ever had much else. It must be eating bitter fruit indeed, I thought, to come here now, where the man Ruth Napier was so mad about lay dead, not fifty feet away from us. Almost as if he were answering me, he uncrossed his legs, ran his two open palms back over his head, drew a deep breath and relaxed back against the soft cushions.

Of the four men in that room—Talbot Seymour the cousin, George Luton the servant, Bill Haines my lodger, and Marshall Yardley, Faith's cousin—two of them hated the dead man; one frankly and for any one who cared to listen to hear; the other bitterly and quietly. Marshall Yardley had never in all his life been free to announce from the housetops that he hated anybody's guts, as the extraordinary Mr. Haines had felt not the least compunction about doing . . . and dammed-up streams are dangerous streams. I've heard that at lots of Commencements, and besides it's quite true. Moreover, I thought, Sergeant Priddy, regarding the various people in the room with a detached and shrewd eye, was just the man to see all that.

"You can tell Mr. Crabtree what you know about this, Luton," he said.

The valet looked at the Commonwealth Attorney—I have to keep calling him that so I don't get him mixed up in my own mind with the boy I've always known, and underestimate his intelligence and honesty, and kindliness.

"I think, sir, I should be allowed counsel," he said, and then, as everybody looked completely flabbergasted, he went on, his pale face quite expressionless. "You see, sir, it was I who found Mr. Seymour's body. I was in the house alone with him all night. The doctor says he was killed between half-past ten and eleven; there was no one in the house then but myself. I should like to point out that my position is definitely equivocal. . . ."

Many Virginians speak with what some people would call a drawl, I suppose, but John Carter Crabtree speaks even slower than most, almost as if he weren't fully awake yet. It deceives a lot of people.

"If you think anybody's goin' to railroad you to the chair, Mr. Luton, you're dead wrong," he said amiably. "All we want to know is what happened around here. I shouldn't think you'd need counsel to tell us that. Would you, Marshall?—You're a lawyer."

"Not unless Luton did it," Marshall Yardley said. "You can't make a man give evidence against himself, of course."

Mr. Luton winced, in a respectful way. Bill Haines left

off his study of the geography of the British Isles, turned around with a grin and attended the remainder of the proceedings, leaning forward, his elbows resting on the high back of the canary-yellow leather chair.

Luton hesitated only an instant. "I went upstairs shortly after half-past nine, then, sir," he said.

I looked at him rather curiously, never having seen much of him before. His head was oddly shaped, large across the skull and tapering to a pointed chin; his ears rather like an afterthought, when the proper size for his head had run low and a larger one had to be used. He was sandy-haired, with mildish blue eyes and a thin upper lip deeply grooved or possibly scarred. His shoulders were narrow, or possibly merely looked narrow beside the broad checked and somewhat padded shoulders of Talbot Seymour, the dead man's cousin, lounging in the window near him.

"Mr. Seymour was expecting a caller."

The valet stopped, and glanced ever so hesitantly at Marshall Yardley.

"He suggested earlier I go to the movie, but he thought of such a number of things he wanted arranged after the colored servants had gone that I was too late for the second show. I went to bed instead. I didn't hear Mr. Seymour come upstairs, but as his hours were always inclined to be irregular, I thought nothing of it until I got up this morning. I saw the lights still on and the front door open, and found him in the library. I called the doctor and Sergeant Priddy at once, sir."

"You didn't see anybody, or hear anything?"

"I didn't hear the shot, if that's what you mean, sir," Luton said a little stiffly. "I've had a very hard couple of days, since Mr. Seymour's engagement to Miss Yardley was announced, and I was glad to get off my feet. I have trouble with my legs, is why I'm in domestic service, sir."

"Did you *see* anybody around?" John Crabtree drawled. "Was there any company yesterday?"

Mr. Luton hesitated again. "As a matter of fact, sir, there were a number of people here all evening.—The last that I saw was Mr. Haines here."

My lodger was absorbed in trying to straighten a bent and mutilated cigarette into sufficient resemblance of the original so that it would draw.

He barely glanced up. "Go on," he said.

Mr. Luton moistened his lips. "I'm sorry, sir," he said. "But I have to tell these gentlemen what I saw."

"Sure," Bill said. "Go right ahead. Don't mind me."

He threw the cigarette into the fireplace and pulled out his pipe and his tobacco pouch. John Crabtree's eyes rested oddly on him, and Sergeant Priddy turned and spat out of the window. Nicotine is very good for roses, as a matter of fact, except that it does spot them right badly.

"Mr. Haines came over about ten o'clock, sir. Mr. Seymour was engaged."

"Doin' what?" the Commonwealth Attorney drawled.

"He was talking to a young lady."

"Name?"

"It was . . . Miss Ruth Napier, sir."

The man didn't look at Marshall Yardley, and Marshall sat there without moving a muscle or batting an eye.

"Go on."

"Mr. Haines didn't come in. He stood out on the porch. I came downstairs and told him Mr. Seymour did not care to be disturbed. He said that was too bad, because he was going to be disturbed plenty. His manner was very . . . belligerent. I presumed he must have been drinking."

"As a matter of fact," Bill Haines said placidly, "I'd had three glasses of Miss Lucy's raspberry shrub. That stuff is mighty powerful."

A hogshead of it wouldn't discommode a fly, except for sheer bulk. I saw the Commonwealth Attorney smile a little.

Mr. Luton's discreet voice went on.

"Mr. Haines's manner was equally flippant last night, sir. I had to call Mr. Seymour. He came out, and I gathered he recognized Mr. Haines, because he said, 'Oh, it's the White Knight again.' Mr. Haines said, 'No, it's the Eagle Scout, and I'm behind on my good deed for the day. That's why I'm here—I couldn't go to bed till I'd got it done.' Mr. Seymour turned around and told me to tell Miss Napier he'd be back shortly, and they went into the dining room and closed the door. I went back to the library, but Miss Napier wasn't there."

"Where was she?"

It was Sergeant Priddy who thrust that in.

The lift of the servant's brows was barely perceptible.

"I didn't attempt to inquire into that, Sergeant. I went back upstairs, undressed and went to bed immediately."

John Crabtree fished a wadded piece of paper out of his coat pocket and unfolded it. "So that, to the best of your knowledge, the last person to see Mr. Mason Seymour was a young man named Haines."

"That's correct, sir."

That statement scrawled on a leaf torn out of Sergeant Priddy's notebook had, I take it, been responsible for my young lodger's being routed out of bed at daybreak. I glanced at him out of the corner of my eye. He looked extraordinarily composed, leaning forward easily, his forearms resting on the back of the chair, a detached and even mildly amused expression on his not handsome but certainly very attractive face.

In fact, it seemed to me he looked almost too composed. It wasn't natural and it wasn't human, and he'd been so extremely both up to this time. I thought back to his barging out of the house the night before, and his coming back, sitting there in the office door, saying, "You said I'd be sorry, and I am." And he'd meant it. If he'd never meant another thing in all his life he'd meant that—I'd stake my own life on it. And yet here he was, letting them go on without putting in a serious word in his own defense, exactly as if nothing of the least consequence had come to his personal notice for days and days.

"Was anybody else here?"

John Crabtree's voice ambled along like an old horse in the shade. "I mean, beside the lady and Mr. Haines here?— How about this gentleman?"

He looked at Mr. Talbot Seymour, who instantly and with great aplomb projected himself into the very center of things.

"I got to town here about half-past nine," he said. "I'm on my way up from Southern Pines to New York. I read the announcement of my cousin's engagement in the Richmond papers, thought I'd drop down and congratulate him. I phoned from the Inn, about a quarter to ten. He said he was tied up for the evening, and that Luton had gone to bed, so if I didn't mind would I crawl in where I was, bring my kit over first thing this morning in time for breakfast, and stay on for the wedding."

Mr. Talbot Seymour made a slight movement with his shoulders.

"And this," he said, "is what I walk into."

I think we all—except Bill Haines—shifted a little uneasily, as if we were each of us, in some way, personally responsible for his unfortunate breach of Southern hospitality. Talbot Seymour lighted a cigarette and blew a long slow column of smoke through his thin nostrils.

"Then you didn't see your cousin at all?"

He shook his head. He didn't, I thought, seem particularly grief-stricken at that fact, but then he wasn't trying to pretend he was, I must say that for him. He did, however, have the air of a man who was watching his own brief with a pretty sharp eye—almost sharper, it seemed, than the occasion demanded. But then he had no way, I realized, of knowing we were all perfectly honest. And after all, his cousin had been murdered. It wasn't as if he had just died of pneumonia, or something.

"And you're staying at the Inn?" John Crabtree asked.

Talbot Seymour laughed shortly. "Well, I stayed there last night. My things are here now. I don't suppose there's any objection to my continuing on. After all, I'm the nearest relative. I suppose I'd be expected to stick around till the mess is cleaned up."

There was an instant silence in the room, not sharp or dramatic at all, but the kind of drawing-room silence that meets a pretty profound breach of good taste. Even Mr. Seymour, whose skin, I should imagine, was fairly thick, felt it.

"Of course, I'd be glad to clear out if the local gendarmes want to kick up a row about it."

"Wouldn't want to put you to any extra trouble at all, sir," John Crabtree drawled courteously. I imagine that only Sergeant Priddy and I, who knew him of old, knew that Mr. Talbot Seymour had made probably one of the biggest mistakes of his life.

The Commonwealth Attorney turned back to Mr. Luton.

"Anybody else here, last night?"

The valet hesitated again, and when he spoke his quiet voice was still more reluctant than it had been. "Several people called during the evening, sir. Doctor Yardley came, just as Mr. Seymour was sitting down to dinner."

He turned to Marshall Yardley, beside me on the gold brocatelle sofa.

"And I beg your pardon, sir.—Mr. Marshall Yardley was here, after dinner. I happened to see you, sir, when I was bringing the brandy and soda from the sideboard."

Marshall Yardley's lips twisted in a wry smile.

"I don't think I've said I was not here, have I?" he asked, a little angrily. "The Commonwealth Attorney knows he can have a complete and detailed account of my movements at any time he cares to ask for it."

He sat forward, his flexible mouth a little grimmer than I'd seen it before.

"In fact, I'd like it to go on the record, John, that I object to all this elaborate air of discretion that Luton's putting on for the simple purpose of damning everybody. My uncle and I both came in the front gate and went out the front gate. If Luton didn't happen to be at the front door to let us in the house, it was probably because he had business elsewhere. I dare say the same applies to both Miss Napier and Mr. Haines. I object strongly to this beating about the bush that implies we all crept in and out through a hole in a hedge."

My heart sank to the bottom of my now dry shoes and lay there, trembling.

Marhsall ground out his cigarette in the ash tray on the Chippendale coffee table in front of us, and added quietly, "I can understand about people not wanting to be seen coming to this house. But as far as I know, nobody seems to have had sense to put it into practice."

"Well," the Commonwealth Attorney drawled, with a slow smile, "it sure looks like somebody did. There's no getting away from that. *Somebody* crawled through a hole in the hedge. Mason Seymour was shot from the terrace through the open window, while he was sittin' at the table writing, by somebody he never expected to do him any harm. You can tell he was surprised by the look on his face, and the way his pen's clutched in his fingers, and his chair pushed back hard, so it caught up the rug—as if he tried to get up all of a sudden and couldn't make it."

My feet and hands were as cold and remote as if they belonged to a woman in Greenland, not to me in Williamsburg.

# 8

I barely heard Bill Haines saying abruptly, "How do you know he was shot from the terrace, Mr. Crabtree?"

"Because the waddin' from the shotgun shell's out there, and you can calculate how far off the fellow was standin' by the spread of the shot."

"Have you found the gun?" Talbot Seymour asked.

John Crabtree shook his head.

"We've got one gun, but it's not the gun that killed Seymour. And that's a funny thing . . . about your hole in the hedge, Marshall."

He glanced at Sergeant Priddy, who went out into the hall. I've often wondered how long any one's heart can stop beating and he still go on living. It's a very long time, I'm sure, because mine had stopped absolutely dead for some time before Sergeant Priddy came back into the room. In his hand was my grandmother's black-beaded reticule. He put it down with a thud on the table in front of the Commonwealth Attorney, the frayed broken cords lying there, burning my eyes as if they were made of molten fire, not ancient rusty silk. I felt Bill Haines's eyes pinioned there too. Without looking at him I could see the blood recede under his deep sun-bronzed skin. Then John Crabtree's hands fumbling at the broken cord blotted everything else out from my consciousness, and then the bag was open, and there on the shiny satin lay my grandfather's old pistol.

I never knew a room could be so still. The only sound in it was the tiny tick-tick-tick of the enamelled French clock on the mantel and the roar of the blood in my ears. And then John's slow voice, each word hour-long, like water dropping from a leaky tap at night when you're sick.

"Sergeant Priddy found this caught in the box hedge this mornin'. Somebody was gettin' through there. The long grass in the Lanes' place is trampled down where they came in, and where they made a bee line back for the street again.—But this isn't what Mason Seymour was killed with."

He turned the pistol over, looking at it intently.

"The interestin' thing about it is that somebody thought they were goin' to kill him with it, and I reckon it's plain enough it's a woman. Nobody else would think of tryin' to kill a body with an old thing like this."

. . . And all the time it kept pounding in my ears that I ought to lean forward and say, "That's mine, John. I didn't really plan to kill him. I don't know what I planned to do."

I should have done it, of course. I even think now John would have understood if I had, that I could have made him understand. But then it seemed that, if I did, now that they knew Bill had been there it would point at some hidden connection, and if I didn't speak they might never know I'd been there at all. First one thing burned in my mind, then the other, and then it was too late. John Crabtree pushed the bag aside. I watched it as I imagine a half-crazed collector would watch a priceless relic being indifferently thrust aside by an auctioneer who had no inkling of its value, biding his time.

And then suddenly I saw Bill Haines straighten up. I knew in one dreadful flash that he was going to speak for me. And then my eyes met his. I don't know what he must have seen in them—or thought he saw—but he turned away silently. Then John Crabtree's voice came in, smooth and slow as molasses in January, saying, "Well, you all can go along now."

He began gathering up his things, and turned with his pleasant grin. "Mr. Haines, it looks like you're goin' to have to do a little explainin' around here, but there's no use puttin' you in jail. I reckon I'll just put you in Miss Lucy's custody instead—if she'll promise to produce you any time you're needed."

He grinned at me. My knees were like water.

"Okay, Mr. Crabtree—I'll see she does," Bill said.

It wasn't till we'd got out in the street that he said, "What he means is he'll put you in my custody. For God's sake why didn't you tell him that was your bag?"

"I couldn't," I gasped.

"You'll wish you had. I ought to have done it myself. What in . . . what did you think you were doing? Those guys aren't fools. If they could see through that glamour boy in the checked coat and through all ten layers of lard on that bird Luton, where do you think you'll land when they start on you?"

"Oh, dear!" I said, and then I didn't say any more, because Marshall Yardley caught up with us just as we got to England Street.

"Aunt Mel wants to see you, Cousin Lucy," he said. He turned to Bill.

"Why don't you go on in with Cousin Lucy, Haines, and as soon as I run over to the courthouse we can do a little checking up on this?"

"No, thanks," Bill Haines said briefly. "I've got to push along."

When Marshall left us at the garden gate I said, "Won't you come in, Bill?"

"I said No, thanks," he repeated rudely.

"You mean they'll see through everybody but you," I said with some heat. "Why, a beetle could see through you! Don't you think the first moment John Crabtree starts inquiring why Mason Seymour called you a White Knight, and why you took it upon yourself to call him out in the middle of a tête-à-tête with Ruth Napier, and why she then disappeared from sight, and why you then turn up with all this elaborate nonchalance that wouldn't deceive a rabbit, they won't instantly connect you with Ruth? And then, as soon as they find out you don't even know her, don't you think they'll go straight to Faith Yardley?"

His jaw tightened ominously.

"I don't know what happened while you were out last night," I went on, "but I do know it must have been a great deal to make a man who yesterday was inventing the most preposterous yarn to get into a girl's house to tell her he'd fallen in love with her, refuse this morning—when she probably needs friends worse than she ever needed them in her life—to accept a polite invitation to step in the place."

"Take it easy," Bill Haines said. His face was flushed a little and quite angry.

"All I have got to say is," I said, "that so long as you're in my custody, you've got to act as if you at least had half sense. Or else I'll insist they lock you up."

He stood there for a moment, his lips compressed, his eyes smouldering and unhappy and resentful. Then he shrugged. "Okay, lady."

He followed me—not with the best grace, I'm afraid—through the white picket gate into the side garden of Yardley Hall. I was so cross that I marched ahead of him well into the grounds before I suddenly felt my steps falter and my heart go quite cold.

In front of me, at my right, beyond the soft jade mountains of box, was the narrow peaked roof of the well-house with its black wheel and oiled chain. And with one sickening flash the whole unreal business of the night before leaped into my mind—the shadowy hand in the moonlight, the thin sound of the moving chain, the eerie splash and dabble of dripping water, and the hollow thud of the bucket hitting the depths of the well. I felt again the awful panicky desire to turn and flee, as I had the night before, but I dared not. I forced myself on, telling myself there was nothing there now in the broad May sunlight; the night was over.

Then I came even with the well and realized I'd stopped short before I knew it, because Bill, coming behind me, bumped into me and mumbled an apology. Then his warm strong hand closed hard on my arm.

"What is it, Miss Lucy?—Are you ill?"

I couldn't answer him. All I could do was stare at the whitewashed board that the raised bucket rested on. There was a brown stain there, against the gleaming white surface. It was blood. I knew it instantly, and with an instinct as sure as death. I felt Bill Haines's hand on my arm tighten in a sharp spasm, and relax. He saw that mark too, and he too knew what it was.

I tried to move, but I could not. All I could do was stand there with it going through my brain:

"There's blood on the well at Yardley Hall. There's blood on the well at Yardley Hall."

That rang through my head, over and over again, until he literally moved me bodily forward, saying nothing, just making me go on toward the house, around to the front, up the stairs to the big closed door. He lifted the polished brass knocker and let it fall.

"If you want to keep anything to yourself, now's the time to start, Miss Lucy," he said, just as Abraham's black face appeared in the narrow opening, and the chain fell, and we entered the dim cool hall with its far-off fragrance of pot-pourri and roses and spice pinks. A big copper basin of California poppies and blue anchusa burned on the sunburst table. Abraham closed the door, and as he did the library door opened quietly, and Doctor Yardley looked out.

He gazed at us for a moment as if we were people from a strange land. Then he passed his transparent hand over his high white forehead, and said, "May I speak to you a moment, Lucy?—You might wait in the parlor, Mr. Haines, if you please, sir."

It was the first time for years and years that I'd been in that old pine-panelled room, with its side walls covered with mellow calf bindings, and high carved overmantel with the dim portrait of the first Sir Robert Yardley, with the tower of the Jamestown church behind his left shoulder and the sails of the little ship with the English flag at his right. The old turkey carpet was still on the floor, and the green corded silk curtains, stained and faded with sunlight and age, were still at the windows. The big globe of a long-changed world was there too, and in the corner the old mahogany press, behind whose close-curtained doors, neatly packed against time and rust, were Doctor Yardley's medical instruments . . . including, I thought with sudden irony, the forceps that had brought young John Crabtree reluctantly into the world, leaving a mark now faded that used to be the source of unwearied interest when he was a lad.

Doctor Yardley sat down behind the walnut Queen Anne table, folded his hands on its tooled leather cover, and looked at me.

"I went to call on Mason Seymour last evening, Lucy," he said quietly.

I nodded.

"I became convinced that you were quite right—it would have been most inappropriate and unsuitable for . . . my daughter to marry him."

I nodded again.

He got up and moved over to the fireplace, and stood, one hand resting on the mantel, looking down into the empty grate.

"Melusina hasn't been as discreet as she might have been,"

he said, after a moment. "But there are things worse than death. We sometimes have . . . obligations to the living that are greater . . ."

He hesitated.

"Well, no matter. Lucy, I only wanted to say that if you hear things that seem very strange to you, just remember that . . ."

He stopped again, and stood there, lost in his own solitary world so long that I thought he'd forgotten me and moved toward the door. He looked up, his face strangely contracted.

"Lucy," he said abruptly, "—has Marshall . . . declared himself?"

I was completely bowled over.

"I'm—sure I don't know," I stammered. "I certainly shouldn't think so . . . I mean——"

"No, I presume he hasn't. Well, no matter. It's most unfortunate—I wish it could have been avoided."

I got out at that point. Unfortunate, I thought, was hardly the word for it. Not even Melusina could approve of Marshall Yardley's marrying a girl who played hide and seek around a bachelor's establishment at ten o'clock at night the very day his engagement was announced. I believe they're broader about these things in the North, but I doubt even if one lived as far north as the Pole one could approve of that.

"Declared himself indeed!" I thought, crossing the hall to tell Bill Haines I wouldn't be but a moment now.

# 9

I didn't get more than halfway to the door before I stopped dead. Voices, angry and subdued with obvious effort, were coming out of the parlor where Lady Anne's portrait with the saber cut in it hung between the windows. One of them —the one doing the talking—was William Quincy Adams Haines's.

"It's just as distasteful for me to be here, Miss Yardley, as it is for you to have me here. After last night I thought I'd never see you again—but I'm not running out till I've done as much as I can to keep them from tying a noose around your neck . . . whether you like it or not. And the sooner I can pass you in the street, and not have Miss Lucy and your father and the local constabulary wonder why we're not speaking, the better I'll like it. Just get that straight, sister."

I don't think I ever got up a flight of stairs quicker or more quietly in my entire life. I know it was the first time in all my life that I burst into Melusina Yardley's room without first rapping and waiting to be told to come in. And it was probably the one time when I should have waited. At least it was if I was to judge by the extraordinary expression on the face of Melusina, propped up on a dozen pillows in the middle of her fourposter bed with its crisp muslin curtains, a crocheted cap on her head, her face covered with cold cream that I knew was there to hide the haggard expression she couldn't keep from looking out of her eyes.

But it was the other woman who was the most overcome.

Hallie Taswell, in her sprigged muslin Colonial hostess gown, with cerise velvet bows on her frilled white fichu and white ruffed sleeves and frilled cap, and paint enough on her face to stop a train, looked as if she'd swoon. She jerked back in her chair—she and Melusina must have had their heads together like a couple of hungry magpies—and batted her eyes.

"Oh, Lucy!" she cried. "*Dear* Lucy—oh, isn't it dreadful about poor Mason!"

"It surely is," I replied stiffly, and I hope I shan't be called to account for it on Judgment Day, because I didn't actually intend to say it, and nobody was more surprised than I was to hear myself saying it. "And they're hunting for a woman who's been slipping through the hedge from Mason Seymour's garden into the Lanes' old place and out. It seems," I said, "some one's been making a practice of that."

It was a horrible thing to have said.—After what I'd said to Bill Haines when we'd seen her, tear-streaked and upset, the day before, about his being an intolerant young man. Especially, of course, as it was me myself they were hunting, not poor Hallie. But the effect of it was even worse than I could have believed! She turned a perfectly ghastly greenish-white, and her fluttering hands were as still as still, until one of them crawled, shaking horribly, to her throat, clutching at it as if she were going to die.

"Oh, my God!" she gasped. "They mustn't, Lucy! They mustn't!"

Melusina, who had stiffened against her pillows in outraged propriety, snapped her mouth shut, and opened it immediately.

"Hallie!—Have you been going to Mason Seymour's?"

"Just once, Melusina . . . just yesterday, after I saw the paper!" Hallie cried piteously. "You must believe me!"

"Then you're an even bigger donkey than I took you to be," Melusina said acidly. "And my advice to you, Hallie Taswell, is to go home and take off that rig, and tell your husband the whole ridiculous business!"

She took a deep breath. "—I *am* surprised!"

I stared at her. It couldn't, I thought, be *possible* she didn't already know all this. Everybody in town knew that Hallie had been making the most extraordinary donkey of herself for months. Melusina must have heard her say a dozen times, with that smug simper, that if she wanted to she could divorce Hugh just like that, and do very much better for herself. And when Hallie got out of the room, which I may say she did with incredible despatch, I turned to Melusina.

"You don't mean this is the first you've heard of all this?" I demanded.

Melusina poured some witch hazel on the pad in her hand and laid it over her eyes, and leaned her head back against the pillows.

"Oh, of course not, Lucy," she said heavily. "But there are times when it's so much simpler not to know too much. Especially as Hallie's been here the last hour trying to get out of me how much everybody does know—or worse, how much they suspect. Twelve hours ago there was not a person in town wouldn't have been too happy for the chance to tell her at length—now nobody will open their heads."

There was no reason why I should have been surprised, and I wasn't, really.

"Just how much do you know?" I asked. "Not about Hallie. About Mason Seymour."

"Not a thing, Lucy," she replied evenly. "—Except that it's a great pity."

"Because of Faith?"

She took the compress off her eyes and looked at me.

"We had decided last night to break the engagement, Lucy —before any of this happened."

She spoke with a kind of even tartness.

"That's for your private ear. My brother proved exceedingly recalcitrant."

"Really?"

"Yes. But that—as it happens—isn't what I want to speak to you about. It was, when I phoned this morning, because I didn't, at that time, know poor Mason was dead."

I stared at her. She met my gaze with perfect—or almost perfect—composure. I thought for a moment that I had never in my life seen anything to equal it. And yet, when I stopped to think, I had no right to doubt her word. Just because I'd known for hours that Mason Seymour was dead was no sign every one else did. But there was something in the way she underlined each word as she spoke it.

"Since it was you, Lucy," she was going on, not taking her eyes off me, "that set my brother against Mason in the first place, I thought the least you could do—for all of us —was to undo the damage you'd done. I didn't at that time know that you had something else in your mind . . . although I suppose I should have suspected."

I must have looked perfectly blank. I certainly felt it.

Melusina leaned forward a little.

"Lucy," she said, almost entreatingly. "Why couldn't you have been frank with me? It would have saved all of us so much . . . so much heartache!"

I just sat perfectly limp in the chair Hallie Taswell had vacated, completely bewildered.

"Why couldn't you have come to me and told me who the young man you sent to my brother was?"

I stared at her. "I didn't send him, in the first place," I literally blurted out then. "And *who* is he in the second?"

Melusina put her head back against the pillows and closed her eyes. There wasn't any cold cream on her eyelids, so that they looked odd and dry, like a mud terrapin's. Her lips were trembling and her hands plucked at the counterpane.

"You're being stupid and unkind, Lucy," she said, controlling herself with an effort.

"About what?" I cried. "I wish you'd tell me what you're talking about!"

"Now, Lucy," she said tartly. "Don't get hysterics. You know quite well what I'm talking about. Hallie went to your house before she came here, and she saw Summers Baldwin's card introducing this young man on your parlor table. She didn't have time to read all of it, apparently—Community interrupted her—but obviously if Summers Baldwin sent him, he must be a highly eligible young man."

She took a deep breath and went on.

"I dare say it never occurred to Summers that we, at Yardley Hall, would stoop to take in a . . . guest, which is why he sent him to you. But there's no doubt the young man was greatly attracted to Faith. Even my brother noticed that, and I must say it was rather clever of you, arranging it all the way you did. It will no doubt be an excellent match for Faith."

I was staring at her open-mouthed, appalled, almost sick, at this extraordinary leaping to conclusions with all the amazing agility of a super-mountain goat. I was *so* appalled that I hadn't seen the door open, nor seen Faith Yardley standing in it—how long heaven only knows but far, far too long—until I saw Melusina's jaw drop and saw her eyes fastened in the dim old Adam mirror over the fireplace. And as I looked at her she seemed literally to shrink.

I turned around, and that's when I saw Faith standing there, her eyes as black as living coals, her face white as death. At first she didn't move, and then she did, coming in slowly, never taking her burning eyes off her aunt. She closed the door behind her and stood against it, her hands gripping the knob, steadying her trembling body. And then she spoke, her voice so cold and distilled with passion that my insides shrivelled like a strip of bacon on white-hot coals. Melusina's face under the cold cream was putty-grey.

"Listen, Aunt Melusina," Faith said. "I agreed to marry Mason Seymour because you made me believe it was what my father wanted me to do. I would have done it, and done the best I could at it. But that's the last thing I'll ever do. And as for Mr. Haines, I wouldn't marry him if he was the King of the Golden Mountains—even if he wanted me to, which it happens he doesn't.

"And there's one thing I do want, and I'm going to have. And that's for you to let me alone and never again as long as you live meddle in my life again. You've done your best to ruin it. Now leave it alone."

She turned slowly to me, almost as if she hated me, at first, until her frozen calm broke and she cried, suddenly and passionately, "Oh, Cousin Lucy, how could you? How could you? I've always thought you were my one friend! How could you scheme and plot with Aunt Melusina and with . . . with him to make a fool of me!"

She turned and fled out the door, almost strangled with sobs.

Melusina and I sat there, dumb and old. It was she, of course, who got her voice back first.

"Well, Lucinda," she said sharply. "You've certainly made a mess of *that*."

And I suppose I had, although heaven knows I couldn't make out where my mess left off and somebody else's began.

I was even deeper in fog when I got home—I don't even know how—and crept into my sitting room, darkened against the glaring midday sun, and collapsed on the sofa and closed my eyes. Then I opened them again, abruptly, and sat up, suddenly aware that Ruth Napier, of all people on earth, was sitting quietly on the needle-point ottoman in front of the fireplace.

I couldn't for a moment believe my eyes. I thought I must be losing my mind.

"You're surprised to see me, aren't you, Miss Randolph?" she said with a twisted smile.

"Very," I said, and thought, "oh, dear, how much like Melusina I'm getting to sound."

"You look all in," she remarked coolly.

"I am," I said.

Then we just sat there, both of us, looking at each other. I don't know what she was thinking. I was thinking how amazingly untouched she seemed by Mason Seymour's death, and how strikingly good-looking she was.

She had on a riding coat, perfectly tailored, of a coarse white stuff, salt sacking I think it is, with tan twill jodhpurs and brown jodhpur boots. Her white silk shirt was open at the throat, and her thick black hair, tied back with a ribbon around her head, hung in heavy wavy masses around her slim brown throat. Her large liquid dark eyes looked apparently untroubled out from under two perfectly arched narrow black eyebrows, and her thin oval face had an exotic kind of beauty I should have thought would have appealed very strongly to Mason Seymour. Only a faint pallor around her nostrils, spreading down around her small scarlet mouth, indicated that somewhere behind all that perfect façade there was anything remotely resembling pain . . . or fear.

"I've been coming to see you a long time," she said. She looked at me, tracing the roses in the carpet with the end of her plaited leather crop.

I smiled. Her eyes tightened. I think it was then she decided to change her method and come to the point, because she said, "This Mr. Haines who's staying with you, Miss Randolph. Was he a . . . friend of Mason's?"

"I really haven't an idea," I said.

She straightened one neat leg, fished in her jodhpurs pocket, brought out a leather cigarette case, flexed her knee again and sat there with the case in her hands between her slim knees.

"And if you had you wouldn't tell me, is that it?" she asked coolly.

"Something of the sort," I answered. "After all, his business is his own, isn't it?"

She took a cigarette out and tapped it meditatively against her knee. "She must be about twenty-five or twenty-six," I thought, "but she doesn't look it—except that she doesn't look as much like a young green sapling as Faith does, and Faith's twenty-one."

"He's very attractive, isn't he?" she said, a slow little smile just in one corner of her red mouth.

"Very," I said.

I don't know why my heart began to sink very slowly. Or rather I do, of course, and part of it was because I heard the latch of the front gate click, and heavy steps on the brick walk until the hinge of the office door groaned.

Ruth Napier's eyes moved from the window to me, the smile in her dark eyes deepening warily. Then, almost at once, the hinge groaned again. Her lithe body straightened, but when my knocker banged perfunctorily she relaxed, and when Bill shouted "Hey, Miss Lucy, you home?" and pushed open the sitting room door, she wasn't even looking up.

Not till he said, "Oh, I'm sorry, I didn't—" and I said, "Do come in." Then she looked up, and her face took on the most pleasant naïve surprise, just as if she were actually saying out loud, "How extraordinary seeing any one so marvellous just walk in a door!"

And Bill, whose reaction time when it comes to young women I knew from experience was anything but slow, went through a short kaleidoscope from annoyance to surprise to a pleased grin. Flesh and blood couldn't have done otherwise.

"This is Miss Napier, Mr. Haines," I said.

She looked up at him with a gay open smile and held out her hand, moving over so he could sit down beside her on the ottoman.

"I hear you're an architect," she said. I glanced at the table. Summers Baldwin's card was gone, but it certainly had done its job of introducing Mr. William Quincy Adams Haines to Williamsburg society, I thought sardonically.

"You've come to the one most marvellous place in the entire world—hasn't he, Miss Randolph?" Ruth Napier laughed. "But of course the people who've always lived here can't appreciate it, they don't know about subways and zoning laws. Don't you adore the supper room in the Palace?"

"I haven't seen it," Bill grinned. "I just got here. I haven't been any place."

"But how thrilling, to have it all ahead of you! You must

see the Palace, I'm simply mad about it! It's *too* lovely! Oh,
do come right now—I adore going with people who're seeing it for the first time! You mustn't wait another minute,
must he, Miss Randolph?"

I'm sure I haven't given a very clear account of just how
that happened. It was all so much smoother and more natural and charmingly casual than it sounds . . . her just
chancing to meet him there, and his being the one architect
in the world who hadn't seen the Palace, and she being so
perfectly just the person to show it to him because she was
so completely mad about it! And of course a riper plum
never sat on a tree waiting to be shaken off.

I heard them laughing and the gate click, and saw them
race across the street to her green open sports coupé that I
hadn't even noticed when I came in, and heard its soft powerful motor whirr. And then I saw it slip away, with Bill at
the wheel. I believe it's considered very subtle flattery to let
a man drive one's car.

People say the early colonists used to stand on Capitol
Landing and watch the ships round the bend for home and
England with very heavy hearts indeed. They couldn't have
been much heavier than mine was, watching that car go
round the curve into Woodpecker Street and out toward the
York Road . . . especially as the Palace was in exactly the
opposite direction.

# 10

Bill didn't, of course, get home to supper. I don't think I really expected he would—there had been something so like carefree escape in the way that car had gathered speed toward the open road. But I should never have admitted it—not openly, the way Community did. And I hadn't even known she knew anything had happened until I sat down at the table and saw the dreary York River flounder in front of me instead of the golden mountains of fried chicken and Sally Lunn I'd ordered because Bill had never eaten either Sally Lunn or enough fried chicken.

For the first time since I'd got used to being the sole occupant of the house, I felt poignantly and intolerably lonely, sitting there at the end of the long mahogany table. My great-great-grandfather looked soberly down at me from the white painted overmantel. My great-grandmother, holding a single damask rose in her pale hands, looked down from the panel over the sideboard. We seemed, just then, all equally of the dead past. Bill and Ruth Napier and Faith—they were the present. And that night—and I'm rather ashamed to admit it, but since the Restoration has come, and manna seems to rain from it instead of Heaven, I'm afraid I've got a little remiss about saying them—I said my prayers not for a patch on the roof, but for Bill and Faith Yardley, and Doctor Yardley. Possibly if I'd included Melusina and Ruth Napier, and Hallie Taswell, and even the dead Mason Seymour and his man Luton, they'd have been answered more readily. But I couldn't bring myself to do that. Or perhaps I was just then learning what I should have learned with its first touch of colic if one of them had been my own child—though I believe children very sensibly don't have colic any more: that each human being's life is his own, and so is his destiny, and no matter how close we are we're still as far apart as the stars . . . and that for each of us pain, especially pain, has an inviolable personal orbit of its own.

I wasn't thinking that then as I sat there at the table, trying to choke down flat bits of flounder fried in coarse white cornmeal. The old blue willow platter and the silver dish with the dab of green peas and mint leaves in the bottom swam in front of my eyes. And then through the flickering unsteady candlelight something else swam too. I had to catch my fork sharply to keep it from falling, and tell myself it wasn't a ghost, no matter how much she looked like one, standing there in the open door with her hair a nimbus of gold-colored light, her wide grey eyes dark like summer dusk.

I pushed my chair back and got up, realizing with a sharp pang that this was why I'd been so unbearably lonely. It wasn't that my loyalties had changed, but because I'd been afraid in my own heart that Bill Haines and Melusina together had driven Faith away from me, and that she wouldn't come back to me, or not soon, and when she did she wouldn't be the child grown up, trudging across the Court House Green to make daily grave little visits of state.

Across the pointed yellow candle tips I saw her gallant little smile and the quick proud toss of her head that was hardly that as much as it was an association in my own brain of a kind of challenge she was meeting, coming here. We went together, without either of us speaking, back into the parlor. My own heart was far too full to speak and still make sense.

"I had to come tell you I'm sorry about what I said," she said softly, pulling up a horsehair gout stool that some early forbear of mine addicted to too much port had brought from England, and sitting down at my feet. "I was . . . very upset, and I was so afraid Aunt Melusina would do something to make this all . . . so much worse. Oh, I suppose she means well, Cousin Lucy, but—that doesn't make it any less . . . embarrassing, and awful. Does it?"

"No," I said, picking up my work. "It probably makes it worse."

She sat there looking straight ahead of her for a long time, her slim brown arms resting across the sock I've been eight months knitting for some Eskimo who'd probably much prefer reindeer hide next to his feet.

"Cousin Lucy, did you ever . . . ever hate anybody almost more than you could bear?" she whispered, suddenly and with so much passion that I should have been alarmed and shocked if I hadn't seen the bright tears glistening on her long dark lashes.

"Not really," I said. "It's too corrosive. It only hurts the person who does the hating. Of course, there have been a thousand people I could cheerfully have boiled in oil, but it never lasts more than a minute or two."

"But I really hate Aunt Melusina," Faith whispered again. "I really do, Cousin Lucy. I've tried to keep away from her all last night and today—even before what she was saying to you. Because . . . oh, no, it's such a dreadful thing to say!"

"In that case you'd better say it, honey lamb, and get it out of your mind, and then we'll both forget it," I said. Which shows, I'm afraid, that Melusina isn't the only one who can mean well and still be very stupid indeed.

"I mean about all my whole life making me do things I hated because Father wanted me to—like marrying . . . Mason to keep from selling Yardley Hall, and all that, because there's nothing I wouldn't do if he wanted me to, and she's known it all the time. And all my life I've just taken it for granted that when she said 'Your father says he wants you to wear your overshoes,' or 'eat your rhubarb,' or 'wear your sunbonnet so you won't get freckles,' . . . that it really meant that, that she'd really, some way, got the orders from him. I didn't care who made fun of my sunbonnet or my funny shoes. I was proud, because I was doing it for him. —You know?"

She gave me a twisted unconvincing smile.

"Yes, I know," I said.

"Well, last night, at dinner . . ." She hesitated, and looked down, biting her red lower lip to steady it. "Father put his napkin down and said—oh, so quietly, the way he does—'Daughter, unless you're very sure your happiness depends on your marriage with Mason Seymour, I strongly suggest that you withdraw from your understanding with him at once.' I couldn't believe my ears . . . not until I saw Aunt

Melusina. She was utterly speechless, Cousin Lucy. You know——"

"Yes, I know," I said hastily.

"Marshall and I just sat there, and then Aunt Melusina broke loose, and said . . . oh, all sorts of things—ending with that we'd have to sell the house to vandals. Father just sat looking at her, and then all of a sudden his eyes were like they'd caught on fire. He got up, and even Aunt Melusina looked frightened. He didn't raise his voice, but he didn't have to—he just said, 'That's enough, Melusina. I'd rather sell my house than sell my soul, but I'd rather sell both of them than sell my daughter.'"

Faith's eyes were like two dark stars.

"It was me he meant, Cousin Lucy!" she whispered—poor hungry lamb!

"Then he said, 'I don't wish the matter referred to again . . . and hereafter I shall expect to be advised of what is going on in this household.'—He hadn't even *known* . . . and he's never known *anything* . . . I mean about the rhubarb, or the sunbonnet, or my doing things for *him*."

Her eyes were suddenly bright with tears, but she blinked them back, trying to smile as if it was all very silly, really. And of course, it was ironic in the extreme that marriage, and Mason Seymour, and death all crowded overwhelmingly together in one pan of the scales were nothing against a fragile childhood sacrifice made for love in the other. But I'm told there are psychologists who think that what happens before one is two is more important than anything else that happens this side of the grave. So perhaps Faith Yardley was quite innocently fulfilling a high law. I'm sure I shouldn't attempt to judge—beyond its very immediate irony.

"Then he left the room, and Aunt Melusina nearly went out of her mind," she went on, in a controlled grown-up voice again. "I just sat there. I scarcely heard what she was saying, except that it was something awful she'd done that they'd send us all to jail for. All I could think of was that I didn't have to marry Mason Seymour now, and it was just as if somebody had taken a lot of heavy chains off me that I hadn't really known I'd had on.

"I expect that sounds very silly, Cousin Lucy," she added, with a sudden flash of her old prim gravity, so that for a moment all I could see was the stodgy little buttoned boots and the snub freckled nose and tight plaited hair, all denying the loveliness of the girl at my knee pulling the hard-won stitches—I don't really like to knit—out of the missionary sock with the pressure of her brown arms across my lap.

"Then I sort of came to—as if I'd been sitting in a dream —and saw Marshall trying to make her be quiet, telling her that they couldn't send Father to jail and that he'd go and see Mason. Oh, Cousin Lucy, it was dreadful! Marshall was white as that paper, and Aunt Melusina was like an old rag that's been wrung out in coffee."

Faith's eyes were wide and almost black, remembering. Her mat brown skin was pale. She gripped her folded hands tighter to keep her arms from trembling on my lap.

"But Aunt Melusina wouldn't let Marshall go. He tried to loosen her hands, but she kept holding him back and he didn't want to be unkind. Then she . . . she sort of flew at me, saying I'd given my promise, it was my duty. Then Marshall jerked away. I've never seen him defy her before. He was terribly, terribly angry.—'It's nothing of the sort, and don't you dare say that to her again!' And out he went."

She sat almost rigid for a moment. Then she got up and moved over to the fireplace, and stood looking down just the way her father had done that morning. The candlelight on her hair made it glow like molten gold against the lead-blue overmantel. When she spoke again there was a note of weariness in her voice that I'd never heard there before.

"It seems that Aunt Melusina had . . . involved us all, much more than we knew—or she knew either, I suppose. Because she came upstairs after me and explained she hadn't dared tell Marshall everything, but that unless I did go through with it Mason could take the house and everything, and leave nothing for . . . for Father."

She drew a deep unhappy breath.

"I never knew I could . . . well, hate anybody so much, Cousin Lucy. It was just as if everything inside me had turned to . . . oh, well, it doesn't matter now—I mean that doesn't."

She turned to me suddenly.

"Have you ever been terribly, *terribly* afraid, Cousin Lucy?" she said softly.

I nodded. In the years before the Restoration I'd been afraid—terribly afraid—of the grim grey sisters who crept with me up and down the rickety stairs and stood beside my bed. Now Old Age had taken on a kinder face since Homeless Poverty had gone. But I had known fear, and I recognized it now as it seeped like a numbing vapor into my heart again as I sat there, my bone needles motionless in my lap, looking at Faith.

"I've got to tell somebody, Cousin Lucy, or I'll go mad!"

I tried to open my lips to tell her not to tell, but they wouldn't move. She stood there silently looking down for a moment, then she sat down on the ottoman where Ruth Napier had sat and moved so Bill could sit beside her, and leaned toward me, her voice hardly more than a whisper.

"I went downstairs to phone Mason. Luton answered and said he was engaged."

She went on quickly, her voice like soft running feet in a distant room coming closer.

"I asked him if it was my cousin. He said he wasn't at liberty to say who was with Mr. Seymour. In just a few minutes I heard Marshall come in and go into the library. I tried to get Mason again, but nobody answered the phone. Then I guess I got sort of scared. I don't know, but the house seemed so still, and at the other end the phone ringing in Mason's house with no one answering . . . I got the sudden feeling that I was the only person in all the world. When I held my breath I couldn't hear a sound. Anyway, I ran down the hall to the library. The door was closed, of course, but I didn't wait to knock—I knew Father would understand and wouldn't mind. But nobody was there, Cousin Lucy . . . just a curl of smoke that hadn't all disappeared yet. The window was open. I ran to it and called, but no one answered.

"It seemed too strange . . . and then I turned around, and there were all Father's things, his glasses on his book, the medicine he'd mixed for Abraham's rheumatism . . . And that's when I decided really I would go on with Mason. I know it sounds horrible . . . but he was getting what he must have thought he wanted. I mean, Aunt Melusina hadn't made him want to marry me, had she?"

I shook my head. That was one thing Melusina hadn't had the least hand in. If the Adam mirror at the end of the room hadn't been so mildewed even Faith herself must have realized it, just then.

"Anyway," she went on quickly, "I tried to phone Mason again, and I still couldn't get him. Then I got a panicky feeling that what if Father and Marshall had gone to see him, not knowing about any of the other—and I knew I had to see him first. That's why I went over. I know it was a dreadful thing to do, Cousin Lucy, but I had to—don't you see? —before anything happened."

"What time was that, Faith, do you know?"

"I know the ten-thirty train went by as I was going down Mason's path," she answered. "But that was . . . later."

She stopped. The color deepened in her cheeks, and something very like resentment drove the fear out of her eyes for the moment.

"When did you meet Bill Haines?" I asked, as quietly as I could.

"He told you?"

I shook my head.

"Then how did you know . . . ?"

"I just guessed it," I said. I couldn't say, "Both of you are as transparent as an April shower."

"He was just coming out of Mason's gate," Faith said steadily. "He closed it and stood in front of it and said, 'What is this, ladies' day at the races?' I suppose it was silly, but I got very angry."

She looked down at the roses and lilies in the carpet.

"I guess I must have sounded just like Aunt Melusina. I said a lot of things I wouldn't have said if . . . well, if it hadn't been for something that happened after lunch that . . . that came back into my mind the minute Father said I didn't have to marry Mason."

I took up my knitting. She hadn't been as impervious to Bill's yarn about the inscription on their table at home— "Whoever loved that loved not at first sight?"—as she'd appeared to be, I thought. Bill's presence there blocking the gate had somehow allayed the fear in my heart . . . but only for a moment, because she went on.

"I told him I was going to marry Mason, and he said, 'But your father says you're not,' and I said Father was mistaken, and anybody else who said I wasn't was mistaken, and that I knew quite well what I was doing, and that I . . . oh, a lot of things I didn't mean, and didn't want to say, and hated myself for all the time I was saying them."

"What did he do?"

"What could he do but tip his hat and say 'I'm sorry,' and stand aside. But he didn't open the gate. I had to do that my-

self, and I couldn't. My hands were shaking. I was so angry
. . . and miserable too, I guess. He said, 'There, you see? A
wooden gate post has sense enough to see it's no good. Even
if you leave me out, Faith, don't go down there tonight. Go
home and sleep on it.' "

"Very sound too," I said.

She nodded.

"I know," she said wretchedly. "But just then the gate
came open and I ran down the path. I was almost in tears,
and I . . . I didn't want him to see me crying. Anyway, I
got to the door, and then I . . . I got cold feet. I would have
gone back then, but I could see Bill still standing back there.
So I went up on the porch. The door was open. I knocked,
but nobody answered. I waited a long time, and called. Then
I thought maybe Mason was in the garden, because I knew
he'd never go away and leave the house open like that—he
was too careful of his things and never understood how we
left our doors open all the time."

She hesitated. She was even paler under her brown skin
than when she'd first come.

"Then I got awfully alarmed, some way. I looked back.
Bill was gone. It was all so terribly still. The only sound was
that little enamelled clock on the parlor mantel, and it
seemed to be going so fast, as if it had to catch up with something that was getting way ahead of it. The library door
was closed. I knocked at it, but nobody answered. I started
to open it . . . and a funny thing happened, Cousin Lucy."

All the color was drained from her face now, leaving only
her red lips and her eyes dark like great subterranean lakes.

"Nobody would believe me, but it's *really* true," she whispered. "As I stood by that door, something touched me on
the shoulder and said, 'Don't go in there, Faith' . . . just as
plain as I'm speaking to you, Cousin Lucy. For a minute I
even thought it was Bill. I looked around.—Nobody was
there, and I . . . I knew nobody had been there."

I put down my sock and looked at her. There was something so translucently lovely in her face that it didn't seem
strange or far-fetched to me that some manifestation of what
simpler people used to call a guardian angel might very easily have spoken to her that night. But the Rector has
frequently complained of my unorthodoxy, and perhaps it
*was* just Faith's subconscious mind . . . although I'm sure
I don't see that it matters a great deal what you call it.

# 11

"What did you do?" I asked.

"I went back out on the porch and along the walk, and stopped. I could see shadows moving all through the garden, it seemed to me, under the mimosas, in between the box. And then, Cousin Lucy . . ."

She paused.

"I saw a woman. I know it was a woman. I don't know where she came from, or where she went—only that the gate was dark a moment, and then I saw the white pickets and she was gone. Then I realized that was what Bill had meant by ladies' day at the races and telling me not to go down. And then I got scared. I hadn't been before, not very, anyway, but I was then, and I ran as fast as I could back to the house."

She stopped again.

"Somebody had closed the door."

I sat there motionless, my brain numb, seeing all this more plainly than she could know.

"I didn't wait to knock, I burst in and through the parlor there. The door of the library was open a little. I called Mason and ran in. . . . And there he was. There was blood all over everything."

She closed her eyes, blotting out that awful memory. There was no use in closing mine. The same dark image was there whether they were open or shut.

"I ran to the telephone. I knew I must call Doctor Harriman, and then I knew there was no use. It was too awful—it seemed to me as if I knew without any one telling me that he hadn't killed himself—not like that. It must have been some one who hated him horribly, who wanted to disfigure him so dreadfully.—And then, all of a sudden, Cousin Lucy, with Central saying 'Number, please; number, please,' I put down the phone . . ."

She looked up at me. I think she wanted me to deny what she was going to say, and was afraid, somehow, that I wouldn't.

"You see, Cousin Lucy, all . . . *all* the people who hated Mason the most live at Yardley Hall."

She waited. There was nothing I could say. I couldn't say, even though it was true, that Bill Haines had virtually shouted from the Palace lanthorn how much he objected to Mason Seymour—because that, of course, wasn't very serious. Or was it? I thought suddenly. I hurried on in my own mind to Hallie Taswell's husband Hugh, and Hallie herself, and Ruth Napier. I'm sure I shouldn't care to trust any of them with a frantic cause and a loaded shotgun. But that wasn't the sort of thing I could say to Faith. What she had said was true enough; and to make it truer still, there was blood on the well at Yardley Hall.

"Anyway, that's why I didn't call Mr. Priddy," Faith said evenly. "And I should have, because——"

Her voice sank to a whisper again. "—because somebody was out on the terrace."

I stared at her.

"Faith!"

"Somebody was watching me."

Her lips were pale under the bright lipstick.

"I was in the light. It was dark out there, but I could . . . I could feel some one looking at me.—And oh, Cousin Lucy!"

She got up abruptly and stood, her hands clenched at her side. "What if it's somebody I know—who saw me, and doesn't know really whether I saw him or not, and keeps looking at me, wondering whether I know? I . . . I'm *terrified!* It isn't that I'm afraid he'll . . . kill me too; it's something else. It's just the knowing—because I heard something outside before I put down the phone, and looked out, and I know somebody knew I was looking at him . . ."

"Faith," I said, very quietly, "do you think you know who it was?"

She put her hands to her head. "Oh, I don't know, Cousin Lucy, I don't know!"

"Sit down, Faith," I said. She sat down on the ottoman, her head bent forward, her hands clasped tightly around her knees to keep herself from trembling from head to foot.

"Listen, Faith," I began—but that's as far as I got. The iron gate latch clicked and two feet—and not two, I realized instantly, but four—came up the path; two heavy, two so twinkling light that if I hadn't been fearing desperately they'd come I should never have heard them. Faith looked up.

"Is that . . . ?"

I nodded. I needn't have, because that "Hi, Miss Lucy!" in the hall meant that the next moment the door would open and there they'd be, not just one as she thought, but two . . . and it did open and there they were—both of them.

Ruth Napier was no longer in jodhpurs but in a sort of dark reddish dress that fitted her slim figure as if she'd just risen from a sea of crushed raspberries, with a crushed raspberry turban on her dark head and a necklace made of the little brass bells that Indian dancing girls wear as anklets. She looked utterly enchanting, and the big young man behind her in the crumpled white linen suit knew it quite as well as she did . . . or did until he saw the other girl sitting on the ottoman in front of the fireplace. Then his face changed. I suspect he must have thought I always kept a female figure, stuffed if necessary, on that ottoman for him to barge in on.

"Oh, hello, Faith," Ruth Napier said, with a sort of "Fancy-meeting-you-here" air and that little snapdragon smile flicking the corner of her red mouth.

"Hello, Ruth. Good evening, Mr. Haines."

"Good evening, Miss Yardley." Bill was like a sullen schoolboy.

"We've come to tell you we're going over to Barrett's to dance," Ruth said. She looked up at him, laughing gaily. "Bill seems to think you ring curfew at nine-thirty. He wanted to be properly checked out so he could get back in again."

"He has the key to the office," I said tartly. "Furthermore, he's quite free to come and go as he chooses."

He gave me a savage scowl. And Ruth, whose command of the situation was nothing less than admirable, unless it was somewhat shocking for Williamsburg's classic repose, said, "Faith, *why* don't you come along with us? Mason would hate all this gloom!—*You* ask her, Bill!"

Well, I'm afraid I'm pretty old-fashioned, I must say. Bill Haines flushed, or maybe it was Ruth's frock reflected in his face—they were very much the same shade.

"No, thanks—I couldn't, really," Faith said.

"Then do let us drop you at home—it isn't a bit out of our way . . . is it, Bill?"

"Thanks," Faith said. "My cousin's coming after me."

And when they'd gone, and the gate had clicked and the sound of the motor was lost, and the frogs and some students harmonizing somewhere in the distance were all the sound left to us, Faith looked at me with an unhappy little smile.

"So that's that," she said, trying to keep the husky edge off her voice.

I'd have given my head to be able to say, "Not at all, my dear," but I wasn't. So I didn't say anything at all. If I should wake up some morning and look out and see that eternal midnight had come, and our Cinderella town had gone back to its old self, and where the Palace is, an ash heap was again, and where the Capitol is, an empty lot with a bronze tablet on a stone, and in place of the blue coach and four, with its liveried footmen, a gasoline truck backfiring down the Duke of Gloucester Street, I couldn't, I suppose, be sicker than I was just then. I hadn't been matchmaking . . . but I had seen the topless towers of Ilium rise glowing in a young man's eyes, and in a girl's now it wasn't even a smoldering ruin, it was just a ruin.

It's not without relief, however, that I can say I didn't get up and make a bee line over to the office and get my father's shotgun out of the old press and set out into the night to do something about it. If I'd even had the impulse, I think I should have hurried down the street and applied for admittance to the State Hospital. Instead I just sat there, hoping that Mr. William Quincy Adams Haines was having the most miserable evening of his life, and that the mosquitoes at Barrett's were as ubiquitously carnivorous as they used to be when I was a girl and went there.

Faith just sat there too. Every line of her young body had changed, somehow, and drooped the way the petals of an iris droop under an unseasonable sun. I don't mean she'd collapsed or anything of the sort, just that a kind of fresh resilient young glory that she had had suddenly dimmed, like a cloud crossing the sun, draining its golden radiance from the earth.

After a moment she got up, slowly, as if it was a hard thing to do to move her weary little feet in their blue-braided sandals, and moved to the fireplace and stood there, the way her father does, looking down, her back to me, her bright head bent forward a little. A firefly that Bill and Ruth had let in out of the night circled its lemon-pale lantern around her a moment and settled, dark again, on the bowl of scarlet roses in the corner. At last Faith raised her head, and when she turned to me again her chin was up, her eyes clear, her slim young body crisp and green again . . . so that I thought preposterously that this firefly must have brought her some subtle elixir—a pennyworth of starch for her heart.

She looked at me with her wide grey tranquil eyes, and then that sudden merry smile that had always punctured her prim gravity with a sharp plop just as people were about to say "What a *serious* child!" lighted her face, not with any cold firefly light but warm and radiant as the sun.

"Oh don't, Cousin Lucy, don't!" she cried. "You look just like Williamsburg before the Restoration!"

It was precisely the way I felt, of course.

"Oh, *please*, darling!"

The Bruton Church clock struck its silver bell. She paused to listen.

"Oh, dear, I've got to go home—it's late."

She picked up the blue straw cartwheel she'd tossed on the sofa and dropped an airy kiss on the top of my head.

"Isn't Marshall coming after you?" I asked.

"Don't be naïve, Cousin Lucy," she said lightly. "Of course he isn't. Poor dear, he's probably sitting moping in the moon-light in Ruth Napier's rose arbor."

She shrugged her slim shoulders.

"We Yardleys are tragic figures, darling.—You know?"

The gate latch clicked again just then, and almost at once, with the casual bang of the brass knocker that old friends give before they walk in, knowing the servants are off, the door opened and Marshall Yardley literally materialized out of the chorus of frogs and ballet of fireflies that make up Williamsburg's spring comic opera nights. And Faith's flip-pancy to the contrary notwithstanding, Marshall Yardley, standing there filling the hall door, *was* a tragic figure.

# 12

If ever in my entire life I saw aching hopeless hunger in human eyes, it was in Marshall's just then. If it hadn't been for the Yardley nose and the Yardley jaw and the Yardley pride keeping it all in an iron strait-jacket, I think I should have wept seeing him. Because I couldn't help seeing at the same time the other man who'd stood in that very spot such a few minutes before . . . the gay dark girl in the raspberry frock and turban laughing up at him. Had Marshall known she'd been there, I wondered, and was that why he'd come?

"Hullo, Cousin Lucy," he said shortly. He turned to Faith. "I've just been down at the Court House. Priddy said you were here.—I thought if you were ready . . ."

He hesitated.

"I was just starting to go," Faith said. And I knew I hadn't just imagined the pain in Marshall's eyes. Faith had seen it too, and her voice was warm and gentle, the way honey tastes that's been standing in the sun. I looked at her with surprise. Perhaps the fragment of love she'd glimpsed herself had done it. Perhaps, I thought, if Melusina had ever had such a glimpse she wouldn't have botched Faith's life the way she had. But Melusina had never loved anything, not even a dog, really. And Faith had always before been a little off-hand and snippish and young about Marshall and Ruth Napier. Her voice just now was a kind of rich apology for all that.

I folded up my knitting and bent down to lay it in the basket beside my chair. I was thinking, "Why don't I ask Marshall if they've found anything out since morning? He's just been down to the Court House. It isn't natural, with the whole town crying Murder and every parlor in Williamsburg buzzing with it, for us to act as if nothing at all had happened."

So I said aloud, "Is there any news, Marshall?"

He didn't answer, not as quickly as it seemed to me he should. So I glanced up—and looked away quickly, too startled to breathe without gasping. He and Faith were looking at each other. Faith's lips were parted just a little, her face had gone quite pale. But it was the expression in her eyes that was the perfectly extraordinary thing . . . as if she'd suddenly and abruptly discovered in that very instant something she'd not been sure of before; something she hadn't wanted to know, that she'd wanted, in fact, not to know but couldn't help knowing now.

Marshall's dark strong face was pale too, and focused and intense. They looked, I thought with dismay, no more like the two pleasant children who'd grown up together than the man in the moon. Then suddenly Faith turned away, and I saw that her lips were trembling and her eyes wide, and almost anguished, it seemed to me. And Marshall, quite as if my question had solidified, and was still there in the air, waiting for him to take hold of it, jerked himself quite literally to attention.

"They've found out that . . . a woman was at Seymour's last night, in the study—either when he was killed, or immediately after," he said.

His voice was hard, as if it was coming out of a mechanical, not a human, throat, except that it jolted unevenly as Faith reached out her hand to steady herself against the wing of the fireside chair.

"Priddy says it must have been after, because he's convinced the shot was fired through the window from the terrace. They're sure nobody went either in or out of the house from the terrace, either before or after the . . . murder. They've put pink roach powder all over the back entrances and the drains. Anybody going in or out would have had to track the powder. And no one did."

He stopped and wiped the perspiration from his forehead with a crumpled handkerchief.

"Somebody," he said harshly—not because he wanted to be harsh, I thought, but because it was the only way he could control his voice, "a man—went back onto the terrace and out again to the front. He didn't go in the house. They've got his footprints in moulage—that's a kind of wax they use. So if Priddy's right and the shot came from the terrace, it's not so bad for the . . . woman. If he's not, and John Crabtree doesn't seem convinced, because they can't find a gun anywhere—then it won't be so . . . simple."

He stopped abruptly. It was just as if I wasn't there, or the room, or the ottoman, or the roses and lilies in the rug, or the unravelled sock for the Eskimo, or the Empire table with the veneer broken off the apron, or anything—just those two speaking to each other across a barren wind-swept plain. Marshall knowing Faith was the woman in the study; Faith knowing then that Marshall must have been outside . . . and the people who hated Mason Seymour the most all lived at Yardley Hall. It was almost as if I was hearing her say it again.

"How do they know it was a woman there?" I heard my voice say. I knew with a sudden sharp intuition that that was the question Faith dared not ask, and that I was asking it not through any free volition of my own, but because the words were there in the room and some one's lips had to give them form.

Marshall looked at Faith, not me.

"The telephone operator says a signal flashed from the phone there shortly after half-past ten. She said 'Number, please' twice without any answer, and then she heard a woman give a . . . a sort of little gasp. She's sure it was a woman. She can't say why, she just knows it was.—And there are a woman's fingerprints, with blood on them, on the phone."

He stopped again. The atmosphere in the room moved like a dark turgid river slow with fear.

"Does John Crabtree know who it was?" I heard myself asking. My voice sounded strangled and unnatural, but I knew it was because it was falling into a choked and unnatural silence, and because my own ears were tortured with dread.

Even in the candlelight I could see the hard muscles of Marshall's jaw working under the heavy blue shadow of his clean-shaven beard. He didn't answer, not for ever so long, but when he did his voice was more controlled than it had been.

"He hasn't said. All he says is that one woman was known to have been in the house at about that time. He thinks it may be that she . . . killed Seymour—for the reason women always kill men—and picked up the phone to tell the police what she'd done . . . and then couldn't go through with it."

He stopped, and added quietly, "They've been hunting her this evening to take her fingerprints. She's out . . . somewhere."

So that was it, I thought. Marshall knew that Faith was the woman who'd been in the study—but suspicion was pointing to Ruth Napier. He stood torn between the Yardley loyalty to his cousin on the one hand, and on the other a more poignant loyalty to a woman dancing somewhere under the soft May moon in another man's arms. And what, I thought, if between those two loyalties was something else, something grimmer and starker than any one knew—the gaunt terrible shadow of murder—sealing his lips?

If Faith didn't speak, he never could. Only one man had gone into the back garden to the terrace, tracking the roach powder as he went, and come again, tracking more than roach powder . . . unless this murder *was* a kind of human roach powder. Which is a very *dreadful* thing to say, and no really nice woman would dream of saying it.

I knew Faith was thinking that too: that Marshall would not dare to speak. I knew she was thinking of the sound she had heard, standing there beside her dead fiancé's body . . . and that she mustn't now move or speak a word to say she knew.

I heard Marshall say, "We'd better be going, Faith. Your father will be worried," and my heart rose in sharp alarmed protest. I saw Faith's body go taut for an instant.

"Why don't you stay all night with me, Faith," I said, and heard myself trying desperately to sound ordinary and casual. I saw her brighten, clutching an instant at a straw, and grow dim again, rejecting it.

"No, I believe I'd better go along home, thank you, Cousin Lucy," she said evenly.

She picked up her blue cartwheel hat and smiled, and the gold tip of her head, like the flame of a candle Marshall was carrying in his hand, was all I saw past his dark solid figure as she went out the door in front of him.

I let my head rest back against the carved rosewood frame of the rocking chair and closed my eyes. I heard the gate click, and followed them in my mind each step of the way down Francis Street, across the Market Square by the Powder Horn, across the Court House Green into England Street, into Scotland Street along under the tumorous paper mulberries, through the garden gate, through the dark mountains of box . . . to the well house. Then in my inner ear I could hear the thin sound of that chain again, and the plop of the oak bucket, and I could see the shadowy hand in the moonlight, and the blood against the whitewashed board.

My heart stood almost paralyzed with fear as I waited, minute after minute dragging hour-long. Then I got up and ran to the phone. At last—it seemed years and years—I heard Doctor Yardley's mild quiet voice at the other end. . . . I'd never heard him answer the phone before.

"Why, no, Lucy, they haven't come. Is anything the matter? She's perfectly safe with her cousin, my dear . . ."

And then after a long silence: "Why, yes, here they come, down the Palace walk."

I hung up the phone, my hand shaking like a sear dead ivy leaf against a closed shutter. They hadn't taken the path past the well, then, I thought, and somehow it seemed to confirm the fear in my heart.

I went slowly back to the parlor door and stood there with a seasick feeling in my stomach, not knowing what I could do, and knowing that whatever I did would be just wrong. I don't know now how long it was that I stood there before an odd scratching sound outside the house got through, like a bad telephone connection, to my conscious mind. It seemed to me that I'd been hearing it, when I finally did hear it, for a long, long time. It came from the garden door at the back end of the hall, which was strange, because Community had been gone for some time and I couldn't think of any one else who'd be likely to be back there at half-past nine at night.

I suppose one of the bad things about fear is that it distorts and stains all parts of one's life, not just a narrow immediate bit of it, and makes warm friendly things cold and unfriendly . . . so that I stood there, hesitating even to go to my own back door. Then after a moment I said, "Don't be ridiculous!" and went back . . . turning on a lot of lights, however. Rather more than the occasion seemed a moment later to warrant, I'm afraid, for when I got the door opened it was George Luton, Mason Seymour's valet, butler, secretary and what-not, who was out there. He was sort of batting about in the dark, hunting a door, the way a tired moth miller hits against a lighted screen.

## 13

He looked startled too, from the way the house was suddenly illuminated, as if I were receiving Lafayette himself. Although, of course, it wasn't our house the gallant French general visited by the garden door. However, that's something else again, and I can't really see that calling it the intimate history of colonial times makes old Williamsburg's gossip any the less. Certainly there was nothing about Luton that suggested Lafayette. He stood there, not as discreetly sure of himself as he ordinarily was, but still with that quality of unobtrusive persistence that had made one always conscious he was in the room at Mason Seymour's.

"I beg your pardon, Miss Randolph," he said in a low voice, glancing over his shoulder down the moon-lit garden toward the kitchen, for all the world like the third conspirator in a play. "I'm sorry to be coming at this hour. I'm sure I wouldn't want it to look . . ."

I pushed the screen door open and said, even more like Melusina than I'd intended, "Come in, Mr. Luton, and don't stand out there stuttering. I'm sure nothing ever looks like anything but what it is, so kindly state your business."

I led the way back into the parlor . . . something pricking at the corner of my mind, telling me to be careful. I sat down, and said, "Well?"

Luton stood in the door. I supposed at first it was the way the light caught him that made his face look jaundice-pale and haggard. Then I saw it wasn't entirely that. He had

changed—just since the morning before he had changed un-
believably. What Bill had called his ten layers of lard had
worn down to hardly one. His eyes seemed to be hunting
corners to crawl into. His hands—not weak but surprisingly
small and feminine—kept moving around the hard brim of his
bowler hat like a green measuring-worm on a rose stem. He
was most plainly laboring under some extraordinary emotion.—And suddenly it occurred to me that maybe this man
was sorry Mason Seymour was dead!

That may sound very odd, but it's quite true. I'd just assumed, I'm afraid, that everybody had taken the philosophic
attitude about Mason's untimely decease that I myself had
taken—namely that everything works out for the best . . .
though I wasn't, unfortunately, able to carry that over to
Faith's problem.

He looked down at me with oddly naked eyes, and said
unsteadily, "I beg your pardon, madam. I have just put Mr.
Seymour's body on the train, going North for burial. I . . .
I hope you will excuse me, madam."

And I felt very much ashamed of myself, and sorry for
this man standing there with me watching him gimlet-eyed
and sour-mouthed, saying stonily, "Well, my good man?"—
in effect anyway.

Actually I said, "Sit down, Mr. Luton."

"If it wouldn't be taking too great a liberty, madam," he
said, almost gratefully . . . so gratefully, in fact, and at the
same time so smoothly that I found myself remembering that
people had said sometimes Luton acted more like the master
than the servant at Mason Seymour's. Then all the other gossip began to seep up out of the cellar of my mind.
That Luton wasn't actually a servant at all, because Mason
had the full quota of colored help. That Mason had some
strange hold over Luton, or conversely that Luton had some
strange hold over Mason . . . the sort of thing I'd always
put down to the fact that we don't have white servants in
Williamsburg and have to have some explanation for any one
who does. Anyway, I'm sure a visitor from Mars would be
rather put to it at times to discover from the way Community runs me that I'm the mistress and she the servant.
Her hold over me is as effective certainly as any black-
mailer's could be, through the simple fact that she's been my
hands and feet so long that I'd probably starve without her.

Yet she's the best friend I have in the world, and would be very sorry indeed if anybody murdered me.

That's why I'd never paid much attention to the discussion of Mason's and Luton's problems, and I shouldn't be doing it now, Heaven knows, if they hadn't been dumped at my feet on the parlor floor by the man sitting stiffly—in spite of his smooth tongue—his hat balanced on his knees, in the last of my great-grandmother's Hepplewhite dining-room chairs, against the wall next to the pembroke table with one drop leaf missing.

"You see, Miss Randolph, my position is equivocal in the extreme," he said.

"I'm sure you'll find both Mr. Crabtree and Sergeant Priddy honest and capable men, Mr. Luton," I said.

"That's not entirely the point, if I may say so, madam," he replied evenly. "If I might explain . . ."

"Don't you think it would be better to explain to Mr. Crabtree?"

His grip on his hat brim tightened. He made a move to rise.

"Perhaps it would, madam."

He put one hand in his coat pocket and took out an envelope.

"But in view of . . . this, and in so much as you seem to have the confidence——"

He had got up and put the envelope in my lap, and got back to his chair, with almost no evidence of motion, some way, and I sat there looking at it.

"If you'll open it, madam . . ."

I picked it up and raised the flap. Inside was a white handkerchief—except that it wasn't white. It had big dry brown spots on it. My hands shook—not at the spots but at the blue letters trailing gaily, like sky writing, across the corner folded so that I would see it first. "Faith Yardley," they said, with a gallant little flourish.

And the awful part of it was that I'd given them to her myself—two dozen of them with her name in red and blue, and in white on red and blue, because she could never keep handkerchiefs at school.

"—The confidence of Miss Faith, madam. I thought perhaps . . ."

I heard Luton's quiet voice as I imagine a prisoner hears

the key turned in a smooth oiled lock behind him. I could feel his steady eyes on me. I closed the flap of the envelope. He got up again and came toward me, holding his hand out for it. I tried not to shrink back, clutching at it to keep it from him, as I wanted to do but dared not do, for fear he'd see how much it all meant.

So I let him take it. He moved to the mantel and held the corner of the handkerchief in the tip of the candle flame, watched it flare up until I thought the flame would eat his hand, dropped it into the fireplace, and stood there, very quietly, watching it burn. Then he took the fire irons and scattered the crisp black ash. I watched him go back to the chair against the wall and sit down.

"What is it you wish to say, Mr. Luton?" I asked.

"Thank you, madam," he said.

I reached down and picked up my knitting and unfolded the towel on my lap.

"You see, Miss Randolph, my position with Mr. Seymour was not precisely that of a servant. At one time I was employed in a bank in Paris. I lost my post . . . through a youthful indiscretion. I was unable to get another position. Some one suggested I might be useful to Mr. Seymour, who had just come abroad. It happened that I was familiar with the Boulevards, and the West End of London. Mr. Seymour had all the facts at his disposal, and when he quit Europe two years later he suggested I come along with him and make a fresh start in the new world."

I suppose anybody who'd not spent her life in Williamsburg, Virginia, with a very rare foray into the metropolis of Richmond, or Norfolk, would have got a great deal more, or possibly a great deal less, out of this extraordinary circumlocution than I. I found myself one moment deciding he'd lost his post, as he called it, for falling in love with a duchess, and the next that he'd made off with the entire French gold reserve. It was all too confusing, and every time I glanced up from my knitting there he'd be with his eyes fixed on me so steadily that I declare I didn't know what to think.

"Then Mr. Seymour bought me a farm in Canada," he continued quietly. "But I found very shortly I hadn't got the physical stamina farm work demands, so I came back to him. I had charge of his household, his accounts, and all except the most personal of his correspondence. I never so

much as answered the door except when he had very . . .
especial guests."

He moistened his lips and hesitated for an instant.

"My position now is very difficult, madam. Mr. Talbot
Seymour, who has taken charge of the house, doesn't understand my previous duties, and acts as if I were a personal servant. The result is that I am unable to stay there any longer."

I looked up. I didn't, I'm afraid, see how any of this was
concerned with me or the girl whose handkerchief still filled
the room with a faint odor of burnt cloth. He apparently
understood at once, because he went on more quickly.

"You see, Miss Randolph, I was planning to leave as soon
as Mr. Seymour's marriage to Miss Faith took place. We had
discussed it. Mr. Seymour felt, and I felt even more strongly,
that Miss Faith, being a Southern girl, would wish to have
personal charge of her own establishment. He made arrange-
ments for me to have a position in New York with a firm of
wine merchants where I could use the knowledge I have, and
where the work wouldn't be too difficult. You see, I was
badly gassed during the last months of the War, and am not
as strong as I should like to be. It's possible for me to take
that position the first of next month, although we had
thought it would be somewhat later."

"That's splendid," I said.

Mr. Luton cleared his throat.

"There is only one thing, madam."

His hands moving on his hat brim were agitated now
. . . and I'd given up all pretense at working.

"It's very difficult to explain—and that's why I felt you
might be able to help me," he said slowly. "You see, Mr. Seymour called me into the study just before Doctor Yardley
came to the house last evening, and said that because everything had gone so nicely—he was very much in love with
Miss Faith, madam—he was going to give me the present
now that he had planned on giving me later. He had his
check book out on the table and had started writing. He was
in very high spirits, and I may say I was surprised to see the
figure on the check."

I thought, "Oh," and picked up my knitting again.

"Just then we heard the knocker, and I went out to see
who it was. Mr. Seymour was anxious not to be disturbed by
. . . certain people."

Mr. Luton's hands were motionless on his hat.

"It was Doctor Yardley. I showed him in, and closed the door. He stayed about half an hour."

I waited, looking at him, keeping back a dozen questions that rushed to my lips.

"Mr. Seymour showed him out himself, and when I went in to take away the glasses I saw the check there, still unsigned. Mr. Mason came back and said, 'Will you see if you can get Miss Melusina Yardley on the phone.' He seemed disturbed, but not seriously so. I asked him if anything was wrong. He said No. I tried to get Miss Yardley, but she was out. Mr. Seymour said to try again after dinner. Then, as I was bringing in brandy—he didn't trust the servants with the key to the cellarette—I saw him out in the garden with Mr. Marshall Yardley."

"In the front garden, or the back garden?" I asked.

"In the front, madam. It was dark, and our front garden is quite private, though I imagine Mr. Seymour would have preferred as little seclusion for his interview with Mr. Marshall Yardley as possible. Mr. Marshall was angry, and even . . . threatening. But that is not the point, Miss Randolph. I don't wish to go into any of that. It's just that later, when Mr. Haines came and I called Mr. Seymour, I saw the check still on the table. I said, 'I hope you won't forget the most important part of a check, sir,' and he laughed and said, 'As soon as I'm through here, George.' "

Mr. Luton paused. His face had taken on an odd determined look, his eyes were terribly bright.

"Well, this morning, madam, when I went downstairs and found him, I couldn't help seeing he was sitting there with a pen in his hand, his check book still open . . . but the check he'd made for me was gone. There was just the blue perforated tip under his hand, Miss Randolph . . . as if somebody had ripped it out, and torn it as they did."

"You mean," I said, "that you never got the check?"

"No, madam. And . . . I thought perhaps you would ask the young lady to give it to me—in return for her handkerchief."

I stared at him.

"You mean you think Faith Yardley——"

"I simply mean, madam, that that amount of money means a great deal to me. And I understand that Mr. Mason's latest will leaves all his property to her . . ."

I was utterly speechless. His voice kept falling on my brain like monotonously dripping water.

"I can't blame her for being incensed at Mr. Mason's philandering, Miss Randolph. Being young and unsophisticated, she hadn't any way of knowing that he was tired of being unsettled and that he regarded his marriage very seriously indeed. It was just the abrupt way the announcement came out, when he hadn't hoped for it for some months, that upset everything."

I got my breath then, and got up.

"Mr. Luton," I said. "I think, if I were you, I would go to Mr. Crabtree immediately."

His face hardened, not very pleasantly; but his eyes dimmed as if a bright light had been turned off behind them.

"I think you're making a mistake, Miss Randolph," he said steadily.

"No, I'm not," I said.

He stood a moment. Then he said, "I'll wait till morning, madam. If you should change your mind, perhaps you'll be good enough to phone Mr. Mason's house."

I heard the knocker give a little bang, the way it does when the door closes, and stood there, my hands quite cold. What, I thought, if I *was* making a mistake? But I couldn't be, it was ridiculous on the face of it. Faith Yardley wouldn't take a check. But what if some one else . . . I stopped. I didn't dare go past that.

I put my hand on the door knob, not to call him back, really, but to tell him I'd let him know in the morning what I'd decided. I turned it and drew the door open, and stopped.

Luton was still there at the gate, and beyond him, just coming in, was the towering white figure of Bill Haines. I saw him stop, and then I heard Luton's soft unholy voice say:

"I don't believe you remember me, do you, Mr. Haines?"

I closed the door quickly. My heart had gone as cold as my hands.

# 14

I knew, without knowing exactly how I knew it, that Luton was referring then to some particular time in the past that Bill Haines didn't remember him from . . . not just that he hadn't at that moment recognized him, coming out of my gate. It's strange, too, how some sounds that just as sounds are quite harmless seem nevertheless to strike deep-rooted memories of fear . . . like a bird hearing a water moccasin, or a dog, they say, coming on a tumble-down graveyard in the woods at midnight. Something in Luton's voice affected me that way then, stirring a forgotten atavistic terror, so that as obediently as if I were obeying an old instinct I stole silently into the parlor and put out the lights and crept upstairs in the dark.

It seemed a long long time before I heard the gate click and the hinge on the office door groan. A little ladder of light through the slats of the shutter climbed up the ceiling above my window. I lay in bed watching it, missing the sound of Bill Haines bursting exuberantly about in the four narrow walls like a Newfoundland puppy in a shoe box. Once or twice a black shadow crossed the yellow slits on the wall, and at last I heard the hinge groan open, and creak shut, and then after a while the light went out and I heard Bill open the window and put the screen in.

To try to say what horrible thousand imaginings were racing through my mind before sleep came would be like trying to describe a mental cross section of a madhouse. And when it did come it was worse. I kept dreaming and waking up and dreaming again that Faith and Bill were caught in the quicksands near College Creek, and that Ruth Napier and Luton were looking on, in some frightful subtle way hindering Doctor Yardley and Marshall and myself from saving them . . . and over it all was Talbot Seymour's brilliant white smile and checked coat, weaving in and out a pattern so sinister and so hopeless that I couldn't bear it.

When I woke up I felt as if I'd been riding all night at a witches' Sabbath, and from the way Community's coconut eyes searched my face as she poured my coffee next morning I knew I looked it too. When she said, "Mr. Haines, he look lak he slep' all night in a thrashin' machine," I saw she was putting two and two together again . . . with what possibly extraordinary results this time I was too distressed to think.

And all the time I kept knowing I would tell Luton I wouldn't speak to John Crabtree, and would speak to Faith, and I hated myself, because there's something mean and degrading about fear. But the more I thought of it the more intolerable the idea of my calling him on the phone became. Finally, to escape being conscious of the phone, I put on my hat and left the house.

The office door was open. Community was in there, running the carpet sweeper over the threadbare rug, her deep religious voice singing over and over—

> "Nobody knows the trouble I've seen,
> Nobody knows but Jesus."

Bill was gone. I knew that because his car was gone from the parking cobblestones under the elm tree. I wondered anxiously where he was and what he was doing.

I got as far as the Powder Horn across the Market Square, and stopped. In front of the old court house in the Duke of Gloucester Street I saw Talbot Seymour sitting bareheaded in his dead cousin's car. John Crabtree the Commonwealth Attorney was standing with one foot on the running board, his arms leaning on the door, talking to him. There was a clatter and clop of horses' hoofs and John looked up. The blue coach and four with its coachman in blue and footman in brown up behind him drove by. Inside was Hallie Taswell in her sprigged muslin gown and frilled white cap. She nodded to John Crabtree, and then, as they passed, I saw her put

her handkerchief up to her mouth. The coach went on toward the Capitol at the end of the street, John Crabtree
watching it go.

I went back behind the Powder Horn and down to the
Travis House gardens, and through that way across the
Duke of Gloucester Street to the Palace Green. Even if I
didn't want to meet John Crabtree face to face just then, I
still think the sight of him had brought me back a little
sanity. I was suddenly quite calm again, and aware that the
only sensible and reasonable thing in the world to do was to
talk to Faith, tell her what Luton had told me, so she'd know
what was coming if he tried to speak to her.

But I didn't get as far as Yardley Hall. A little crowd of
colored boys and dogs and a few colored women in neat
house dresses had gathered across the Green where the lane
runs down by the Palace wall at the end of the Canal. Sergeant Priddy's car was there, at the side of the big door lead-
ing to the Palace kitchen courtyard. I hesitated. Obviously
something had happened . . . but equally obviously I was
not in a position to join the group of goggle-eyed colored
boys to find out what it was. Then a boy on a bicycle who
delivers for the butcher reluctantly separated himself from
the crowd and pedalled across the circle. The meat on his
basket had soaked through the paper, so I knew he'd been
there some little time.

"What's going on over there, Fred?" I asked.

"I dunno, Mis' Lucy," he said. "They's down there in the
Canal huntin' somethin'. Dunno what it is."

I doubt if the hounds of hell could have kept me from doing what I did then. I crossed the Green. The little group
broke apart and I went through, down the rain-guttered path
that runs along the Palace garden wall, until I got to the
level aqueduct where a little brook drains into the Canal.
Then, seeing the gate was open just a little way along and
nobody was there to stop me, I went in and through the
shrubs to the Canal.

There I stopped. On the rustic bridge, under the long pale
streamers of the weeping willow, and to the intense annoyance of a mother duck whose nest, I suppose, was near by,
was Sergeant Priddy, with a couple of other men I didn't
know. Standing in the water, in hip boots, was still another
man. He was fishing in the green spirogyra, among the lily
roots and swamp iris, with a long rake. And just as I peered

through the bay and laurel bushes I heard them all exclaim, and I saw the man under the bridge pull something up.

It was a shotgun. And I heard one of the men on the bridge say, "I figured that's how it was—I was at the other end just before eleven and heard something splash. They musta thrown it over the fence from outside."

I didn't wait for any more of that. I don't think any woman of fifty-five, used as I am to the mildest and least active kind of existence, ever traversed the length of the Palace Green and crossed the green of the Market Square as rapidly as I did. One of the ladies of the Auxiliary says she said good-morning to me and I told her I'd bake a cake for the sale Saturday, but I have no memory of that. I only know that I got back up Francis Street and through the white picket gate and to the office door very quickly indeed.

I didn't knock. I hurried straight in and to the old press in the corner, and opened its door.

My father's shotgun, that had stood there since he put it reluctantly away thirty years before, was gone.

I turned around. Community was standing in the door. She'd known it, of course, since the morning she cleaned Bill Haines' shoes. I leaned against the foot of the sleigh-back bed and closed my eyes. Then I opened them. A car had stopped at the gate.

"It's Sergeant Priddy and Mistah John Crabtree, Mis' Lucy," Community said.

# 15

I didn't realize, not until I saw the swift change in the expression on John Crabtree's face flash into Michael Priddy's, how revealing my own must have been as I came into the parlor. For an instant all three of us stood perfectly motionless, their eyes on me, mine on them, until mine moved and fell on the shotgun lying on a damp newspaper across the ottoman. Brief as that instant was, it was long enough for a whole new pattern to shape simultaneously in both their minds . . . for until that instant, the possibility that I—their own Sunday school teacher, one of the town's most respectable spinsters —could have had any connection with the murder of Mason Seymour had never even faintly occurred to them.

I felt rather than saw their eyes follow mine to the gun on the ottoman, and to my father's name, "J. P. Randolph," burned in the polished wood of the butt.

John Crabtree wrinkled his face up and wiped his moist forehead. It was hard to know where to start—even I recognized that. So I said:

"If it's that shotgun you're worrying about, John, it belongs to me. And I knew it was gone, because I was passing the Palace when you all were pulling it out of the Canal. I thought it looked familiar—that's why I rushed home to see if mine was missing. It is—or was. But how long it's been gone, or who took it, I haven't an idea."

I saw a heavy weight rise miraculously from the Commonwealth Attorney's almost comically furrowed brow. As his old Sunday school teacher I was glad it didn't so much as

occur to him to doubt my word—and relieved too, I may
say. As a voter it seemed to me he ought to be a little more
cautious about accepting people's statements. That was before he went on, he and Sergeant Priddy together, asking me
a thousand more questions—when I'd seen the gun last,
where did I keep it, how many people knew I kept it
there . . .

I tried to think when I'd seen it last. The nearest I could
come to it was in March when we were spring cleaning and
I had Community's brother clean and oil it. I always did
that, two or three times a year.

"Was it loaded, Miss Lucy?"

I shook my head.

"Who knew you kept it in the office?"

"I've been trying to think," I said, which wasn't true . . .
I'd been trying desperately to think that Bill Haines of course
knew, that Faith Yardley knew, that Marshall Yardley knew.

"It's always stood in the corner press," I said. "I suppose
everybody I've ever showed the office to must know that,
because I always open the cupboard—it's considered very interesting by antiquers. I mean, practically anybody might
know, if they were interested in knowing."

John Crabtree nodded slowly.

"For instance, if any of us stopped to think, I expect we
could remember a dozen houses in Williamsburg where they
have old arms of some kind . . . not counting either the
Powder Horn or the Palace. Mason Seymour himself had a
lot of bowie knives and tomahawks and blunderbusses in the
room over the coach house. You remember he collected old
weapons."

I didn't go on to say the Yardleys had a whole armory in
and around the iron chest in the old wine cellar of the Hall.
They knew that, both of them, as well as I did, because they
used to play pirates down there with Marshall when they
were boys.

They both nodded. My heart began to rise, and sank
abruptly as Sergeant Priddy said, "I'll go ask Community—
she might remember."

I heard his heavy steps along the hall, and Community's
hymn stop. Then I saw that John Crabtree was watching me listen, so I sat down, trying not to look concerned at
all. He sat down too, and leaned forward, his elbows on his
knees.

"Miss Lucy," he said, very kindly, really, "what all's goin' on around here?"

"—John," I said abruptly, without really knowing until I got it out that I was going to say it at all, "Luton told me that Mason Seymour had written him a check, fairly large he said, and that when he found Mason in the morning, his check book was there, but the check was gone.—Is that true?"

He looked at me. "Did he tell you that?"

I nodded, a cold feeling that I'd made a ghastly mistake creeping about my heart.

"It's funny he didn't tell me about it," he said slowly. "There was a check, all right. We got a picture of the one underneath it. You can trace the name, and the amount."

"Was it signed?" I asked. If it hadn't been signed, and Luton had taken it himself to cast suspicion on . . . I didn't need to go any farther, for John Crabtree's slow voice wiped all that—wishful thinking, I suppose you might call it —right out.

"Oh, it was signed, all right, Miss Lucy. You can see the signature plain. In fact the tail of the 'r' runs onto the piece somebody tore off, gettin' it out from under his hand."

I said, "Oh," noticing the quiet glance he gave me through a cloud of blue-grey fragrant smoke and wishing I hadn't said anything at all. Wishing that, it seems almost perverse that I should have then gone on the way I did.

"How much was the check for, John?" I asked. "Luton said it was right good size."

"It was for $2,500.00," John Crabtree said. He looked at me. "—You wouldn't reckon the reason he came to you about that check, instead of comin' to me or Priddy, was he thought maybe you could help him get it back quicker'n we could, would you, now, Miss Lucy?"

He drawled that out with a kind of cheerful guile, like an amiable and definitely homey sort of serpent.

It must have been in my imagination—that sudden faint odor of burnt cloth in the room. "Just how would I be able to do that, John?" I asked tartly.

"That's just what I was goin' to ask you to tell me, Miss Lucy," he answered placidly, blowing a wreath of blue smoke above his head.

"He can never smell anything through that," I thought—

sharply denying an impulse to look toward the fireplace. I
didn't of course need to look there to know that the scattered black ash of Faith's handkerchief was still there. I'd
noticed the minute I came downstairs in the morning that
Community hadn't touched the fireplace. In fact, I'd even
thought, for an instant, of setting fire to the accumulation in
it myself.

And now, sitting there with the unmistakable odor of
burnt cloth in my mind at least, I realized I'd been very stupid indeed. Not for not setting fire to the melange in the fireplace, though that was stupid too, but for mentioning Luton
and the check. If the fact of the check was true, what other
conclusion could the Commonwealth Attorney draw than
the one he had drawn? I kept asking myself that, knowing all
the time that I'd done it because I hadn't believed the fact
of the check—I hadn't actually believed Luton's story at all.
I'd just been frightened by it, and by Faith's blood-stained
handkerchief . . .

John Crabtree said placidly: "Findin' out who murdered
somebody isn't just takin' the first fellow you don't happen
to like and sayin' he did it."

"No, I suppose not," I said. I reached down and picked up
my knitting, knowing that this last was just a friendly inter-
polation to help me save face, and that he was still waiting
for me to answer his question about why Luton should have
come to me about the check instead of going to him.

Just then Sergeant Priddy came back, the change in his
kindly familiar face so sharp and alarming to me that
the sudden tension in my throat was almost strangling. It was
incredible, and terrifying, seeing him so, his jaw set like
granite, his mouth a hard grim line.

"Tell me what you know about this young fellow Haines,
will you please, Miss Lucy?" he asked curtly.

He sat down on the ottoman, grim-faced, watching me.
He'd forgotten he'd ever sat there eating ginger cookies, trying to learn the Ten Commandments—especially the one
that says "Thou shalt not bear false witness against thy
neighbor." Surely, I thought, wondering desperately what he
had found out, what Community had told him, that was
what was happening now, only with inanimate objects doing
it . . . Bill Haines never liked Mason Seymour!

I said, trying to give my voice the conviction that had

melted to nothing in my heart, "I don't know anything about him except that he's a splendid person, that he was sent to me by an old friend."

I didn't say that he'd known Mason Seymour and his man Luton somewhere and didn't like them, that he fell in love at first sight with the girl Mason was to marry, that he was now involved with another girl of Mason's, that he was at Mason's the night he was murdered, that he tried to keep Faith from going there . . .

"Who sent him to you, Miss Lucy?" Sergeant Priddy asked.

"Summers Baldwin," I said.

The two looked at each other.

"Did you get a letter from him?"

I shook my head. "He brought a card."

"May I see it, please?"

I went to the tea caddy where Community puts all cards two days after they're left. There weren't but a few in it. They dated back to Easter—mostly left by people who come from a distance and like to see a restored house that's being lived in, so they can go back home and say, "And that lead blue really isn't *too* dark, my dear . . . not when you get *used* to it." I looked through them. Summers Baldwin's card was not there.

In the Adam mirror I saw John Crabtree and Sergeant Priddy exchange glances behind my back.

"Never mind," John said. "Did you recognize Mr. Baldwin's handwritin', Miss Lucy?"

"Yes," I said. And then I stopped short. I hadn't seen it for years, of course; and I thought suddenly just as I answered that question, "Did I recognize it—or was it just his name on the card?"

I saw Michael Priddy's lips tighten still more at the look that must have been on my face.

"Anyway," I said, "it's quite simple to prove, if you doubt he sent Mr. Haines. I'll telephone him, if you'd like."

"Except he's in Europe," John Crabtree said. "He's been there over a month."

I just said "Oh," rather miserably.

"Do you know where Haines is now, Miss Lucy?" Sergeant Priddy asked.

I shook my head. "I haven't seen him this morning," I said,

and realized, from the quick glance they gave each other, that I was foolish to have said that.

I suppose that's why I don't have as clear a picture of how what happened next exactly did happen as I should have. I mean, I was so worried about Bill . . . or not Bill personally so much as the whole pattern surrounding him . . . that I didn't pay any attention to Sergeant Priddy actually—until he'd suddenly just catapulted from the ottoman across the room and was down on his knees in front of the fireplace, and in a flash had reached his arm into it and held up, covered with the furry coagulated dust of Community's carpet sweeper, the black cord with the frayed ends that had broken from my reticule.

I stared at it, my eyes rivetted, remembering it as one would remember a nightmare if it suddenly materialized in front of his face. I could feel their eyes—John Crabtree's as they moved incredulously from the frayed silk to me, and Michael Priddy's searching my face, not incredulously like John's but as if appalled at the death of an illusion . . . one of the few, I imagine, that he still had left about people, now that he was a policeman.

It was the Commonwealth Attorney who recovered first. "It looks like you'd have to do a little explainin', Miss Lucy," he drawled.

"It looks like Miss Lucy and this Haines are goin' to have more than explainin' to do," Sergeant Priddy interrupted brusquely. "Community says that shotgun was there last week. And you never use pink cockroach powder—but the sweepings in the office fireplace are full of it."

I stared at him, literally with my mouth open.

"But—that's not possible!" I cried. Marshall Yardley's words beat like crashing hail on my inner ears: "They'd put pink roach powder all over the back entrances . . . they've got his footprints in moulage . . ."

Michael Priddy nodded. "There's pink powder in the fluff from the carpet sweeper all right, Miss Lucy."

He was smiling grimly. He was somebody I'd never seen before in my life.

"Where is Haines, Miss Lucy?"

I shook my head. "I don't know," I whispered. I knew, looking at him, that he didn't believe a word I'd said. He swung the fluff-covered black silk cord of my reticule between his fingers, that grim half-smile still in his eyes and on his mouth.

"Tell us about this, Miss Lucy."

I shook my head again. "There's no use. You wouldn't believe me if I did."

John Crabtree got up, almost abruptly for him. "Don't you let Mike get you all upset, Miss Lucy," he said gently. They moved toward the door. "I'm goin' to ask you to stay here till I come back, Miss Lucy—hear?" John said.

I nodded. I heard very well indeed. I also heard them go out, and then through the open window I heard Michael Priddy's voice: "I'm goin' back and see what else is in that fireplace, before Miss Lucy sticks a match to it."

"Okay, fella—but go easy. No use raisin' too much stink around here. That guy Seymour wasn't worth it."

All I had time to do was grab a bit of blackened cloth where Faith's handkerchief hadn't entirely carbonized, thrust it into the Eskimo's sock and get back to my chair before Sergeant Priddy came back.

He gave me an odd look. " 'Scuse me, Miss Lucy, but you understand I've got my duty to do."

"By all means, Michael," I said stiffly. "I'm glad to see you've improved so much."

It was astonishing to see what all he got out. Two cigarettes with bright lipstick on them, part of a card that at first I thought triumphantly was Summers Baldwin's but that was only the one to Mason Seymour's party I'd thrown there so Bill wouldn't see it, the coffee spoon that had been missing two weeks, a button off the sleeve of a dress that Community swore I'd lost at the moving pictures. Eventually he wrapped his dreary loot in his handkerchief, picked up my father's shotgun and said, "Good-bye, Miss Lucy—please don't do nothing else foolish, hear?" I nodded again as he went out.

When Community came in to announce lunch I was still sitting there. She looked at the fireplace, and then at me. She said gloomily, "Was roach powder on Mistah Bill's shoes. Wasn' none on yours."

I nodded. "When did you notice the shotgun last, Community—really?"

"When Ah took Mistah Bill's breakfas' the fust mo'nin' he here. He was aimin' out th' do' at that moth-eaten ol' squirrel. Ah says, 'Yo' bettah put that ol' gun down, Mis' Lucy she don' lak nobody tech nothin' don' belong to 'em.' He jus' grinned, but he put it back in th' press. That's the las' Ah seen of it."

"Did you tell Sergeant Priddy that?"

"No *ma'am*. Ah didn' tell him *nothin'*, ceptin' we don' have no ol' cockroaches roun' this house, an' ain' nobody goin' roun' say we does."

So that, I thought, was how he'd found out we didn't use pink roach powder. Which was ironic too—because we've had a cockroach named General Sherman who has lived in the office wood basket as long as I can remember—or I presume he's the same one and was still there unless the powder Bill tracked home was too much for him. It would be odd, I thought, if Community's pride, based on the erroneous assumption that she's a neat housekeeper, should wind our lodger up behind the bars in England Street.

I didn't say anything, and when I went over to the office after lunch she was there, brushing up the hearth after a man who'd come and taken away the fluff from the carpet sweeper and some dust out of the fireplace. They'd gone through Bill's things too, without attempting to put them back in order.

# 16

It's odd how the mere fact that you're not free to leave a place makes it a kind of prison even though there's no other place you'd rather be, actually. That's how my parlor seemed when I went back to it. I thought I'd never be able to stay there all afternoon. Yet when I started roaming around I felt Community's miserable eyes following me like a yellow hound's.

I suppose actually that like a great many other people I'm only law-abiding when it doesn't conflict with my own sense of freedom. Or maybe it was because, after those two had left, something my father used to say when he was Commonwealth Attorney kept picking at the locks of my mind:

"Mark you me, Lucy—nobody has ever yet committed a murder without leaving his signature on the deed. The law's problem is to find it and read it . . . and read it correctly."

And now John Carter Crabtree obviously regarded the pink powder as Bill's signature . . . and I knew—no doubt because I wanted so passionately to know—that it was really a bitter unconscious forgery. And whether I thought now that if I went back to Mason Seymour's I could find that where the others had failed, I don't know. I do know, however, that I slipped out of the house without a word to Community and made a bee line for the house in Scotland Street.

I kept thinking how I'd explain my coming if it was Luton I met, hoping it would be one of the colored servants, because it would be simple that way. And when I got there

Joe was sweeping the brick walk. He said, "Step right in, Miss Lucy, you'll find 'em in the liberry." And I did—only I didn't go into the library. I stopped abruptly in the sitting room, and stared, definitely open-mouthed, at the extraordinary scene in the overmantel mirror.

For an instant it simply didn't make sense; then I realized that it was not the study, but the reflection of the study in the girandole between the front windows that I saw, and that if he looked, Mr. Talbot Seymour could see me as plainly as I saw him. Only he wasn't looking. He was totally absorbed in going through the contents of the safe, which I'd never known was a safe before, because it looked like any other painted panel of the wall, even to the print of the dashing Colonel Tarleton hanging on it.

But it wasn't the fact of the safe that was extraordinary. It was the desperate and furtive haste in every line and every movement of the man's body, and the way he kept glancing over his shoulder at the other door and at the door into the hall. Even then he missed the exact instant that the figure of his cousin's man appeared there.

Luton halted abruptly, stood there for a fraction of a moment, stepped silently back, hidden, and stood, cat and mouse fashion, watching Mr. Talbot Seymour stealthily going through bundles of documents neatly held together with green rubber bands.

Then, as if he had seen enough, he took a step into the doorway and cleared his throat. Talbot Seymour jumped, recovered himself and turned sharply around, his face dark.

"I thought I told you to pack and get the hell out of here," he said evenly. His eyes were dangerous; so was his clipped quiet voice. And so, in fact, in a different way, were Luton's. He had changed again. There was nothing subdued or respectful or discreet about him, as there had been the first morning I'd seen him after Mason Seymour's murder, or alarmed and cornered as there'd been at my house. Whether it was that he'd cornered Talbot Seymour, so that in some way he now had the upper hand, or whether something else had happened to give him confidence, I don't know. He certainly had it.

"I'm not taking either orders or suggestions from you, Mr. Seymour," he said quietly. "You're as much of an outsider here as I am. More, I'd say, until I've finished the month I've been paid for."

They stood for a moment measuring each other with hostile wary appraisal across the mahogany desk where Mason Seymour's shattered body had sprawled. It was Talbot Seymour who gave way. He raised his eyebrows, took a cigarette, tapped it for a moment on his gold case, lighted it, and blew a long insolently meditative stream of smoke through his nostrils. He said: "I suggest it's time we get together, Luton."

His voice was quietly suave. "You stand to lose a good deal too, don't you, Luton?"

The valet looked at him steadily for an instant. "I don't know what you're talking about."

"Oh yes you do," Talbot Seymour said. "Look here. We're both in this. If you hadn't written me, I'd never have known Mason was even thinking of getting married, or about that old Jezebel trying to rope him in."

"That was before I'd realized Mr. Mason was so taken with Miss Faith's fresh charm," Luton said evenly.

"Baloney," Talbot Seymour said. "Taken with her Waterford lustres and all the other antiques, and the itch to be squire of Yardley Hall and snoot the people who know his money came from a phoney patent medicine. You don't mean her fresh charm—you mean her decayed ancestors'."

Luton said nothing. Talbot Seymour came around the desk up to him.

"That's not the point. If that second will holds, you lose what?—twenty-five thousand and a farm in Canada. You get a kick in the pants. You say he was writing a check when he was bumped off. Maybe you can collect it if the gal wants to believe you, and coughs up as a reward to the faithful servant."

"You forget Mr. Mason arranged for me to have a position in New York," Luton said quietly.

Talbot Seymour laughed.

"Fifty dollars a week, six days a week, in a New York cellar—when you've been your own boss and lived on the fat of the land for fifteen years!—And just how long do you think you'd hang on to a job with Mason dead? You're too old, you're too soft. Some clerk would walk off with the petty cash first thing—and who would they pin it on, because he's got a record? And Mason wouldn't be around to give you a character."

Mr. Seymour laughed again. In the girandole I could see Luton's eyes resting steadily on him.

"You're sunk, and you know it. If you didn't, you wouldn't have written me to come up and try to break up the match—get the old boy to Paris till he got the spring and the magnolias out of his blood."

Talbot Seymour flicked the ash off his cigarette.

"The same holds for me, Luton. I was figuring on twenty thousand a year myself. I get two thousand and a letter to my congressman saying Mason will appreciate anything nice in the way of a WPA job he can wangle for me."

There was a moment's silence.

"I'm just pointing out, Luton, that if accidentally that second will——"

Mr. Seymour lowered his voice.

"—should fall in the incinerator with the morning garbage, both our futures would be considerably pleasanter to look forward to . . ."

"You're not suggesting I should destroy Mr. Mason's second will?" Luton asked coolly.

Talbot Seymour nodded. "Unless, of course, you've done it already." He added softly, "I don't think you have. Have you, Luton?"

"No."

Seymour nodded again. "You get the will—I'll do the trick."

"No," Luton said coldly.

"You mean you don't know where it is?—After all you've done the last fifteen years for my honored cousin, he didn't consult you when he made it out?"

"That's not what I mean at all," Luton said. "I merely mean that since I've been with Mr. Mason, I've gone absolutely straight. I'm not taking any chances on you turning up after you've run through your money and saying 'Luton killed my brother and burned his second will so he'd get twenty-five thousand and a farm instead of a present of twenty-five hundred and a lousy job he knew he couldn't keep.'"

I could see Talbot Seymour's body tense.

"I lived long enough with your cousin," Luton went on slowly, "to know any Seymour would double-cross his grandmother. And I'll get along very nicely, thank you. And the idea of your having to work for a living isn't going to bother me at all."

He paused for an instant, and went on very deliberately.

"On the other hand, I don't think I'll tell Crabtree you didn't know about the second will until you got here.—He might think you shot your cousin thinking the first will was still in effect."

Talbot Seymour's face in the mirror was terrifying.

"You dirty rat," he said softly . . . and I never heard so much sheer hatred in anybody's voice.

I shrank back involuntarily toward the hall—but not before I saw Luton's eyes shift quickly to the mirror opposite the one between the windows, and back again. My heart was as cold as ice as I realized that he'd seen me, he'd known all the time, probably, that I was standing there in the next room, hearing every word. Then he said, as Talbot Seymour must have started to speak, "Sssh—some one's coming up on the porch."

He was out in the hall and to the door just as I got the screen open and myself outside. There wasn't the flicker of an eyelash in his pale face to suggest he'd even suspected I'd been inside.

"Will you come in, Miss Randolph? Mr. Talbot Seymour is here."

I tried wildly to think of something, and went back. There was nothing else I could do. Talbot Seymour came into the sitting room from the study and closed the door behind him.

"How do you do, Miss Randolph?"

He gave me a gleaming smile. Possibly if his face weren't so suntanned and his hair weren't so sleek and shiny black, his teeth wouldn't have looked so white and numerous—or perhaps it was just his extraordinary air of physical well-being that got me down—what with the astonishing scene I'd just listened in on—and made me feel suddenly very grey and drab and definitely not worth having so much sheer brilliance wasted on me.

"So kind of you to come," Mr. Talbot Seymour said.

"I took the liberty of suggesting to Miss Randolph, sir, that she might come and pick out the old books Mr. Mason borrowed from her when we first came," Luton said.

I should have been grateful, I suppose, but I wasn't. I was frightened. The steady look behind Talbot Seymour's smiling eyes was frightening too.

"Perhaps we can have a little chat first, Miss Randolph," Seymour said. He glanced at Luton. "Just leave the door open as you go out, please." And after Luton had gone, quiet and respectful as ever, he turned to me with what I presume was meant to be a disarming candor.

"You know, I don't think you liked my cousin, did you?" he asked.

"Not particularly," I said. "Why?"

He looked a little dashed. "Because I'd hoped maybe you'd help me find who did this ghastly thing."

He leaned forward, his hands folded between his white linen knees, his smiling face suddenly sober, and even troubled, I thought.

"May I be frank with you, Miss Randolph?"

I moved uneasily in my chair.

"I'd rather you'd be frank with Mr. Crabtree, Mr. Seymour."

"Oh, I know I've no right to ask anything of you, Miss Randolph," he said, with an odd kind of buoyant chagrin. He hesitated an instant and went on. "You see, there's no use my pretending Mason and I were like *that*."

He held up two close fingers.

"Because we weren't. But after all, blood is thicker than water, or even Scotch for that matter, and Mason couldn't ever resist giving a good-natured sermon along with a hand-out. And frankly, Miss Randolph, I was sorry to see him get married."

Mr. Seymour glanced very casually at the door that had closed behind Luton's back.

"In fact, the chief reason I rolled in at this time was to get on the right side of the lady—so supplies wouldn't be entirely cut off till I snared some kind of a job."

I'm afraid I looked more shocked than I was, really, having heard what he'd said to Luton. And after all, living off one's relatives is in the gentleman's tradition, and Virginians have always been gentlemen.

"But you see, I can't very well go to your Mr. Crabtree and say, 'Hey there, my cousin's supposed to have made out a new will, making his fiancée his heir and leaving me in the soup, and now he's dead, and I want it proved that that's not the reason he's dead before I shove off to starve.' Because, you see, Mason always said he'd set up a trust fund, so I couldn't touch the principal but still wouldn't have to marry some widow for her yacht."

He pulled his thin gold cigarette case out of his pocket and flashed me a fine smile. "I'll bet a hundred dollars you've never smoked a cigarette in your life!"

"No, thank you," I said. I was beginning to be awfully annoyed at the obviously designed-to-be-interesting Mr. Talbot Seymour, but it apparently did ·not occur to him that a middle-aged spinster could have such glamorous changes rung for her without falling.

Suddenly he was the frank disarming young man again.

"You see, Miss Randolph, if I went to Mr. Crabtree and said any of this to him, when he finally got around to figuring it out, he'd have me in the stocks up there behind the Capitol—for the murder of my cousin."

I looked at him.

"Don't you see?" he went on, not realizing that I saw very well indeed. "Here I am. If my cousin marries, I lose an income for life that I've been pretty damn well figuring on. Nobody thought old Mason would marry anybody, not at his age, and loving peace and comfort, and . . . well, say variety, the way he did."

"But I understood you didn't see your cousin last night," I said. "I mean, that you had a—what do they call it?—a perfect alibi."

"I have."

Mr. Talbot Seymour's voice was easy and smooth, but there was a little movement in the pupils of his eyes as if he hadn't expected me to know about such things as alibis.

"I was at the Inn. The bell boys can all swear to that."

"Then why are you worried about Mr. Crabtree?"

"I'm not, not really.—What I'm worried about, Miss Randolph, is . . . my cousin's will. Luton tells me he drew one up leaving his money in some screwball scheme for Faith Yardley and the restoration of Yardley Hall. It was signed and in order, and in the safe in Mason's study."

Mr. Seymour glanced around again.

"Well, it's not there now. The old will's there, but the new one isn't. So that my position is——"

"Is equivocal in the extreme," I suggested, quoting the rather more literate Mr. Luton.

He gave me a sharp glance. "That's right," he said briefly.

"You're sure it was . . . signed and in the safe?" I asked. "Did Mr. Luton tell you that?"

"No. My cousin's local attorney. A young fellow in his office witnessed it, with one of the local ladies. The only thing in the safe now is a rough draft my cousin typed himself. That's how I first knew about it.—And I want to find it, Miss Randolph."

"Doesn't Mr. Luton know where it is?"

He smiled. "I think not," he said coolly.

"In fact," I wanted to say—and almost did say—"you think if he did he would have destroyed it himself before now."

Instead I caught myself and said, "Do you think I know where it is?"

He lighted the cigarette he'd been holding in his hand for some time, and looked oddly at me. Then he said—and not as pleasantly as he'd sounded up to now—"I thought possibly you might suggest to your friends at Yardley Hall that if that will should happen not to turn up, it would make things . . . well, shall we say simpler—for everybody."

# 17

"You're suggesting, I take it," I said, with as much self-possession as I could muster, "that some one of the Yardleys has the will in his or her possession?"

He looked at me coolly as I got to my feet. Then he flicked the ash off his cigarette and got up too. There was something lithe in the way he moved his body, as if he were part jungle-cat. He stood looking down at me, all the glamorous pretence forgotten.

"I just suggest it might be pleasanter—for everybody—if we got together some way, Miss Randolph."

Then he smiled again, and followed me out onto the porch and up the garden path to the gate. He held it open.

"You see, Miss Randolph, I'm not going to sit back quietly and lose a comfortable income for life. I might even be forced to marry Faith Yardley myself—and that doesn't fit in with my present plans."

At just that moment I saw a slim white figure at the end of the street turn and stop, seeing me, and my heart sank.

Mr. Talbot Seymour saw her too. His eyes lighted with what I took to be quite genuine feelng. "Boy, oh boy!" he said. "I'll just walk along with you, Miss Randolph."

I tried to protest, but I couldn't, some way; and then we came up to Faith. She stood there, hesitating, no sign of recognition on her face. They hadn't met, then, I thought. She had on a chalk-white sports frock and a white open-crowned turban that made her honey-rich skin darker and warmer, and her deep fringed grey eyes almost black under her straight perfect brows and her crown of burnished gold. She looked too lovely—and too exciting, standing there. I didn't need Talbot Seymour's delighted brilliant smile to tell me that.

"This is Mason's cousin, Mr. Talbot Seymour, Faith," I said. "Miss Yardley, Mr. Seymour."

Faith held out her hand. "How do you do," she said, and her voice . . . I never seemed to have noticed until the night before how warm and rich it was. Mr. Talbot Seymour noticed it instantly. And watching him, it seemed to me that he and Ruth Napier must have been raised in the same school. I couldn't tell exactly how *he* did it, either. I don't even know now what he said, besides the usual pattern of condolence—nothing, I'm sure, that any one wouldn't have said under the circumstances, even barring murder. But in some way he managed to convey to her that she was the loveliest thing he'd ever laid eyes on, and how on earth had she happened to be in Williamsburg, just as Ruth had done to Bill, in practically nothing flat.

Only Faith was more reserved than Bill had been. The only sign that she understood was a deepening of the warm color in her brown face and her eyes darkening under their long gold-flecked lashes.

"I hope you'll let me call," Talbot Seymour said, implying richly that the pleasure would be infinitely greater than the duty he'd be performing for his dead cousin. He started back to the house, stopped and turned to me.

"Let's skip everything that's been said, shall we, Miss Randolph? Good-by."

"What *has* been said?" Faith asked, when he'd gone.

"A lot of things that can easily be skipped," I answered. I was tired, and I was trying to remember whether, when I was a girl and a young man did the things young men used to do, like pressing a rose from one's hair to their lips, it hadn't been all just a dreadful waste of time. They seemed to do it so much better now, without doing a thing that one could point to and say, "That's how he did it."

Faith walked slowly along with me. It occurred to me that Talbot Seymour might be a rather dangerous stimulant, but I didn't undertake to tell her so, nor did I offer any comment on her next remark.

"Mason always spoke of Talbot as a sort of glamour boy just out of college," she said. "Why, he must be thirty-five

anyway. Mason sort of regarded himself as Talbot's guardian. I guess that's why I always thought he was younger. I
mean, it seems silly to rail about anybody being irresponsible
after he's got old enough to look out for himself, doesn't it?"

I looked at her. Talbot Seymour was old enough, and
shrewd enough, to look after himself very well indeed, I
thought. Then I said something I really hadn't planned to
say to Faith at all.

"Faith—what about Mason Seymour's will?"

She looked at me, puzzled.

"His—will?"

I nodded.

"How should I know anything about his will, Cousin
Lucy?"

"I just wondered," I said.

She looked at me again with her grave tranquil eyes, still
puzzled. Then she said, suddenly, "—Cousin Lucy . . . who
do you think did it?"

I shook my head.

"They're saying in town that they've found some of the
pink powder in your office. Is that true?"

"It seems to be," I said.

She was silent a moment. Then she said, "They say he's
gone, Cousin Lucy . . . skipped town, without paying you
his rent. And they've searched his things, because three rings
—one of them a very valuable star ruby that Cartier's sent
down for Mason to . . . to choose from—are missing. And
they say Mr. Baldwin never sent him to you at all; he's been
in Europe over a month."

I don't know whether I'd got to the saturation point, so
that nothing else anybody told me about anything that had
happened at Mason Seymour's house the night he was murdered could surprise me, or what. All I know is that I just
walked along perfectly calmly. When Faith was through I
said,

"Do you believe any of it, my dear?"

She didn't answer for a while. Then she said, looking directly ahead of her, "Aunt Melusina says it's clear now that
he's a . . . a gentleman thief. Raffles, or something, she
called him. He gets somebody like Summers Baldwin's card,
and presents it to somebody who doesn't know his handwriting, and worms his way in. She says that's why he didn't
come directly to our house, because she'd have recognized

the phoney handwriting at once. She says look at the flimsy
excuse he made to get around father, and then he walks off
with Heaven knows what. She can't find a 1692 wine cup
we've always had. And . . . and then he gets into Mason's
and takes the jewels——"

"Murdering Mason first, or afterwards?" I asked.

She looked at me with her grave serious face.

"I wish he hadn't gone away," she said, in a dull aching
voice.

I wished so myself, but I wouldn't have thought of saying
so. We'd come to my house. Bill's car was not there by the
picket fence where I knew I'd hoped to see it. I didn't say
anything at all till we were inside and she'd dropped down
on the ottoman. Then I said, "Faith—has Luton been to see
you?"

She shook her head, surprised. "No. Why?"

"Did you see a check on the table in front of Mason . . .
that night? Try and remember, Faith—it's terribly important."

Her face had gone quite pale. I knew she was seeing again
that bloodstained figure of the man she'd been going to
marry, sitting lifeless at the desk. She closed her eyes. After
a long time she opened them again. They were pale too, from
that awful journey.

"I think there was, Cousin Lucy," she whispered. "I'm
quite sure there was. Though I wouldn't have thought of it
if you hadn't spoken of it. It's so horrible—I can see it all so
clearly whenever I shut my eyes, and think I've got to remember it's wrong of me just to have it all gone from my
mind as if it had never happened."

"I'd let it go," I said. "I wouldn't try to remember."

She got up wearily, turned toward the door, and then
turned half-way back to me.

"Is it true the shotgun they found is the one you keep in
the office, Cousin Lucy?"

She didn't look at me.

"Yes," I said. "It is."

"Couldn't anybody have taken it—I mean anybody except
. . . him?"

"I don't know, Faith. I wish I did."

"You were over at our house that afternoon. Community
wasn't here. Couldn't somebody have gone in and taken it?
Have they tried to find out if anybody was seen coming in?"

I got up and went to her, put my hands on her drooping shoulders and looked into her face.

"Faith," I said gently, "tell me—are you trying to prove he didn't do it because you think he didn't, or because you think he did?"

She raised her head, and then she buried it against my shoulder, her body shaken with sobs. "Oh, I don't *know,* Cousin Lucy, I don't know!" she cried wretchedly.

And then she'd gone, leaving me still standing there, my shoulder wet with her tears, my heart torn with doubt, yet clinging to a hopeless hope that it couldn't be true. And then I sat down suddenly as two things popped out of my mind like a couple of grotesque and totally unrelated jack-in-the-boxes . . . one grinning like a zany and the other not grinning at all. The first was Melusina's 1692 wine cup that her gentleman Raffles had stolen. I'd seen it less than a month before, being sold, by what the English call private treaty, to a collector for a Philadelphia museum for some perfectly unbelievable sum. And the second, which wasn't nearly so amusing, was Summers Baldwin's card that Hallie Taswell had seen on my parlor table.

I reached out and pulled the bell cord. Community, just leaving for the afternoon, heard the silvery jingle and came into the parlor, in a starched lavender percale dress and a white straw hat with a red rose on the crown, a paper of scraps for her chickens under her arm.

"Community," I said, "—when did you see the card Mr. Haines brought last?"

"Yes'dy evenin', 'fo' Ah wen' home, Mis' Lucy. It warn't there when Ah come back. Ah look fo' it to show Joe nex' do', they's always braggin' 'bout havin' sech grand comp'ny ovah theah."

"But you didn't see anybody here? I mean when you came back?"

"No, *ma'am.*"

—And Hallie Taswell, I thought, had told Melusina she couldn't read all the card because Community interrupted her.

"Has Miss Hallie been here lately, Community?"

"Ah ain' seen her 'ceptin' in that there coach once or twice lately," Community said.

When she'd gone I sat there, thinking. Hallie Taswell had been to my house. We'd seen her, Bill Haines and I, coming out of Mason Seymour's place through the Lane garden, almost beside herself; and that couldn't have been much later. But why had she told Melusina a story about not reading the card because Community had interrupted her? Why had she been so distraught at my wicked and unchristian thrust about people slipping through the hedge, when she couldn't help knowing that Bill and I had seen her come out? Why had she sat so stoically until the blue coach passed John Crabtree talking to Mason Seymour's cousin in front of the old Court House and then pressed her handkerchief to her mouth after she'd got past them?

# 18

While I was thinking all that I was only vaguely aware that a car had stopped in front of the house and that the gate latch had clicked . . . and then I heard the door bang and a voice shout "Hi, Miss Lucy!" and my heart almost burst with joy as I turned and saw Bill Haines in the doorway, looking more like a drowned rat than either a gentleman thief or a murderer trailing clouds of pink powder. He had a bath towel around his neck and a damp pair of bathing trunks in one hand.

"Where *have* you been?" I demanded.

"Out to Yorktown for a swim. Why?"

"Why?" I said, tartly. "Only that you've practically been convicted of murder in the first degree while you were out there—to say nothing of larceny, theft, burglary, jumping your board bill and parading under false pretenses."

He stared at me for an instant. Then he said, "Oh, gee!" and sank down on the ottoman.

And when I went to the phone and called the Commonwealth Attorney and said, "John, Bill Haines is here, you'd better come and talk to him, alone if you can," I didn't really expect he'd leave Sergeant Priddy behind. I suppose it's just as well he didn't, the way it turned out, because while Michael Priddy never did much in school he was born with considerable more mother sense than a great many schools could give. It didn't, apparently, strike either him or John Crabtree as odd in the least that Bill should have taken the morning off to go swimming. In fact, the impression I got

was that they wished he'd let them know so they could have
gone too. The business of Summers Baldwin's card seemed
reasonable enough too. He'd given it to Bill just as he was
sailing, the first of March when Bill was coming to Williamsburg. Then a man in the office had done something to his
sacroiliac so that Bill had to put off his trip till the man came
back from Florida. He'd kept the card and used it when he
came. They could cable Mr. Baldwin at Nice if they wanted
to, unless he'd already left for home. As for the rest of it,
sure he'd seen the shotgun. He was nuts about guns, and always had been. But he hadn't shot Seymour with it, if that
interested them any.

And from that point on he refused to be drawn.

"This here pink cockroach powder, Haines," Sergeant
Priddy said.

Bill's jaw went hard. I looked at John Crabtree. He tipped
his chair back, regarding Bill and the Sergeant with the kind
of deliberately benign glance that an old setter would give
a pair of haggling pups.

"It looks to me like you've got yourself out on a limb,
Haines," he said peaceably, in that slow ambling fashion of
his. "You can see how it is yourself. You go around to Seymour's, have a quarrel with him. He's found dead. The shotgun was in your room, you admit knowin' it's there, and
bein' familiar with guns. Then it comes out that only one
person went back on the terrace through cockroach powder,
and there's a lot of it in your room. And your shoes just
fit the tracks comin' and goin' through it. Looks to me like
you'd want to explain how come."

Bill's lips shut like a steel trap. He shook his head. I could
have shaken him. Instead I turned to the Commonwealth
Attorney. "John," I said, "—if I went through the hedge
from the Lanes' garden, is there any reason some one else
couldn't have done the same thing?"

My lodger glowered at me savagely, yet with a kind of
relief . . . thinking, poor lamb, that I'd made a clean breast
of the whole thing. He didn't know that instead I'd mired us
both completely, especially him.

John Crabtree shook his head. He also smiled a little.

"Nobody but you went through there, Miss Lucy. You,
and another woman a good bit earlier."

He glanced at my shoes.

"Your heel marks aren't as square as hers and are on top of

them. Hers just fit these pumps the ladies wear with these colonial costumes."

"Oh," I said weakly. He knew about Hallie Taswell, then. And Hallie, I thought abruptly, had been an old flame of his eldest brother, and Hugh Taswell was some kin to the Crabtrees. That's the worst of Williamsburg—you scratch the grocer's boy and you find a cousin.

John's face was an amiable mask turned back to Bill Haines, sitting there tight-lipped and rather pale in spite of his fresh sunburn.

"I'm goin' to ask you not to leave town, Mr. Haines," he said. "I'd like you to keep an eye on Miss Lucy here. Wouldn't want her to get into any more mischief. Hear?"

When they'd gone I said to Bill, "Why don't you tell them the whole thing from the beginning?"

He shook his head.

"Then will you tell me one thing: did you know Mason Seymour and this man Luton before you came here?"

He nodded. "I met them one summer crossing the Atlantic. Once after that in New York. And I don't like Luton any more than I liked his boss.—And if you don't mind I'm going to get dressed."

He went out to the office, and I went to the phone and called Faith.

"He's back, darling," I said. I told her that the Commonwealth Attorney and the City Sergeant had seen and talked to him, and he wasn't in jail, and that was that, and to give her Aunt Melusina my love.

Her voice over the phone seemed strange and rather choked to me as she said, "Thanks, Cousin Lucy." There was a long silence after that, but I knew she hadn't hung up.

"Are you all right, Faith?" I asked sharply.

"I'll tell you when I see you, Cousin Lucy," she said. Then she added, almost in a whisper, "Is it . . . true, about the powder and the . . . the footprints?"

"He doesn't bother about denying it," I said. "—Or explaining it."

"I'm coming over, Cousin Lucy," she said abruptly. "Do you mind?"

"Of course not, darling."

I hung up the phone. I could hear Bill Haines banging around in the little office. I glanced out to see if the walls

were still standing. Then I went to the door, waiting for
Faith. Maybe if the two of them could talk to each other, I
thought . . . and then my heart collapsed like a punctured
toy balloon. Ruth Napier's car had just drawn up behind
Bill's, and she was getting out. She looked perfectly ravish-
ing with her long dark hair in thick loose curls around her
slim throat framing her vivid face. She had on some odd
kind of yellow dress that made her look like a dark flame-
wrapped star, and she gave me a quick smile.

"Hello, Miss Randolph! Is Bill here? I see he is."

She came through the gate and started for the office. "Do
you mind?"

I smiled—or I tried to. I found myself hoping she'd think
it was prudery she'd so obviously seen on my face that made
her ask if I minded. As I stepped back into the hall and
pushed the door to, I heard her tap on the office door, and
heard the hinge groan. "Hello, Bill!" she called. "You home?"

And after a little while, standing by the window, I saw
Faith Yardley come up Francis Street, look at Ruth's car,
glance ever so slightly at the office and at my closed door,
and go on by as if she'd never intended stopping in at all.

When Community rang the supper bell, Ruth's car was
still in front of the house. I went in the dining room and sat
down, wondering what I'd do if Bill came in and asked if
she could stay for supper. Then I looked up. He was in the
door, alone, and evidently planning to stay, because he sat
down and unfolded his napkin, and grinned at Community
and the golden mountain of fried chicken she brought in on
his heels.

When she'd gone he looked at me.

"Miss Lucy, would you like me to get a room somewhere
else?" he asked soberly.

I was probably nearer tears than I've been for a thousand
years. I shook my head. "Not unless you want to," I answered.

"I don't," he said. Then, when he'd eaten more strawberry
shortcake than it seemed he could possibly envelop, he said,
"Will you do something for me?"

I nodded.

"Take me around to Yardley Hall. I've got to see Faith—
I'll go crazy if I don't . . ."

If only the ceiling had dropped just then, or there'd been

a flood, or anything, so we'd never gone to Yardley Hall
that night! But it didn't, and we went. Abraham showed us
into the library.

"Doctor Yardley, he's upstairs, Miss Melusiny's took bad
again," he said. That alone should have warned me. "Ah'll
tell him you all's come, Mis' Lucy. It's mighty close in here,
Ah'll jus' open th' window."

He put up the window and pushed open the Dutch doors
into the garden.

"Is Miss Faith here, Abraham?" I asked as he went out into
the hall.

"Ah'll see d'rec'ly, Mis' Lucy."

I sat down, and Bill moved restlessly up and down the
floor, absorbed, I've no doubt, in what he was going to say
to her when she came, constantly turning toward the door
to see her there. And all of a sudden I saw him jerk to attention. He was near the open garden door.

Out of the soft night, alive with fitful firefly lanterns,
lemon-pale, I heard a man's voice, more charged with passionate longing than I knew one could be, saying, "I've loved
you all my life, Faith . . . you'll never be sorry, darling . . ."

I sat there, my mouth open, my body turned to water and
ice.

"There's never been any one in all the world but you. Oh,
Faith, Faith, I love you so . . ."

And I realized that it was Marshall Yardley saying that.
It was his own cousin that he loved—it wasn't Ruth Napier.
Melusina had been wrong. All the rest of us had been wrong.
Only Doctor Yardley had seen it. That was what he had
meant—I saw it now—when he'd said to me, "Has Marshall
declared himself?" . . . and that was what Faith had seen
in Marshall Yardley's face last night in my parlor. It wasn't
Ruth Napier he'd come for, it was Faith herself, and she'd
known it, seeing the pain in his eyes.

I looked at Bill. For an instant that seemed a thousand years he stood there, rooted to the floor, turned utterly
to stone. Then suddenly he wrenched himself loose and
barged out of the room, and into the hall, and out into the
night.

# 19

I just sat there, utterly limp. Over and over again, as if they were on a phonograph record that had got stuck and kept repeating the same line, Marshall's voice—"You'll never be sorry, dear; Faith, Faith, I love you so!"—and Bill's tortured retreat marked step by step through the dark lanes of box until the gate banged, ground round and round in my ears. Then Doctor Yardley's gentle voice from the stair landing:

"I don't know where Miss Faith is, Abraham. I presume she's in the garden with Mr. Marshall."

He came in the door.

"Good evening, Lucy."

He looked around. "Abraham said young Haines was with you."

"He was, but he left," I said.

A disturbed shadow crossed Peyton Yardley's transparent finely chiselled face. He touched the bell on the old mahogany table. "Bring some sherry for Miss Lucy, Abraham.— You look ill, my dear. Has something distressed you?"

For the second time in years, and all in less than three hours, I could have wept, long and bitterly. I just shook my head. I did take the sherry Abraham poured me from the delicate blown-glass decanter, and drank it slowly while Doctor Yardley sat in his old faded leather armchair behind the table watching me, his grave, faraway eyes clouded with anxiety.

I put the glass down and managed a smile.

"I'm just a romantic fool, Peyton," I said ruefully. "As the young say, skip it."

The shadow dimmed his face again.

"Have Faith and Haines had another——"

I shook my head.

"It didn't get that far," I said. "Marshall seems to have led the field."

He was silent a moment. He'd seen it coming, of course, with clearer, more understanding eyes than the rest of us had had . . . but it was a kind of stopping for him, even at that.

"Melusina's very upset about it," he said at last. A faint almost sardonic smile moved his face. "Melusina is undoubtedly the world's least successful fixer."

He sat there tapping his fingertips absently on the green tooled leather table cover.

"Marshall may be, and undoubtedly is, in love with Faith, Peyton," I said. (It's extraordinary how nothing will ever teach me to mind my own business.) "But she isn't in love with him. I'm a pretty bad fixer myself, but that doesn't keep me from knowing that Bill Haines is head over heels in love with Faith, and Faith is madly in love with him. Normal people don't go about acting like lunatics unless there's *something* wrong with them."

Doctor Yardley got up, his eyes troubled—almost as troubled as they'd been the afternoon I'd blurted out my pent-up rebellion against his daughter's marriage to Mason Seymour.

"Have they been going about acting like lunatics, Lucy?" he asked at last.

"Worse," I said flatly. "Bill Haines is practically certain to be locked up for the murder of Melusina's precious Mason. God knows he may even have done it—but if he did it was because Faith goaded him to it."

He was standing there, his finger tips balanced on the table top, and not lightly but very hard, to keep his tall body from swaying. I could see how white and bloodless they were.

"I don't understand you, Lucy," he said, almost sharply— very sharply for him.

"I don't understand all of it myself," I replied. "But it seems plain enough to me that Bill tried to stop Faith from going to see Mason Seymour, and she went anyway, and found him dead, and . . ."

I didn't get any farther. Doctor Yardley held up his hand,

his face paler even than it was from years of seclusion within
these four panelled book-lined walls.

"I think I'd better speak to Faith at once, Lucy," he said
quietly. He went over to the open Dutch door, slowly as if
his feet were weighted with lead, looked out and called,
"Faith! Daughter!"

As he called there was a sound of some one stumbling up
the front steps and a man's voice swearing softly. Doctor
Yardley turned back, and frowned. Then his face cleared as
Abraham opened the door and the dim hall light fell on the
perspiring face of the majesty of the law in the person of
Sergeant Michael Priddy, and behind him, looking even less
majestic because he was grinning like a schoolboy, the Commonwealth Attorney, Mr. John Carter Crabtree.

I glanced at Doctor Yardley. If I'd expected—and I'm not
sure that I had—that he'd be annoyed or disturbed at their
coming to Yardley Hall without a formal by-your-leave-sir,
I was wrong. He seemed not the least surprised—almost relieved, in fact, as if he could now get a little first-hand information.

He held out his hand. "Good evening, John; good evening, Michael."

I saw the whimsical flicker lighting his eyes for an instant.
If you've brought two children into the world, given them
the first whack on the back to make them howl and exist, it
must be rather amusing to have them confront you thirty-
five years later as guardians of the law under which you live.

"Good evening, sir," the Commonwealth Attorney said.

"Good evening, sir," the City Sergeant said.

Then they both said, "Good evening, Miss Lucy," and at
just that moment Faith and Marshall came in from the garden—Faith pale and lovely, Marshall as if with star dust still
drunkenly in his eyes. Faith looked quickly at her father,
and at me. I shook my head. She looked relieved, though I'm
sure I don't know either what she thought I meant, or what
I did mean, actually, except that it was all right, whatever it
was.

"Won't you all sit down," Doctor Yardley said, with that
grave courtesy that invested each chair with a canopy of
royal purple like the governor's pew in Bruton Church. "I'm
sorry my sister can't come down, John. She's not well."

For an instant John—as Commonwealth Attorney—

looked as if he thought possibly justice was being ob-
structed, and then immediately as John Crabtree his face
brightened, as at one less ordeal. But they were both wrong,
however, or rather all three—Doctor Yardley, John Crabtree
attorney, and John Crabtree gentleman . . . for nothing
short of death or two broken legs would have kept Melusina
Yardley upstairs when Abraham, replying to her querulous
command, told her who all were downstairs. I saw the faint
ironic gleam in Peyton Yardley's eyes, and caught the tightened glance his daughter gave me. Sergeant Priddy mopped
his forehead, and so did John Crabtree, and Marshall did
nothing but just gaze at Faith, as if he'd never seen her before and wouldn't again for a long, long time.

Then Melusina arrived, her astringent quality heightened
by an obvious suspicion that we'd all rather she'd not come,
and also by her very hasty toilet. She looked frightened, too,
in an odd sort of way, as if something more fundamental
than she'd known existed had suddenly tottered and collapsed in the foundations of her life.

John Crabtree cleared his throat. "Of course, you all understand that we don't want to make any more trouble for
you all than we can help . . ."

Doctor Yardley leaned back in his worn leather chair.

"I think we all understand, John," he said quietly. "We
realize that the unfortunate publication of the announcement
of my daughter's engagement to Mason Seymour involves
us in the investigation you're bound to make. I'm very glad
you've come like this. We know we can trust your and Michael's discretion as gentlemen, as well as your honor as
officers of the law. You understand, of course, that we're not
asking any favor not entirely consistent with your duty as
such."

John Crabtree mumbled something. Doctor Yardley shook
his head. "All you have to do, John, is find out the truth,"
he said. "We shall be entirely content with that."

He passed his hand across his high forehead.

"The first thing for you to know—and this is where I ask
your discretion as a gentleman—is that my daughter was
not engaged to Mason Seymour."

The room was like a forest pool with a stone dropped
abruptly into it. Faith's pale calm rippled and was still again,
Melusina's breath came sharply. Her brother turned to her.

"I think it's only fair to Faith, Melusina, to have the onus for this sickening tragedy taken off her shoulders."

Faith's eyes were fixed like two rapt stars on her father's face; her red lips were parted a little, waiting. It was the first time the onus for anything had ever been taken from her, except for Marshall's clumsy childhood attempts that had never deceived their aunt, only convinced her more firmly that Faith was a spoiled wilful child.

"The announcement was made impulsively by my sister, who, I don't doubt for an instant, thought she was doing the best thing. When I learned that my daughter was not in love with Mason Seymour, I went to him and told him frankly that there had been a misunderstanding, because of my sister's overzealousness, and that I would only consent to my daughter's marrying when I was convinced that her heart, and not any other consideration whatsoever, counselled it."

Peyton Yardley looked at Faith. He was talking to her, not to John Crabtree. He was talking about Marshall, not about Mason Seymour. His grave understanding eyes were as steadfast as the day. The pallor under Faith's honey-gold skin deepened. She closed her eyes. Marshall got up abruptly and moved over to the window, his dark face drawn, his hand trembling as he lighted a match and held it to his cigarette.

Melusina seemed to me to have shrunk down into herself, completely wretched. I think she must have viewed her brother as a child building a castle in the sand, having it washed down and building it up again and again until it at last seemed eternal, must view the final wave that takes it utterly away. Certainly her brother had seemed permanent enough in all the years after the lapse of his marriage, and now he was entirely out of hand again, as he was saying to the Commonwealth Attorney,

"You would, I expect, John, like each of us to give you an account of his movements night before last. We would like to do it, whether you require it or not."

Sergeant Priddy took out his notebook. I think he was glad to have a job of any kind to do . . . there was something pretty overwhelming in the shabby grandeur of Yardley Hall and the impressive dignity of the white-haired cavalier sitting there under the three-hundred-year-old portrait of the first of his line to come to Williamsburg.

"I left the supper table and went to Mason Seymour's a little before seven," Doctor Yardley said evenly. "I was there, I should judge, twenty-five minutes or so. Our interview was entirely amicable. I was surprised, therefore, when I got home to find that my sister was greatly upset and that my nephew here had followed me over. I hadn't met him on the way because I didn't return directly; I walked around to Nicholson Street, to the Palace Green, and back to the Hall that way.

"My nephew came in about half an hour after I returned. We went out into the garden here." He pointed to the curving stone stairs that led down to the path from the Dutch doors. "We had a good deal to talk about. Neither of us noticed the passage of time until the night train went by. We came in shortly after that, about eleven, I should judge. I had a glass of port and we went upstairs."

It was just before eleven, I thought, when the watchman heard the gun being pitched over the fence into the Canal. It was after that—ten minutes or so—that I myself stood at the garden gate in Scotland Street, afraid to come on into Yardley Hall, seeing the shadowy hand and hearing the chain on the well house.

The Commonwealth Attorney looked at Marshall Yardley.

"I went to see Seymour because my aunt felt she'd involved Faith more deeply than my uncle knew," Marshall said shortly. "She felt Seymour wouldn't be as reasonable as my uncle found him."

"Luton says the two of you quarrelled?" John Crabtree drawled.

"We did. I took the opportunity of telling him a few truths. Not that I thought it would do much good, but I had the satisfaction of getting a lot of spleen out of my own system. I went over there about eight. I was back here at eight-thirty or quarter to nine at the latest."

"You didn't go back after that?"

"No. I stayed here in the garden, talking to my uncle."

"And you didn't go in the back garden over there at Seymour's, any time?"

Marshall shook his head, and John Crabtree turned to Faith.

# 20

She might have been carved out of old ivory, she sat there so motionless. Only her eyes were alive, deep black pools, liquid and unafraid.

"You see, the trouble is," John Crabtree said—and I don't think he knew quite how important what he was saying was to her—"it happens this is simplified to a certain extent because we found the shotgun. The Sergeant and Captain Callowhill from Newport News—he's a ballistics expert—they made some tests after dinner, and there's no two ways about it. Seymour was shot at a distance of about twenty feet through the open window from the terrace. Now it happens we can check pretty well on everybody that was in the back garden. Because they've had a plague of cockroaches and waterbugs over there, and they had powder all around the house, along the sills, and the drains, and the gutters, so anybody goin' from the front of the house to the back, or anybody goin' out of the house onto the terrace, was bound to track the stuff. Joe, the gardener, put it down just before supper, and they locked the doors so's nobody'd go trackin' it in."

I heard myself saying: "What if somebody who *was* in the house knew it was there, John—couldn't they have avoided it?"

He shook his head. "Not the way Joe put that powder down," he drawled. "Not less'n he was an aerial trapeze artist. I told you that wouldn't wash, Miss Lucy."

He shook his head at me and went on.

"We happen to know, now, that three people were in the back garden—two of 'em after the powder was put down, one before. A lady with flat heels was there. There's powder in the print of her heel by the pool. A lady with high heels left her mark by the pool too, only afterwards. She went up to about fifteen feet of the house, and turned and ran. Now, maybe she fired that shotgun."

I stared at him in horrified amazement.

"We don't really think she did, because her neighbor across the street says she didn't leave her house till past eleven. Of course, maybe Mason Seymour didn't get shot till after eleven."

Everybody in the room was looking at me, and I was appalled and speechless. And then suddenly I saw through the whole thing, but it was too late to do anything about it. Faith had turned to John Crabtree, and she was saying, very quietly, to save me, "Mr. Seymour was dead before that, Cousin John."

She'd fallen into his miserable transparent trap as innocently as a week-old fawn.

Her father's shoulders stiffened; Marshall Yardley let his head drop on his open palms.

"It was I who started to telephone there—a doctor first, then you—and . . . didn't . . . because I was afraid, all of a sudden . . ."

The kind of innocuous triumph a child's face shows when he's succeeded in snaffling the largest piece of birthday cake beamed in John Crabtree's face, and I could have shaken the life out of him.

"I went to Mason's after my father and my cousin came back and were out in the garden."

Her calm grey eyes touched mine as they passed.

(And I remembered: *But nobody was there, Cousin Lucy . . . just a curl of smoke that hadn't all disappeared yet. The window was open. I ran to it and called, but no one answered.*)

Yet Doctor Yardley, not raising his quiet voice, calling, "Faith! Daughter!" a moment before had brought her and Marshall in from the garden . . . I didn't bat an eyelash. Perhaps all the Yardleys were standing together. Heaven only knew.

"I decided I'd go explain to Mason myself," Faith went on,

just as calmly. "After all, it was my problem. I went to his house. The door was open."

(*You're forgetting the young man standing there in Scotland Street,* I said to myself; *and the gate that wouldn't open, and the young man saying, "Even a gate post knows it's no good, Faith—don't go down there."*)

"I called, but he didn't answer. The study door was closed. It seems to me now that the room was dark—I mean I didn't see a light through the keyhole or under the door—but I didn't notice it then. I just somehow didn't make any attempt to open the door."

(*As I stood by that door, something touched me on the shoulder and said "Don't go in there, Faith" . . . just as plain as I'm speaking to you, Cousin Lucy . . . I looked around.—Nobody was there, and I . . . I knew nobody had been there.*)

"I started back, up the garden path. Then I must have got scared. I suppose I did—it was awfully dark under the mimosas, and everything was so terribly silent, even the frogs, and I hadn't noticed it before. I suppose it was the contrast after the train roared by. Anyway, I went back. The door had swung shut, but it wasn't locked. I opened it and went in. The library door was open . . ."

She stopped for a moment, and went on.

"I saw Mason sitting there, dead. It was long before eleven o'clock."

"It was ten-forty-one when you picked up the phone, Faith," John Crabtree said gently. "—Why didn't you call Sergeant Priddy? That was the thing to do."

"Because I was afraid," Faith said.

(*And then, all of a sudden, Cousin Lucy, . . . I put down the phone. You see, Cousin Lucy, all . . . all the people who hated Mason the most live at Yardley Hall . . . that's why I didn't call Sergeant Priddy . . .*)

"I thought I heard some one on the terrace. That frightened me more . . . it was so light, and horrible, in there!"

She hadn't once looked at her father or her cousin or Melusina. After that one level glance at me her eyes had rested on the Commonwealth Attorney's and stayed there.

"I should have called. I was too . . . too horrified."

Doctor Yardley leaned forward and rested his head on his hand. Faith got up suddenly and ran to him, and put her arms around his head, her lips pressing against his hair.

"Oh, forgive me, Father! I should have told you, but I . . . I couldn't!"

Doctor Yardley put his arms around her, his head close against her young heart. "I've failed you so often, Faith," he said softly, and she put her fingers on his lips, shaking her head. "Never," she whispered. She sat down on the arm of his chair, her arm around his shoulders, his arm around her slim waist—closer together than they had ever been in their lives.

Melusina pleated and unpleated the hem of her handkerchief. She was like a rag that had been wrung out in coffee, Faith had said before, and she was like that now. I glanced at Marshall. He was sitting hunched down in his chair, looking as if he'd been an hour-long eternity in hell. It seemed to me now I'd been blind as a mole not to have seen he'd been in love with Faith ever since they were children. I remembered now that when he was at the University he'd always got a job in the summer instead of accepting invitations from wealthy Northern boys to spend his vacation abroad or in New England. Melusina had glibly attributed it to the Yardley pride and scolded about lost opportunities to meet desirable girls with rich fathers.

And what he must be thinking now I could only guess. "It won't be so bad for the . . . woman," he'd said the night before.

In any case it seemed more important just then to wonder what John Crabtree and Sergeant Priddy were thinking. I saw them exchange a quick glance. They must have a signal code, I thought, remembering that that's what I'd thought up years ago to account for their spontaneous devilment in Sunday school class. Maybe the old signals still worked, I thought, as John said,

"If you don't mind, Miss Melusina, I'd like to hear what you've got to say."

I think a desperate struggle must have been going on in Melusina's soul. For the first time it occurred to me that the Yardley pride she talked so much about was a bitter cloak she'd wrapped herself in to cover up the disappointments of her own life, her own loneliness and the struggle with poverty and fear. The fierce tenacity with which she clung to Yardley Hall, willingly sacrificing Faith to Mason Seymour —even Marshall, whom she loved certainly more deeply than she loved anything—was the last desperate stand for self-preservation. The rest of us had taken the easier way, there was no doubt of that. Whether it wasn't also the better way didn't change the fact that we'd given up a kind of autonomy that Melusina had hung on to, and would, I thought, looking at her gradually drawing her wiry, almost gaunt, frame together, hang on to till the death.

"I have nothing to say whatsoever, John," she snapped at last. "Except"—it was against reason and Melusina's nature to let it stop there—"that there was none of this nonsense about Faith's marriage until certain people began to interfere"—she looked directly at me—"in something that was definitely no business of theirs—from whatever motive; whether it was plain ordinary malicious dislike of a charming and eligible gentleman"—that was me and Mason Seymour—"or whether, having no experience with the world, her head was turned by this young adventurer who calls himself Quincy Adams Haines"—it was my head she was talking about—"I don't know. It may even be that knowing Mr. Seymour was no fonder of her than she was of him, she realized that Faith's marriage would cut her——"

"*Aunt Melusina!*" Faith said. Her eyes were black as coals. Melusina raised her brows.

"You've never realized, Faith," she said coldly, "that Lucy Randolph has stood between you and me since you were a baby—so that we could never come to any' real understanding, you and I."

Had I, I wondered, without being conscious of it—been paying her out for the trouble she'd made the other Faith?

"You shan't talk that way!" Faith cried passionately.

Peyton Yardley tightened his arm around her waist. His face was stern and implacable, his lips hard. "That will do, Melusina. John didn't come here to witness a family row."

He turned to me, his eyes burning coals like his daughter's.

"I know you'll forgive this intolerable discourtesy, Lucy —for Faith."

Which Faith he meant I didn't know—the girl who'd stood with him at the chancel in Bruton Church, or the one who'd stood by Mason Seymour's murdered body, her hand on the telephone.

John Crabtree and Sergeant Priddy were silently watching us tearing at each other's throats this way, like mongrel dogs. It was too horrible. I got up.

"I think I'll go home, Peyton," I said.

"You'd better ask her, John, before she goes," Melusina snapped—she was beside herself with rage—"who this young upstart she's harboring is, and what he's done with the jewels he stole from Mason Seymour."

I'm really a very mild woman, but I think I could have strangled Melusina Yardley just then with my bare hands and rejoiced at the job. And perhaps I should have tried to, I'm sure I don't know, I was so angry, if John Crabtree's slow voice hadn't ambled into the breach:

"Bill Haines is Summers Baldwin's ward in the Massachusetts courts—his father was Mr. Baldwin's partner. Mr. Baldwin just telephoned the Governor from somewhere out in the Atlantic this evenin', the first he'd heard anything had happened down here.—And as for the jewels you're talkin' about, Mason Seymour sent 'em back to New York two weeks ago. Luton sent 'em by registered mail. He's got the post office receipt and the jeweller's receipt filed in the safe."

He looked at Melusina.

"It's always a good plan to know the facts before you do so much talkin', Miss Melusina," he drawled evenly.

Melusina's face had gone the color of old putty. I saw the mildewed reflection of my own face in the old Chippendale mirror by the door. I was grinning like a spotty triumphant cat. In the silence—there was something almost triumphant about that too, it seemed to me—I heard John Crabtree's deliberate voice going on.

"It wouldn't have been you, would it, Miss Melusina, that tore the check out of Mason Seymour's check book on the desk in front of him, now—would it, Miss Melusina?"

# 21

I didn't wait to hear any more. I had to get out of Yardley Hall. As Bill had said about himself, I'd go crazy if I didn't. But I might as well have stayed, as I was practically crazy anyway before I got home, and if I hadn't been, as it turned out, my getting home in itself would have finished the job.

I never would have dreamed that the familiar streets, silent except for the chorus of croaking frogs, dark except for the pale circles suffused from the old street lamps, and the fitful glow of a million fireflies, could be so full of menace. I ran down the stairs and out the drive to Palace Long Wall Street. Then, instead of hurrying down the Palace Green as I probably should have done if I'd stopped to think—even though it is the longer way—I turned left again into Scotland Street. I was thinking so many things, and trying to keep from thinking so many others, that I didn't notice, not until I almost fell over it, that the white wicket gate into the garden was standing open.

I came to an abrupt halt. In the pale glow from the cloudy moon I could see the little peaked roof of the well house again. My heart went cold. For the first time it struck me, with the force of a blow, that I'd never honestly tried to think who it was I'd seen there the night Mason Seymour was murdered . . . or what I thought he'd been doing there . . . or why there'd been blood on the well at Yardley Hall. I'd stopped it all on the threshold of my mind, even before Bill had said "If you want to keep quiet, Miss Lucy, now's the time to begin."

Was it, I wondered, because so many things had been happening in a life where nothing except the Restoration had
ever happened before? Or was it because I was just down-
right afraid to think about it? And now that I did think
about it—if a whole series of things flashing into my mind
at once can be called thinking—I realized that I'd assumed,
in some dark way, that . . . some one—I hadn't given him a
name, I swear I hadn't—had thrown a weapon down there.
And that's why my mind had been in such a turmoil when
they'd fished that shotgun out of the Palace Canal. So it was
clearer now, when I came to think about it. Some one had
thrown the gun into the Canal, and had come back—it would
be less than the distance from the Powder Horn to Travis
House—slipped in the garden gate where I was now standing, drawn up the bucket from the well and washed his
hands. That's why there was blood on the whitewashed
board, and then . . . I stopped. Had he crept on into Yardley Hall?

All around me the great black clumps of box swelled
and moved. The mulberry trees reached out their liquid
arms. *Who am I talking about?* I thought desperately . . .
and I said to myself, "Some one you've known all his life . . .
people your people have known for three hundred years
. . . maybe longer, back on the bowling greens of England,
before Jamestown and Middle Plantation and the Palace and
Yardley Hall and the United States of America." And then
—and I'll never know why I did what I did, except that I
couldn't then have done any other thing—I crept through the
gate, along the brick path between the eerily fragrant, softly
murmuring mountains of box, toward the peaked well house
with the long ghostly fingers of wisteria moving sinuously
in the night air.

I felt the dry flaking whitewash on my hands, and heard
it crack against my body as I leaned against it, putting out
my hand to take hold of the chain to draw up the bucket. As
I touched its cold black links I heard a sound near me, along
the path toward the house.

My knees dissolved in a cold sickening stream, my heart
pounded, suffocating me in my throat. I steadied myself,
clinging to the chain, and forced myself to turn.

Standing in the path, dark against the darker box, was a
man. His voice came quietly but with a controlled undertone
that I'd never heard in it before.

"What are you doing, Cousin Lucy?"

It was Marshall Yardley asking that.

"Nothing," I gasped, my hand frozen to the well chain, my body pressed against the dry brown spot on the whitewashed board that had been red and moist two nights before.

"If you want a drink of water, I'll get it for you from the house."

"No, no!" I cried—frantically, I suppose. "I must hurry home, I really must!"

I ran back to the white wicket gate without turning my head, my hand still aware of the cold black links of the chain, the sound of its thin song in my ears again. I was still running, and very breathless now, when I got to the corner of England Street under the old mulberry tree. Its great tumorous boles seemed to me to swell and move. I stopped, and the terror in my heart died abruptly, and a new terror grew in its place . . . more than terror, terror and that creeping unholy fear I'd known the night before. They say a horse senses a rattlesnake in the grass beside the road; and I, frozen there, knew even before the dark figure disengaged itself from the mulberry tree that George Luton was there, behind it, stepping into my path, blocking it . . . and that I was too much of a coward to simply turn aside and go on to my home without speaking or answering him when he spoke to me.

He said: "Have you got the check for me, Miss Randolph?"

For a moment I couldn't make my voice work, nor my lips; and when they did finally, I didn't recognize them, nor what they said, as mine:

"No—she hasn't got the check."

I could see his eyes glint in his narrow sallow face. I started to move. His hand shot out, pinioning my wrist with a grip of steel.

"Miss Randolph . . . tell them to give me that check . . . or I'll tell all I know . . ."

He must have let my wrist go then, but I didn't know it, I could still feel that grip—I can still feel it now—the way they say a person feels a hand or a limb that's been amputated, as if it was still there, still aching. All I know is that suddenly I was fleeing across the Court House Green, the grass wet with dew around my ankles, more frightened than I'd ever been in all my life or ever hope to be again.

I'm afraid, thinking back, that it must seem dreadfully as if all I did those days—and nights—was fly back from some dreadful place or another to sanctuary in my own white clapboard house with its bower of silver moon roses set in the fairy circle of white picket fence trailing with scarlet rambler and woodbine and honeysuckle. In fact, it rather was all I did . . . except that my house wasn't always sanctuary. And it certainly wasn't now, with Hallie Taswell sitting in my chair, her head back against the carved rosewood frame, looking like death on a pale horse.

The effort of pulling myself together, I suppose, made me brusquer than I should ordinarily have been, although Hallie has always, it seems to me, brought out the worst in me. I sat stiffly down on the sofa and took a deep exasperated breath.

"Oh, Lucy, you must help me," she moaned, rocking back and forth, ignoring the fact that she was ruining the sock that that Eskimo is still waiting for in his igloo in Alaska. I could hear the bone needle crack.

"I'll be glad to do anything I can if you'll quit yammering and act like a sensible white woman," I said, waspishly.

Hallie looked at me with her big brown eyes, dark circles all over her face. In her ordinary clothes she lost, I'm happy to be able to say, a great deal of the arch coquetry that velvet bows and sprigged dimity paniers—to cover the fact that she needed to diet—seemed to bring out in her like a strawberry rash.

She glanced at the door and leaned forward, gripping the arms of her chair.

"What am I going to do, Lucy?" she whispered, almost like a mad woman. "—What if Hugh finds out that I . . . I saw so much of . . . Mason?"

"You should have thought of that a week ago—or a year ago," I answered. I really didn't mean to sound as unpleasant as I did, but I haven't much sympathy with the eat-your-cake-and-have-it-too school of wives who think husbands' chief function is to pay the bills. Anyway, if Hugh Taswell didn't know by now what everybody else in town had known all winter, he probably never would. I said as much, but Hallie shook her head, still frantic.

"Oh, you don't understand, Lucy! It's this man Luton! He doesn't like me, he never did, not when Mason first got . . .

interested in me. I'm afraid he'll make trouble. He was over to the house this morning—I didn't open the door."

A crafty little smile—except that putting it that way makes it sound more theatrical and less real than it was—flicked the corner of her mouth.

"He came over to the Raleigh Tavern then when I was on duty, and went through with a party I had. Honestly, Lucy, I could hardly go through my speech. Every time I'd point to a piece of furniture I'd find him looking at me. I'm almost out of my mind, Lucy! I made Hugh go to a movie tonight so he wouldn't be home if he came, and I waited. I thought I'd just have it out with him. But he didn't come, and I just couldn't stand it any longer, so I came over here."

I looked at her. She was scared green, and I'm not sure I blamed her, remembering Luton sitting in the chair by the door looking steadily at me. And yet—she wasn't telling me the whole truth. She was holding back as much as she dared. I knew that from the way she'd hesitate a little and glance at me to see how I was taking it.

"What does he want, Hallie?" I asked quietly.

She went pale.

"I don't know, Lucy, honestly I don't!" she said quickly. "You mustn't think I'm not telling you the truth!"

"But you aren't, are you? I mean, not all of it."

She gave a little gasp.

"What do you know, Lucy? You must tell me—you've got to, or I'll go crazy!"

She almost screamed the words at me, if any one can scream and still remain practically inaudible.

"I don't know anything," I said, "except that you're acting like a complete fool, and that if you don't stop it, and quit dramatizing yourself and your affair with Mason, you're going to land in——"

I stopped, utterly amazed at myself. I had almost said, "—land in the cooler." I thought wretchedly, "Oh dear—how *have* I picked up such awful language just in the three days Bill Haines has been in this house."

"—You're going to have to explain yourself to the Commonwealth Attorney," I ended more primly.

Hallie closed her eyes. I don't think she'd heard a word I'd said.

"If Hugh should divorce me, Lucy, what *would* I do?" she said.

"Don't be absurd," I retorted sharply. "Just because you haven't any sense is no sign Hugh has lost his. He hasn't any grounds, actually, for divorce, has he? Or has he?"

"Oh no, Lucy . . . but if Luton should go to him! I tell you he hates me!"

"If Luton goes to Hugh, he'll get a thrashing within an inch of his life," I said. "I think you've been associating with Mason Seymour so long you've forgotten the sort of man your husband is, Hallie. If I were you, I'd go home and find out."

She dragged out of the chair and moved miserably toward the door. Then she hesitated, her hand on the knob.

"Lucy . . . have you . . . heard any more about the jewelry that was stolen?"

I looked at her, too disturbed by the way she asked that question to answer it immediately. But I didn't have to, she went quickly on.

"Lucy . . . if you hear anything about . . . about me, will you come and tell me—please? I mean I'd rather go jump in the river, or turn on the gas, than . . ."

"Nonsense," I said. Then I added, not looking at her, "By the way, did you take Summers Baldwin's card off my table the other afternoon?"

She didn't answer. I glanced up at her. She was standing there clinging to the door knob, her face as white and congealed as death, her mouth open, her eyes perfectly awful.

"Hallie—what *is* the matter?" I demanded.

"Then he did tell you!" she gasped.

## 22

I didn't know whether I should run after her, when she'd
darted down my path, and stop her and make her tell me
what all this insane nonsense was about, or just let her go
and jump in the river, if she wanted to—she was a very capable swimmer and a cold douse would probably do her a
lot of good. Anyway, I was too tired. I closed the door and
picked my knitting up from under the rocker and took the
broken needle out . . . and then—which I suppose shows I'm
as unstable actually as Hallie—I threw the whole business,
sock, wool, needles and all smack into the fireplace and set a
match to it, and sat down and kicked off my shoes, and put
my feet up on a chair and took a long deep breath—the first
one I'd had, it seemed to me, for hours.

But I only took one. The gate clicked. I heard leaden unhappy feet dragging slowly up the path, and by the time I'd
got my own pretty leaden feet down and my shoes on, my
lodger was in the doorway, looking as if he'd spent nine days
and dewy nights in the lowest circle of hell.

He sat down on the ottoman, his elbows on his knees,
holding his head in tense widespread fingers. All the comical
tragedy that had characterized his other dejection was gone.
This was nothing but misery—stark, utter misery.

"Oh dear, Bill," I begged, "*please* don't take it like this! Let
me phone to her, or wait and go see her tomorrow."

He straightened up, shaking his head.

"I've just seen her."

"What did she say?"

"She's going to marry Marshall."

"But she . . . she *can't!*" I cried. "She doesn't really care anything for him. Her father knows that—he won't give his consent, and she won't ever marry without that!"

"Well, I don't know about that," Bill Haines said heavily. "Maybe there's . . . more to it than we know. I think she's got it into her head she's destined to make some kind of sacrifice for her family, or . . . or something. Marshall's been in love with her for years. She says she never knew it till the other night. Says she can't bear to make him unhappier than he is."

He got up and stood in front of the fireplace, staring down unseeing at the smoldering wool.

"She admits she doesn't love him. She's sorry for him, and fond of him, and he's always been swell to her—standing between her and that old warhorse Melusina. But it doesn't make sense, Miss Lucy!"

He gave my andirons a violent kick.

"Yes, it does, if you know Faith Yardley," I said. "It makes too horribly much sense."

He stood there, then sat down on the ottoman, his broad rumpled white linen back to me. After a minute he turned around, straddling the ottoman seat.

"She *can't* marry him, Miss Lucy," he said doggedly. "She can't do it. You've got to stop her before it's too late."

I shook my head slowly. I'd much rather it had been some other way, but Faith knew now what she was doing. I was sure of that. There'd been a new gentleness in her face, pale as it was, when she came in from the garden. The two men in the library, her cousin and her father, were hers . . . a part of a deeper life that one had to have known the grave tranquil-eyed little girl with tightly drawn plaits and stodgy button shoes in another Williamsburg to understand. I shook my head again.

"Look, Miss Lucy—you won't think I'm just a damned cad, sore because I'm licked, punch-drunk and hitting below the belt, will you, if I tell you something?"

"No, Bill," I said. "No one would ever think that."

And I tried not to remember Marshall Yardley standing in the path near the well, saying with such ominous calm, "What are you doing, Cousin Lucy?" I didn't want ever to think that again, not if Faith was going to marry him.

Bill hunched forward urgently.

"Well, look. This is the way I've had this business doped out from the beginning . . . only I figured it was the Napier woman sent Marshall off his base. I thought, when she told me it was Faith he was nuts about, she was just making time, and explaining why she felt perfectly free to go all out for Seymour—pretending to lend Marshall a helping hand on the home team."

I folded my hands in my lap, wishing I hadn't been so reckless with my knitting. It would have been convenient to have something to study so I wouldn't have to look into Bill's drawn unhappy face.

"You see, I figured Ruth was a sort of tramp, but the kind that could get a guy like Marshall so he didn't know whether he was going or coming. So that night when Faith's engagement had been announced the day before, and he went over there and found Ruth there, he simply went off his nut. Because she was there, all right. She was still there when Faith went down——"

He stopped abruptly, a shocked unguarded look in his eyes.

"That's all right, Bill," I said wearily. "Faith told me all about it—about you and the gate post. She told the Commonwealth Attorney all about it tonight, leaving you and the gate post out, and Ruth Napier too. So that's when you went back to the terrace and ploughed around in the cockroach powder?"

He was staring at me.

"You mean she told Crabtree she was at Seymour's?" he blurted out.

I nodded. He got to his feet instantly. "I guess I'd better go see Crabtree myself."

"Sit down," I said. "He'll come to you soon enough. Did you tell him——"

"I told him I saw Seymour and left the place without seeing anybody else, or . . . hearing anything."

"Did you hear something?"

He sat down on the ottoman again and began fishing about in his pockets, and eventually pulled out a mangled pack of cigarettes.

"I don't know," he said at last.

As with Hallie Taswell, I knew he wasn't telling me the whole story. And yet it was different. It wasn't himself he was trying to shield.

"Was Marshall down there, Bill?" I asked.

He hesitated. He seemed torn between a kind of conviction and a kind of dubious sense of honor that made it hard to say what he wanted to say.

"Look, Miss Lucy—somebody got into the back garden and shot Mason Seymour, and got out and tossed that shotgun into the Canal. It wasn't you, because he was dead before you got there. It wasn't me, because he was dead before I went barging back—having . . . well, maybe I still had some cockeyed notion that Faith would see the light, and was just telling myself something else."

He gave me a rueful grin.

"Maybe I was just still fooling myself that it was because Seymour was such a bounder that I didn't want her to marry him, not because I was crazy about her myself and saw red every time I thought of him having her. I don't know. I know I'd have been glad to strangle him myself. I almost did, when he was telling me in the dining room, with that most superior smile, that he thought Miss Faith would make up her own mind by morning without advice or assistance from me, in that who-the-hell-did-I-think-I-was sort of tone that burned me up so it was all I could do to keep from sorting one out on his chin.—He said Doctor Yardley had agreed to leave the decision up to his daughter, and he thought I could quite safely do the same."

His lips twisted in a mirthless sort of grin.

"That bucked me up," he said, and after a moment he added, without looking at me, "that's why meeting her five minutes later, on her way down there, handed me such a wallop. That and knowing Ruth Napier was still there, and they'd be sure to meet. I guess that's why I followed her, I don't know. But as soon as she disappeared and the train went by screaming like a banshee, I had a hunch something was wrong.* I wasn't just sticking my nose in. When I got back  there and looked in, and saw him sitting there like a goldfish in a bowl, looking like he'd faced a firing squad . . . well, I've been telling myself I had a hunch all along that something like that was on the cards."

"Was Faith there then, Bill?" I asked.

He nodded.

"She told John Crabtree she heard some one outside."

* The author's apologies to Miss Booth.

He looked up and grinned.

"I guess that makes William the guy with the maroon eyes," he said.

"She thought you'd gone. She looked back up at the gate and you weren't there. She didn't know you'd followed her down."

He nodded.

"But you see what that does—unless somebody else was in the back garden: me and the shotgun and the cockroach powder and all the rest of it. I don't have any yen to take the rap for Cousin Marshall, Miss Lucy—not and let him get Faith too. I mean, that's too much."

He grinned at me, not too pleasantly I may say.

"You see, I've been looking over that back garden, where it runs down to the railroad. If you'd been brought up around here, and played Indians up that ravine, there's a mighty good way you could get up there from the back of Yardley Hall without going through the jungle next door, the way you and the colonial dame did."

I looked at him. The shadowy hand on the chain, the blood on the whitewashed boards, Marshall Yardley saying "What do you want, Cousin Lucy?" . . . I couldn't keep them out of my mind now . . . nor Faith saying, "I went into the library—there was only a curl of smoke . . ."

"What if she's marrying him to . . . to pay for something, Miss Lucy?" Bill Haines said. "Because of what she knows . . . or because of what—he knows?"

The clock in Bruton Church struck ten.

"It's funny about Seymour," Bill said. "He was an odd sort of guy. Maybe he was going to settle down and cut out the middle-aged Casanova stuff. He always paid for his fun. More than that, he was as generous as they come. I was talking to his cousin today. He says Seymour gave him five hundred a month, and was always good for a touch if the wrong horse came in. He's pretty down in the mouth about that second will. He says it leaves everything as a sort of endowment to Yardley Hall, with enough for him to buy a pack of cigarettes twice a week if the tax doesn't go up."

"How does he know that?" I demanded.

Bill shook his head.

"Has anybody seen that will? John Crabtree didn't mention it tonight at Yardley Hall. Maybe Mason wasn't signing it until after the wedding."

"No, it was signed all right," Bill said. "Ruth Napier was one of the witnesses, some lawyer here in town was the other."

He tossed his cigarette toward the fireplace.

"Well, it works out swell for Marshall. Mason bites the dust, I take the rap, he gets the girl and Yardley Hall plenteously endowed. Neat, I call it."

I shook my head. "That's not like Marshall," I said.

(*There's blood on the well at Yardley Hall.*)

"And anyway, how would he have ever got the gun?"

Bill looked at me. "He was here the day before. He was coming out of the house when I came. He said you weren't here. I didn't know who he was then, of course. He had a newspaper in his hand."

"That would be the announcement of Faith's engagement," I said. "But anyway, the gun was here after that. Community says you were aiming it at my squirrel who lives in the pavlovnia tree."

He grinned.

"I recognize that shotgun as my problem, Miss Randolph," he said. "Gosh, maybe I did shoulder it and march down the Green—but I sure don't remember doing it. You're sure it wasn't you? Or what about your lady in the fancy dress? There's room enough under that paniered skirt to carry an arsenal."

"Don't be preposterous," I said sharply.

"That's not as preposterous as it sounds," he replied calmly. "You know about hell hath no fury like a woman scorned. She's certainly got the wind up about something."

"She's scared out of her skin that Luton will tell her husband what an idiot she's been, that's all," I said.

Bill nodded. "I think it's time somebody gave that fellow a break, by the way," he said seriously.

"Who—Luton?"

"Yeah. Talbot Seymour says Mason picked him up when he was down and out, in Paris. He'd been a customer's man in a private bank there, doing a little bucket shopping on his own, and he got caught out. He took hold of Mason's affairs and cut off all the servants' pipe lines, and saved about ten grand a year just in petty cash. He knew all the tax dodges, and never tried to chisel for himself."

I thought back, a little ashamed of myself after a minute. If I'd ever had a check for two thousand five hundred dollars snatched from my fingers I wondered what I would have done . . . I glanced at the fireplace where Faith's flaming handkerchief had fallen to ashes. Luton could have taken it to John Carter Crabtree just as well. The check had been his—it had his name on it and Mason Seymour's signature at the bottom . . . like the signatures people used to write for the devil, only it was Mason's blood had wet the paper, not the pen. "That money means a great deal to me, Miss Randolph," he'd said.

Then suddenly it occurred to me that maybe he hadn't been so sure Faith had taken it, had just guessed that because he'd found her handkerchief there, spotted brown with blood. Maybe that was why he was dogging Hallie Taswell's steps too, and if . . .

"I mean, you've got to give the devil his due," Bill Haines was saying earnestly. "He had his job to do, and I don't suppose it was his fault that the guy that gave him a break when he needed it was a louse."

He got up. A sudden alarm gripped my heart. "Bill," I said, "—what are you planning to do?"

He gave me another mirthless grin.

"Me, Miss Lucy? I'll tell you. I'm going over to Yardley Hall, and I'm going to tell Marshall Yardley that it's his cousin or his life. If he don't give up the gal, I'm going to show his old friend Johnny Crabtree the hole in the back fence. Boy, oh boy—am I going to tell him plenty!"

I got up too. "Please don't, Bill—wait till morning anyway!" I cried. "You don't know what you're doing!"

"Yes, I do, Miss Lucy," he said, his voice suddenly very gentle. "You know the base Indian that threw a pearl away richer than all his tribe? Well—that's not me, Miss Lucy. We Haineses always get our girl."

"The last of the Haineses will be getting a bullet in his head if he doesn't start using it," I said sharply.

He grinned, and put his head back in the door just before he closed it. "Cheerioh!" he said.

I leaned my head back against the carved rosewood frame of my Victorian rocking chair. It was definitely the place I belonged in, and I didn't care just then whether I ever moved out of it or not. Tomorrow I'd have somebody get me some more knitting to do, and I'd hereafter sit there and do it—the Haineses and the Yardleys and the Taswells and the Lutons and the Talbot Seymours, and the entire universe of men and angels, could go their several ways without help or hindrance from me. I'll get a cat and a parrot, I thought, and a little darky to wind my wool . . . and Bill Haines's long legs are crossing the Court House Green into England Street, I thought, and now he's passing the old mulberry tree by the cutting garden. . . . In a moment he'll be in Scotland Street by the white wicket with the cannon ball on the chain to keep it closed. He'll see the long dark alleys of box and the peaked roof of the little well house with the long fingers of wisteria and the brown spot of blood on the whitewashed board.

I closed my eyes. The carved pear on the back of my chair pressing against my head made it ache suddenly as it had never ached before . . . but it wasn't my head that was aching, or the carved rosewood pear on the Victorian chair back that made it ache . . . it was my heart, and the last of the Haineses, and the last of the Yardleys.

And just then the phone rang. I don't know why it sounded so urgent and peremptory, except that the house was so still and dead. It rang again, sharp and long, and I ran out into the hall and took down the receiver.

"Hello," I said.

"*Oh, Cousin Lucy!*"

It was Faith; her voice was all agony.

"*Oh Cousin Lucy, come quickly . . . it's Marshall . . . he's dead!*"

# 23

Faith's voice, all agony, crying through the night *"Oh Cousin Lucy, come quickly . . . it's Marshall, he's dead!"* was still throbbing in my numb brain as I hurried, too tired to even try to think, into Scotland Street. When I got there I stopped abruptly. Across the middle of the road was Sergeant Priddy's car. It was turned so that the long white fingers of its headlights reached in through the white picket fence and groped among the dark branches of heavy box up the path, past the well house to Yardley Hall. I ran forward to the wicket. It had been propped open with a rock, the black cannon ball on its chain hanging ominously across the beam of solid light. Then I saw ahead of me in the path, grouped silently and terribly about the little well house, four motionless figures, their white-linen backs all toward me, looking down at something on the ground.

I turned quickly and ran up to Palace Long Wall Street, and down the elm-shaded drive to the high pillared porch of Yardley Hall. The door was ajar. I pushed it open and went in. Death was there already. I felt his cold soulless silence touch my face and creep into my heart as I had felt it another time in those same dim walls. I closed the door softly and stole into the library. Faith was sitting there in her father's chair, her face as pale as old alabaster, her eyes wide and tearless, her hands folded in front of her on the green-gold leather table cover. She didn't move as I went to her and pressed my lips to her cold forehead. Then she closed her eyes.

159

"They say he killed himself, Cousin Lucy," she whispered. "I'll never forgive myself, Cousin Lucy."

She clung to me quickly, desperately, her voice choked in a dry awful sob, her whole body shaking like a leaf.

"Please, honey, please!" I implored, holding her tight against me.

"Oh, how could he, Cousin Lucy, how *could* he? I did love him, really—in a way I did. I was going to marry him, I truly was."

I looked up. Melusina Yardley was standing in the door. Faith must have sensed it; she clutched me more tightly, and I her. Melusina's face was terrible. It was calm and set as if nothing had happened. I couldn't believe my eyes. I'd expected she'd be a fury with all hell loose in her eyes and in her serpent's tongue. I shrank away from her hard level gaze, holding my child tightly in my arms—for she was mine, more mine than any one else's, except her father's, and she'd been mine for years and his only four short days.

"I think you see the tragedy you have brought on this house, Lucy," Melusina said, with horrible evenness. "Seeing it, I should think you'd have the decency to stay in your home, not come here to triumph over us."

Faith held to me tighter, her young arms giving back the strength that drained from my body like blood from a horrible wound.

"Oh Melusina, how can you?" I whispered.

"You've been against me all my life, Lucy," she said, still with that same dreadful calm. "I see it now more clearly every day. And now you've taken Marshall—the only person I've loved, or who ever loved me."

"*I've* taken him . . . ?" I gasped.

"Yes, you." Her voice was so deadly cold that even Faith shrank from it. "If you hadn't brought Haines here to turn Faith's head, Marshall would never have had to raise a hand against . . . against himself."

In one swift intuitive flash I realized she'd been going to say "against Mason Seymour" and had stopped just on the verge of it.—Then Bill had been right, and Melusina knew it: Marshall *had* killed Mason Seymour, for Faith . . .

I leaned weakly against the table, my limbs shaking almost unbearably. So it was Marshall, in the end, I thought, who'd made the sacrifice for the Yardley's, not Faith who'd seemed so destined to be the one who made it. And in a sense it seemed right that he'd done it, right that it should have been he who killed Mason, right that having done it he should pay for it with his own life. And yet it wasn't right! Everything inside me cried out against it! Marshall was too good a person to go like that—and what right had this thin bitter woman with her overweening pride, clinging with such fierce tenacity on the shell of a dead past, to force any of them to the point where they had to sacrifice themselves—Faith and Marshall—to keep her from sacrificing her pride! It wasn't right, there was nothing right about it; it was cruel and selfish and wrong!

I looked at Melusina. In all the years I'd known her, seeing her almost daily, putting up with her riding roughshod over me and every one else, and over her brother's child, I'd never opened my mouth to her or against her. My dingy parlor, the little stool at my feet, the canton ginger jar full of sugar cookies with a bit of candied watermelon rind in the center, a safe haven for a little girl with tight carrot-gold plaits and grave grey eyes and a warm sensitive mouth—these were all I'd ever set up against her. But now, standing there, the child grown up clinging so desperately to me—shocked, too profoundly hurt to cry out,—I turned on Melusina.—But not quickly enough, her tongue was so much more limber from years of indulgence than mine was from years of abstinence.

"You'll see you've not been as clever as you think, Lucy Randolph. We'll see who wins in the end, you or me."

Then all the anger that had boiled up in me dissolved. It seemed to me too horrible for us, two old women, to be in that silent house, fighting like a pair of hungry buzzards over our own dead lives.

Faith, sensing the struggle, and the end of it in me, relaxed her hold against my body.

"You were always a spineless coward, Lucy," Melusina said.

Just then her brother stood behind her in the door. God knows how much of this scene he'd heard. His face was almost unearthly, and terrifying, it was so pale and so stern; and when he spoke—"That will be enough of that, Melusina"—his voice was blue steel sheathed in velvet.

Melusina shrank, her face crumpling like an old paper bag. Peyton Yardley looked at me.

"Thank you, Lucy, for coming to us. The others will be

here in a moment. I'd like you to stay, if you'll take Faith upstairs and come back."

Faith raised her head. "I'd rather stay, father," she said quietly.

A sharp spasm of pain crossed his face.

"You must do as you think best, daughter."

He turned to his sister and gave her a searching glance. "I advise you to go to bed at once, Melusina."

He passed his frail transparent hand across his eyes, and turned back, drawing the door to. We heard the slow muted steps of the men bringing Marshall Yardley back to the Hall. Faith closed her eyes and hid her face against my side. After a little the muffled steps were silent, and then I heard the men coming down, quietly still but individually, their terrible burden no longer unifying them.

John Crabtree came in first, behind him one of the Palace watchmen; and then—and my heart rose, and sank numb again—Bill Haines. His face was as white as his linen coat, his blue eyes sick as they met mine and moved, with a quickening dumb ache in them, to the girl beside me. I was so concerned with him that I didn't see it was George Luton coming in behind him, between him and Michael Priddy, looming in the doorway as tall as Bill himself, both of them a full head and shoulders taller than Luton and twice as broad.

They sorted themselves out in the room, Bill farthest away, his eyes drawn, in spite of his efforts to keep them away, constantly back to Faith. Luton edged to the side of the door and stood there, his back to the old Chippendale mirror. The room was as silent as the tomb as we all waited for John Crabtree to speak. And he was finding it very hard to do. Marshall was younger than he by several years, but they'd been friends, close friends, since Marshall had been admitted to the bar and John had been Commonwealth Attorney.

It seemed such pitiful irony, some way, that we should all be so much more shattered by this than Melusina, whose heart he had been. I saw the quick glance she darted at me. She was going to take the offensive, I thought—knowing just how desperately offensive she could be. . . . But her brother cleared his throat, and she subsided as John Crabtree said,

"There'll be an autopsy in the morning, sir. We've got the revolver he killed himself with. Maybe he left a message.— Mr. Haines here was almost up to him when it happened."

He took a rumpled handkerchief out of his pocket and wiped his forehead.

"There's just one thing I want to ask about, Doctor Yardley. This will that Mason Seymour made out . . . It was witnessed by Miss Napier and Jerry Matthews in town.— Have you any idea what's . . . become of it?"

I glanced at Luton. There's the man you should ask about that, I thought, uncharitably—or possibly, and I don't know why the idea hadn't struck me before, the man you should ask about that would be Mr. Talbot Seymour. After all, it was Talbot Seymour who inherited his cousin's property by the first will. And having thought of that, I looked eagerly at John Crabtree, just as Doctor Yardley, standing very erect, and really beautiful, in front of the carved mantel, the portrait of Sir Robert Yardley above him, three centuries of dignity and honor linking them together, inclined his head gravely.

"I don't know how the law will regard what I did, John," he said quietly. "I explained to Mr. Seymour, when I saw him at his house that night, before his death—and I think he understood me perfectly—that such a will as his, drawn before he had either a moral or legal claim or obligation to my daughter, was an intolerable impertinence—ill-advised and misguided in the extreme. I tore the document up, in front of him, and put it in the fireplace, and set a match to it with my own hand.—I don't know how the law regards that act . . . but so far as my daughter and I are concerned, Mr. Seymour's second will never existed."

I think the silence in that room then was as profound and breathless as any silence could have been. Faith's hand tightened in mine. I didn't want to look at Melusina, but I couldn't help it. The most extraordinary change had come over her. She was as rigid as granite, her eyes were terrible. She got up—I don't see how she did it—and stood, one hand out in front of her as if to ward off some dreadful injury, looking first at her brother, who met her gaze calm and unflinching, and then at me, anything but either . . . and then she turned without a word and went from the room. At the door she tottered, her whole body sagging, her knees buckling, and pitched forward in a miserable heap on the floor.

Her brother's calm voice cut the shocked silence. "My sister has fainted—will you carry her upstairs, please, Michael?"

The rest of us sat perfectly still, unable to move for a moment. It was all too dreadful. Then Faith released my hand and followed her father and John Crabtree up the stairs. The Palace guard said, "Jeez, what come over her so sudden?" but nobody answered him, and he went out. I saw him stop on the porch and light a cigarette. The flame shook and the cigarette shook, but at last I saw smoke and heard him go down the steps. I looked around at Bill. He'd stepped out into the garden through the dutch door. Mr. Luton and I were left alone. I should have apologized to him, I suppose, for what I'd been thinking. I certainly wasn't prepared for his apologizing to me instead.

He took a step into the room toward me.

"I hope you didn't misunderstand my seizing your wrist this evening, Miss Randolph," he said earnestly. "You were so agitated, and you looked so shaken, I thought you were going to lose your balance. I'm sorry if I alarmed you."

"Not at all," I said curtly. I didn't mean it to sound that way, but I was really upset, because I *had* misunderstood him. I hadn't thought of how I must have looked, barging off up the street.

"Thank you, Miss Randolph," he said. He hesitated and glanced around. My heart sank again as I thought, "What's coming now?"—the old alarm springing up, constricting my throat.

"I wonder if you'd do one thing for me, Miss Randolph," he said, so quietly that it was almost under his breath. His hand went to his inside coat pocket. He glanced back into the hall again.

"Oh, dear, oh, dear!" I thought desperately. "Why doesn't that wretched William Quincy Adams Haines come back in here!"

Luton drew out a thick packet of pale blue letters held together with a red rubber band.

"Will you give these to Mrs. Taswell?" he said, in that same preternaturally quiet voice. "I've tried to get them to her myself, but I've been unable to do so. I hesitated just to leave them at her house, or send them through the post. From portions of them Mr. Seymour used to read aloud to me, madam, I expect she would prefer they didn't fall into . . . any other hands. If you'd be so kind . . ."

I almost snatched them out of his hand.

"Thank you, madam," he said. "Good night."

What a beast Mason Seymour must have been, I thought, and what a fool Hallie was! I thrust the packet down the neck of my dress and turned around. Bill Haines was bending down to clear the window above the dutch door. He came on into the room and took hold of my arm.

"Let's go home, Miss Lucy," he said. Then he said, "What's the matter? Are *you* going to faint?"

"I shouldn't be at all surprised," I said. But I didn't. Though I nearly did just as we were crossing the Market Square. Bill hadn't said a word since we'd left Yardley Hall, just trudged along silently, holding my arm in his big hand, bearing most of my weight as we went along. As we cut across beside the Powder Horn he said, not abruptly but as if he'd thought it all out and decided finally to say it,

"Miss Lucy—Marshall didn't kill himself. Some one shot him, when he was standing by the well. Don't ask me who it was, because I don't know. And just keep this under your hat till we decide what to do."

I couldn't go to sleep that night. I got up half-a-dozen times and wandered wretchedly about the dark house. Outside it was pitch-black except for the fireflies bearing their pale lanterns up and down the streets. The grotesque idea that there was a plague in Williamsburg and they were showing their lights, calling "Bring out your dead!" came to me as I sat by the window in my room watching them.

I found myself watching one of them especially, under the old mulberry tree across the street, glow redder than others and go down, and up and glow again. Then my heart suddenly sank cold and heavy to the pit of my stomach and lay there like a stone. Fireflies are lemon-pale, and glow upward, never more than once in the same place. That wasn't a firefly. It was a cigarette. Somebody was standing under the tree across the road, watching my house . . . or my office, rather, where Bill Haines was sleeping . . . if he could sleep.

Some one else knew, too, that Marshall Yardley had been murdered.

# 24

If Sergeant Michael Priddy hadn't come to the office before
Bill was dressed the next morning and waited while he
shaved, and left with him in the police car before Community had come to get breakfast, I shouldn't probably have
done what I did. But all night the chain of circumstantial
evidence that bound Bill to Mason Seymour's murder kept
going around and around in my head. The gun from the
office; his footprints in the cockroach powder; the definite
knowledge that Mason was shot from the terrace and that
Bill was the only person on the terrace; his ridiculous be-
havior in trying to keep Faith from marrying Mason in the
first place, his trying to shield her from the consequences of
her presence at Mason's house, her folly to deny his presence
there . . . it was all too frightening.

Now, added to that, Marshall Yardley was dead . . .
Marshall who Bill had thought murdered Mason Seymour.
God knows whom he may have told that beside me, or who
might have heard him tell me. Or what if some one else had
possibly heard him say what he was going to tell Marshall?
My doors and windows are always open—if the man with
the cigarette under the mulberry tree had cared to listen outside . . . And the Commonwealth Attorney had said Mr.
Haines was almost up to Marshall when he shot himself.

All night long I'd gone over that in my mind, and at the
end as at the beginning, I knew it was at least in part my
fault. If I'd told John Crabtree everything from the beginning, if I'd told him about the shadowy hand on the black

chain, and the blood on the well at Yardley Hall, Marshall might not have died . . . and Faith would have married him, I had to add . . . ashamed because I did.

Nevertheless, it was all too serious now for me to do anything to shield anybody—no matter who it might be—but Bill. I dressed and went downstairs before Community had brought my coffee, and phoned John Crabtree's house. He was gone. He'd left early, his wife said; I could probably catch him at his office. But he wasn't there either, he wouldn't be there until nine. At a quarter to nine I went upstairs and put on my hat. As I came down some one lifted my knocker and rapped. I opened the door.

Ruth Napier was standing on the stoop. She'd been crying. Her face was a mess. Her long loosely curled hair was raven black against the thick sprays of silver moon roses over the door.

"May I come in, Miss Randolph?" she said. I glanced at the office. Had she been there first, I wondered? I held the door open. She went straight across the parlor and dropped down on the ottoman.

"Tell me about Marshall, Miss Randolph!" she demanded. "Is it true he . . . killed himself?"

"That's what Mr. Crabtree said last night," I answered.

"Oh, that little *fool!*" she cried suddenly. "She doesn't deserve all this!"

"What are you talking about?" I asked sharply, astonished and bewildered by her violence, and by the great hot tears that drowned her dark eyes.

"Oh, you know as well as I do—he adored her, and it's her fault . . ."

"Look, Miss Napier," I said. "I think Faith wouldn't care if I told you that she had—just last night after supper—told Marshall she'd marry him."

She stared at me, her great eyes blank, her red lips opened. "Then why . . . why did he . . ."

"I don't know," I said.

"Oh, it's not true, then!" she cried passionately. "It doesn't make sense, Miss Randolph!"

She got up and stood confronting me, challenging everything.

"You don't understand . . . none of you did. Marshall was absolutely mad about her. It was killing him, having to let Mason Seymour have her because he didn't have anything to offer her—no money, I mean. He was almost desperate, living there in the same house with her, with that horrible old woman always talking about keeping the Hall, not caring what she did to people's lives just so that awful house could live!"

She threw back her dark loose curls, her eyes blazing.

"I suppose I was in love with Marshall. I don't know— he certainly never knew it if I was. I would have done *anything* to help him get away from here and make a name for himself! But he couldn't bear not seeing her.—I didn't want Mason Seymour, but I couldn't bear seeing him marry that kid and get tired of her in six months and make a wreck of her, because I knew if he did Marshall would kill him!"

I sat down weakly. If the whole place had gone up in a pillar of fire and a cloud of smoke, I shouldn't have been the least surprised. This girl was a flaming torch.

Then suddenly, as violently and passionately as she'd flared up, she collapsed in a broken heap on the ottoman, sobbing bitterly. I got up, went out and closed the door. Community was in the hall.

"Take that girl some coffee," I said. "And get her quieted down before she goes out of her mind."

Community looked at my hat and gloves, and glanced up at the hall clock.

"You sho' you ain' done gone out a' yours, Mis' Lucy?" she inquired darkly.

"On the contrary, Community," I replied sharply. "I'm convinced that's exactly what I have done."

"Yes, *ma'am*," Community said.

She watched me as far as the gate.

I went down Francis Street and up the walk to the new red brick courthouse and upstairs to the Commonwealth Attorney's office. Mr. Crabtree wasn't in, the girl in the bare outer office told me, but he was expected any moment.

"If you'd like to go in and wait, I'm sure it will be all right, Miss Randolph," she said.

I went in. His desk with its swivel chair set in the dormer was like a vacant niche in an empty church. I sat down in the chair in front of the littered desk to wait. Whatever doubts I might have had about the wisdom of my course before Ruth Napier came had been entirely dissipated by her passionate avowal. I was a little chastened too. I'd been wrong about the blood on the well at Yardley Hall, apparently. I'd certainly been wrong about Luton, and about Ruth Napier herself. What if I'd been equally wrong about . . . well, say about Bill Haines, I thought dismally? What if the circumstantial evidence that surrounded him *was* true? What if it was true that the Haineses always got their girl—let the chips fall and the blood spout where they may? What if I'd been trying my level worst to marry the child I loved better than my own life to a cold-blooded murderer?

"Oh dear," I thought; "I wish John would come!"

And then—and I suppose I ought to be ashamed indeed to admit it, and certainly shall never tell it any more after I have admitted it—I did a perfectly inexcusable thing, or rather a continued series of perfectly inexcusable things. John Crabtree's desk was piled—even more piled than littered, when I got to looking at it—with stacks of typed reports. I had only to crane my neck the least bit—at first—to see that the top one was a statement in the Seymour case. Craning my neck a little more I could read it quite plainly—and I did.

It was the report of a colored boy named Craddock who was a member of the C.C.C. camp working on the archeological diggings at Jamestown. He had heard a shotgun being fired in the woods near Jamestown the evening of Mason Seymour's death, at about four-thirty o'clock. He was curious, and ran out to see what was going on. He didn't see who fired the shot, but he heard a car leaving the place hurriedly. It was gone by the time he got to the road. He could however show the place where the gun had been fired.

Attached to that statement was a photograph of a lot of shot marks against a group of loblolly pines. I couldn't, of course, see that by just craning my neck. I had to reach out and pick it up, which is exactly what I did. After that the rest was quite simple. I went through the whole case without batting an eye, my conscience, heavily drugged with curiosity, slumbering profoundly.

The next was a statement of five members of the staff of the Inn. Mr. Talbot Seymour had arrived by motor car at the Inn at eight-fifty. He had inquired the way to his cousin's house, registered, gone to the phone booth by the desk, not in his own room, and phoned his cousin. He had then come out and gone to his room. At about nine-thirty he had left the hotel without taking his car. He had returned, talked to the desk clerk a few moments, and retired.

The report of Talbot Seymour's conversation with the desk clerk followed. He had been in Southern Pines, was returning to New York, had seen the announcement of his cousin's engagement to a Williamsburg girl and decided he'd come down and look her over. He'd left Richmond about two o'clock, but he'd got mixed up on Route 60 and gone the wrong way, and then, to make everything worse, he'd had a flat that had taken him a long time to change. That's why he'd arrived so late, and that's why he didn't go directly to his cousin's house. He would however be checking out the first thing in the morning. Williamsburg was certainly a dead hole, and personally if he'd been Mr. Rockefeller he'd never have sunk fifty cents in it, much less fifty million dollars. He had looked at his watch, set it with the clock on the mantel, said he'd like some ice sent to his room so he could have a drink and turn in. He phoned from his room at nine-forty-five, asking for a boy to get his suit and have it pressed by morning, and get his shoes to clean—he didn't want to unpack his bag. The boy had got his suit and shoes, which were in the valet's room until Mr. Talbot Seymour phoned for them at eight-thirty the next morning.

He had had a room on the first floor in the west wing.

Attached to that report was a floor plan of the Inn. An exit into the garden was marked on it in red ink.

Next came a complete dossier of the life of Mr. W. Q. A. Haines, from the service station on the Richmond Road where he'd stopped for a hot dog at four-forty-five, from the Information Booth by William and Mary College where he'd asked the direction to Miss Lucy Randolph's house in Francis Street, to his arrival, and to my arrival—through the eyes of my neighbor across the road.—"I thought for a minute she wasn't going to let him have her room," she said. "You know, Miss Randolph's right peculiar at times, and she don't take in everybody."

Under that was a whole batch of cards with a lot of ill-assorted fingerprints on them. One of them, from the telephone in Mason Seymour's study, was labelled, "Miss Faith Yardley; picked up the phone at 10.41, uncompleted call, by own admission."

Next was a complete photographic statement of the crime. I put that down quickly, sick at my stomach and my heart, and picked up the report of Joe Sanders, colored gardener at Mason Seymour's. Joe had put down ten pounds of pink cockroach powder. Roaches and water bugs were what Mr. Seymour and Mr. Luton "mostes' didn' like." They always kept a quantity of powder in the cellar, but it had got wet, so Mr. Luton had sent him for a fresh supply that day, and he'd put it around. Joe himself didn't see that a few roaches and water bugs made any difference, and grumbled considerably. The other servants had grumbled too, because the time before it had got tracked into the house and Mason Seymour had raised Cain.

Joe admitted too that he had oiled and cleaned Miss Lucy Randolph's shotgun, and that he had borrowed it once or twice without her knowledge to go hunting, but he'd always put it back in the cupboard in the office. He admitted buying shells to use in it, but he hadn't any at the present time.

After that was a statement from Ray Byers at the hardware shop in the Duke of Gloucester Street. Joe had bought ten pounds of pink cockroach powder about three o'clock the same afternoon. He had bought shells from time to time, in duck season mostly. The roach powder was charged to Mr. Seymour's bill. The shells he had always paid for himself.

Next was an envelope labelled, "Sweepings from Miss Lucy Randolph's office, occupied by W. Q. A. Haines."

On the card under that was part of the sweepings from Miss Lucy Randolph's house occupied by herself, I suppose. It was Mason Seymour's card with the invitation to supper written on it, torn in two, the two pieces pasted on a mount about half an inch apart. Under it, attached to the same card, was an envelope that said, "Contents of Miss Lucy Randolph's fireplace." I didn't look into that. "I must make Community be more careful," I thought, passing it by to look at a long and complicated report that meant nothing to me. It was signed "E. C. Callowhill, Ballistics Expert, Newport News, Va."

Under that was a long grey envelope entitled "Last Will and Testament." I didn't open that either, much as I'd have liked to do . . . knowing it was not the last will and testament of Mason Seymour, that his last will and testament had been torn up and burned by the man whose house and whose daughter profited most under it. Yet I couldn't put it down at once; I stood there with it in my hand, unable to get it out of my head that perhaps Mason Seymour, in signing these instruments, had signed away his life. And not this one so much as the other one, the one that Peyton Yardley had burned.

I put the grey envelope down at last and started on the next report, and passed it over without much interest, thinking it was just a silly waste of time. It was about Hallie Taswell's husband Hugh, who apparently had been in Richmond attending an insurance salesmen's get-together the night Mason was killed. And following that was a whole batch of drawings clipped together with a ticket labelled: "Diagrams illustrating wounds produced by shotgun fire at varying distances.—Gun belonging to Miss Lucy Randolph, Francis Street, taken from Palace Canal, 19th May, 10.15 A.M."

And just as I bent down to study the first diagram, feeling again a little sick at my stomach, I heard the jangle of the phone in the outer office, and I heard John's secretary say, "Yes, sir. She's here now, waiting for you. Yes, I'll tell her, Mr. Crabtree."

I hastily stacked the Commonwealth's accumulated evidence against a person or persons unknown—or were they unknown, I wondered; I had a curious feeling that all this mountain of detail wasn't without some subtle and pertinent direction—back the way I'd found it, and got back to my chair. I was there, calm I believe, if a little flushed, when the girl put her head in the door.

"Mr. Crabtree says he's awfully sorry he's kept you waiting, Miss Randolph," she said apologetically. "He's got to go over to Yardley Hall right away. He wonders if you'd mind meeting him there instead."

"Not in the least," I said.

"I'm awfully sorry you had to wait."

"That's quite all right, my dear," I said.

She smiled. "I expect maybe the rest did you good, Miss Randolph."

"Yes, I expect maybe it did," I replied.

# 25

I wasn't so sure of it myself, however, as I crossed the Court House Green into England Street and turned there at the cutting gardens behind the Archibald-Blair house into Scotland Street. There'd been too many ballistics reports on my father's shotgun, and too many references in one way and another to Miss Lucy Randolph's house in Francis Street to reassure me very much. It did serve, however, to heighten the immediate necessity for me to tell John Crabtree I'd seen somebody at the well—when Bill Haines was safe at home.

I turned in the garden path from Scotland Street. John Crabtree and Sergeant Priddy, and another man, were standing talking, half-way along between the gate and the well house. I could see its peaked roof with the long full fingers of wisteria moving delicately in the air. John and Michael lifted their hats.

"This is Captain Callowhill from Newport News, Miss Lucy," John Crabtree said. "—This is the lady whose shotgun you've been trying out, Ed."

Captain Callowhill's face had all the best features, I thought, of a brace of working ferrets. He was lean and keen and wiry, and as he looked at me I had a sudden panicky picture of myself in a diagram, all neatly plotted and subdivided with dotted lines running from my eyeballs to infinity.—Or to the well house; because I said quickly,

"John, I should have told you before that some one . . . some one was here at the well house a little after eleven o'clock the night Mason Seymour was killed—and that brown spot on the well is blood."

They looked at me as if they thought the sun had addled my brains. Then they glanced at each other as much as to say, "Gently, now—let's not get Miss Lucy excited."

"It's just Bill Haines I'm trying to—to get off," I said quickly. "I mean, he was at my house by eleven o'clock or a minute after, so he couldn't have been pitching a shotgun in the canal. And I was back there at the wicket, after I left Mason Seymour's garden . . . and I heard some one washing his hands at that well . . . and I saw blood there the next morning."

They looked back silently at the little peaked roof and the black wheel and delicate chain. Then they looked at me, and at each other again, and at me again. Then John Crabtree went slowly back toward the well, and we all followed him.

"I came out here last night," I went on. "On my way home. Marshall caught me here. He seemed . . . annoyed, I guess, though that's not quite the word . . . as if I was meddling. That was less than an hour before he . . . shot himself."

John didn't look at me. He said quietly, "Marshall didn't shoot himself, Miss Lucy. He was shot from right behind that clump of box there."

He pointed to where a broken branch, its leaves limp in the morning sun, hung down to the ground. The periwinkle and scylla under it were tramped in the earth.

Michael Priddy didn't look at me either, only Captain Callowhill, so I knew they'd been saying that Bill Haines must have done this too. My heart sank dismally, but I didn't let go. I said, "It still doesn't explain the blood on the well, John," as if they'd actually said what they were avoiding saying because I'd said I wanted to get Bill Haines off. John turned then.

"What blood, Miss Lucy?"

"The stain there on the board."

They moved aside for me to show them, and I stopped, my jaw dropping in spite of myself. The brown stain that had been red still when Bill and I had seen it was gone, the well house was fresh and clean, newly whitewashed.

I just stood looking at it, John and Sergeant Priddy looking at me. I glanced up, hopelessly, through the leafy canopy toward the house. A curtain in the transverse hall moved ever so gently back into place. A sharp anguished protest sprang up inside me. Bill shouldn't be sacrified the way Marshall had been, to save Melusina's pride—not if I could help him!

I turned crazily to John. "But it was there, I tell you!"

"There, there, Miss Lucy!" he said, maddeningly soothing.

"Listen, John Crabtree," I snapped.

"Now, now, Miss Lucy," Sergeant Priddy put in. "You just keep your shirt on a minute. If the well's been white-washed in the last day or so, we'll find it out. You just leave it to us."

I was so angry I could have snatched them both bald-headed.

ı He stepped up to the well. Captain Callowhill and John Crabtree moved around behind it. "Is this in use?" Captain Callowhill asked.

(*"If you want a drink of water, I'll get you one from the house," Marshall had said to me.*)

"It's just decoration," John said. "The Restoration goes in for wells and smoke houses. I expect that's why Miss Melusina's refurbished hers—tourist season's just started."

They still didn't believe me. If a lady can ever be said to snort, I snorted at that . . . if indeed I hadn't, in the last day or so, entirely ceased to be a lady. Certainly no one had ever before presumed to tell me to keep my shirt on.

Sergeant Priddy looked at me—a shade less patronizing than he had been. I suppose there's something impressive about tenacious and determined conviction. He put out his hands and took hold of the well chain. It squeaked a little salutation, and then began its thin song as he drew it, hand over hand, around the black pulley wheel in the little peaked wisteria-festooned belfry. Deep below in the old well we heard the clupaclupaclup of the oaken bucket in the cool water at the bottom, and the splash drip-drip-drip as it came above the surface.

Sergeant Priddy drew steadily. He waited. Something of my own suspense seemed to communicate itself to them. I told myself that the blood—if there had been blood—would all be gone, it would never show on the ancient moss-covered bucket that had been submerged in the well.

Sergeant Priddy leaned over, peering down. I heard suddenly a deep "Plop!" as something fell . . . and it wasn't the bucket, for the chain was still heavy in Sergeant Priddy's hands and the next thing we knew it was out, full of water, there in front of us. Sergeant Priddy swung it over onto the washboard, and looked at John Crabtree.

"Something fell off," he said. They looked at me.

There was something too ridiculously ironic in the gleam of triumph I realized was in my faded blue eyes. Heaven knows I didn't dream what a bitter backhanded triumph it was to appear to be. And I have no doubt Melusina was entirely right in saying I revealed my true colors as a vulgar curiosity seeker and the commonest poor white trash, staying out there the way I did for almost an hour, watching them work.

They brought an old oyster rake from the cellar and lashed a pruning hook from the toolshed to it. Doctor Yardley came out, and Bill Haines, who must have been in the house with him. The watchman from the Palace, who'd helped bring Marshall's body in, was there, and a couple of colored gardeners from the Palace gardens, and old Nance the Yardleys' outdoor man. And me—and after they'd worked half an hour or so Faith crept out and slipped her hand in mine, and stood beside me, bewildered and distrait, not daring to ask what none of us could have told her anyway.

It wasn't until Sergeant Priddy had sent old Nance around to the colored school in Nicholson Street to get his great-grandson that they got anywhere, actually. Then they emptied the water from the bucket and put the boy in it, explained about the rakes and all, and lowered him, dubious and putty-colored, down the narrow shaft, Sergeant Priddy and Mr. John Carter Crabtree and old Nance and the Palace watchman and the two colored gardeners all shouting contrary directions down after him. Then suddenly the rope that John Crabtree held gave a jerk in his hands, and Sergeant Priddy started pulling the boy up again by the rope attached to the cradle they'd made for the bucket, slowly so as not to disturb the balance of the oyster rake lashed to the pruning hook.

And finally the shaved kinky head appeared, paled to the color of old chocolate bonbons after a summer in a showcase, and Sergeant Priddy seized the handle of the pruning hook, toppled the boy and the bucket out onto the ground with less than scant ceremony indeed, and began drawing carefully on the hook. Then they unlashed that, leaving him only the rake.

And I wasn't the only one there who was breathless now, as the long handle came up and up, never ending, it seemed, until at last it did end, almost abruptly, as if we'd all expected it to go on forever, never revealing its secret . . . and its secret lay, wet and astonishing, across the wooden moss-hung teeth.

We all stood motionless, staring stupidly, the whole lot of us . . . all except Captain Callowhill the ballistics expert from Newport News. He gave a sharp excited snarl—like a terrier spying a rat—and sprang forward, his eyes bright as buttons.

"What did I tell you, Priddy!" he shouted.

He picked up the old bell-mouthed pistol lying balanced on the teeth of the rake. All my life before I'd seen it balanced on the gun rack above the old iron chest in the cellar at Yardley Hall.

Faith's fingers tightened on mine. I glanced at Doctor Yardley. His white delicate face was shocked a little, his body taut, as if he'd been rocked back on his heels and had balanced himself again quickly so nobody would notice.

I looked at Bill Haines. His face had gone the color of old parchment, the cigarette half-way to his lips must have been burning his fingers. It still stayed there, motionless.

"I told you the fellow was shot from inside the room, with some kind of a contraption rigged up to make it look like a shotgun was used," Captain Callowhill said. "And here we are. Get hold of that girl—she knows plenty."

I heard Faith gasp.

Bill Haines took a quick step forward. "You're crazy, all of you."

His voice was hard and clear.

"It was that shotgun. I ought to know—I killed Seymour."

John Crabtree smiled. Faith's fingernails biting into my hand went perfectly dead. It was all I could do to hold myself up, much less her. I saw her raise her eyes desperately, imploring, to her father. Peyton Yardley straightened his tall stooped figure.

"I think we need counsel, all of us, John," he said very quietly. "I suggest you dismiss this crew and come inside a moment."

# 26

At the door of the library Doctor Yardley turned around to me.

"Will you and Faith wait in the parlor, please, Lucy," he said, and when Faith gave a little cry of protest he put his arm around her trembling shoulders and said, very gently, "For just a few minutes, child."

The rest of them, John Crabtree and Sergeant Priddy, and Captain Callowhill with the old bell-mouthed pistol in his hands, and Bill Haines, his blue eyes a mixture of all the unhappy tragic things life holds, followed Peyton Yardley into the panelled library. They closed the door. Faith and I went into the darkened parlor, heavy with the complicated perfume of fresh roses and peonies and potpourri and old damask draperies and polished mahogany and rosewood.

I sat down in the short Chippendale sofa with its cherry-red brocatelle faded and worn on the arms and across the back. Faith opened one of the inside shutters and stood by the window, looking out into the rose garden through the screen of crape myrtles toward the Palace. After a long time she came slowly back and drew up a little round needlepoint stool. She sat down and leaned her head wearily against my knees.

"It's dreadful to say, Cousin Lucy," she said softly. "But I'm glad Marshall didn't . . . do it himself. I couldn't understand it—he seemed so happy, even after Father talked to both of us, after everybody left, and I made Father see . . .

the way it was, and that I'd be happiest that way. That's why
it seemed so awful, as if Marshall hadn't believed me, and
thought I was just being noble, and he'd rather be dead than
have me that way. I couldn't have stood it, Cousin Lucy."

"I know, lamb."

"He was always so good, all my life," she whispered. She
was silent a long time, rocking her bright head back and
forth against my knees as if it ached too profoundly to rest.

The door to the library opened. In the mirror under the
Empire side table in front of the door I could see Doctor
Yardley's quiet feet come out and turn up the stairs, and
Sergeant Priddy's black leather puttees come after him and
turn out the door. It was very strange. I never knew I could
recognize so many people by their legs and feet, reflected
from the knees down . . . and that was all I could see of
them in the plate glass backing of the heavy ornate table. I
was glad Faith's back was to it, though I doubt if she'd have
noticed it, she was so absorbed in her own misery. She didn't
even notice the involuntary start that jarred my body as I
heard steps on the stairs and saw her father's feet appear
again, and beside them, the full black skirt and rusty black
kid slippers of her Aunt Melusina as they paused at the door
and went in, closing it after them.

"It doesn't seem real, any of it," Faith whispered.

I patted her slim dark shoulder gently.

"Maybe it isn't, Faith," I murmured.

She raised her head, listening. "Who's that?"

"Never mind, dearest," I said.

She rested her head against my knee again like a tired
child. In the mirror I saw Sergeant Priddy's black puttees
again, and a pair of twinkling feet in high-heeled brown and
white pumps, and two slim elegant legs and an inch or so of
dark red spun silk. Why was Ruth Napier here, I wondered
anxiously? And why those knife-creased white palm beach
trousers above a pair of white buckskin brogues?—Mr. Talbot Seymour was as buoyant and snappy from the knees
down as he was from there up. I could almost see his gay
white smile and sleek curly black hair.

The library door opened, and they went in, Sergeant
Priddy holding the door for them. In a moment another pair
of feet appeared, quiet, discreet feet. George Luton's feet;
I'd seen them neatly together on the faded lilies and roses

of my parlor rug. Then I heard more people outside, and saw Sergeant Priddy's black puttees go to meet them.

"I know Bill says he killed Mason because he thinks I did it," Faith's voice was far away, down there at my knees.

"Hush, honey," I whispered. I was frightened at all these people going into the library, with Faith left outside. In the crystal-clear mirror I saw the wide swish of sprigged muslin, and two little black square-toed feet with square buckles on them, and a flash of white cotton stocking. For a moment I thought maybe the ghost of a colonial Lady Anne had come back in broad daylight, until I saw a pair of brown shoes and a grey worsted trouser leg, and Sergeant Priddy again.

My hand on Faith's shoulder turned cold. Why had Hugh Taswell come with Hallie?

I closed my eyes. They were all in there—everybody who'd been connected with Mason Seymour for the last few days . . . everybody except Marshall Yardley, and he was asleep upstairs, and Faith, secure there for the moment against my knee. Then some one else came. There was another pair of black leather puttees in the hall. Sergeant Priddy's were shabby and worn beside them. They disappeared almost instantly, and in a moment another and slower pair of feet appeared, feet I didn't know, in polished brown shoes under a fine light English tweed. They went through the library door too.

"I would have liked to marry Bill, Cousin Lucy," Faith said softly. "Now I'll just grow old here in Yardley Hall, like Aunt Melusina . . ."

Then her voice raised poignantly. "No—not like Aunt Melusina . . . like you, and father."

"Oh, no, Faith!" I cried. "Not like us—not wasted, like us!"

And the door opened again, and Sergeant Priddy's feet came across the dingy lovely old hall and into our door.

"Miss Lucy—will you all come now?"

It was odd, and rather terrifying, going into that embattled room, with Faith's cold fingers gripped in mine. Doctor Yardley was at his table, John Crabtree on one side of him, Melusina on the other. I caught my breath as I saw her. She'd changed so extraordinarily since last night—too extraordinarily for me to believe at once, seeing her suddenly that way. Her snowy hair, carefully waved, was piled loosely on her head the way she dresses it on special occasions. She had on her best black gown with the high lace collar closely covering her thin neck. She really looked quite regal, and handsomer than I'd ever seen her, even on days when she was pouring tea, or showing Yardley Hall off to the few especially selected Garden pilgrims from the North. That should have told me something, but it didn't; it just made me think she'd gone quietly insane, primping while Rome burned.

Then I turned to find a chair, and saw, sitting just behind Bill, his arm resting, affectionate and reassuring, around his shoulders, a tall bony man with thick grey hair and beetling grey brows in a craggy, rugged sunburned face. And I stopped dead.

"It must be me, not Melusina, that's gone insane," I thought. "Or is it?"

He rose and bowed, and smiled, a quick amused smile that I'd forgotten years and years and years ago. And there was no doubt about it now . . . Melusina's Great Sacrifice had come back to Williamsburg. Summers Baldwin, economic royalist and son of the livery stable on Buttermilk Hill, had returned to the house where he'd had his ears soundly boxed under the magnolias, forty-four years ago.

I looked at Melusina. Maybe it wasn't rouge on her cheeks, or belladonna in her eyes. She smiled, ever so faintly triumphant. The great man might send his harum-scarum unhousebroken ward to me, but he himself came to Yardley Hall . . . that was very much the gist of Melusina's smile.

I said, "Touché," though not out loud, and sat down with Faith in the seat Sergeant Priddy pushed forward. I found, pleasantly, that I didn't mind that at all—that all I felt was a vast relief that now Bill would be safe whatever happened: the last of the Haineses might not get his girl, but at least he wouldn't end in the electric chair.

He hadn't looked at me, or at Faith, and Faith hadn't looked at him. Of the rest of them, Ruth Napier and Talbot Seymour were sitting together in the window seat beyond the faded old globe, Ruth distraught under her lacquered perfect finish, Talbot Seymour confident and a little bored, as if he wished they'd get on with it so he could settle things and get back North in time for the spring meetings. You ought to look grateful, my friend, I thought; if it hadn't been for the courteous old gentleman behind the table, you'd be hunting a job instead of driving your cousin's car and looking so impatiently at his platinum watch on your wrist.

Luton, discreetly by the window into the garden, edged a little nearer it as the shift necessitated by Faith's and my entry brought Hallie and Hugh Taswell closer to him. Poor Hallie, I thought; her letters were still at my house. No wonder she looked scared to death. And yet in some way she also looked awfully to me as if she'd managed to convince Hugh it was his neglect and his get-together dinners in Richmond, and no doubt his secretary, that had been the cause of her wretched escapade.

John Crabtree wiped his forehead with his handkerchief.

"There's been a lot of talk goin' around," he said, in that slow ambling voice of his. "I thought I'd get you all together, and tell you where we're goin', in this case.—You can hear anythin', in a town like this, if you want to listen. Why, people are sayin' all kinds of things. That Mr. Talbot Seymour here, for instance, hot-footed it to Williamsburg the minute he heard his cousin was goin' to get married, because he was scared he'd have to go to work."

I thought Mr. Talbot Seymour looked a little startled, to say the least.

"I don't know why people figure work would be distasteful to Mr. Talbot, now, but that's what they're sayin'. Others are sayin' Mr. Talbot Seymour didn't have anythin' to do with it, it was Mr. Luton."

The valet by the window turned the color of a green peach. I thought he edged a little closer to the gardens.

"Some of 'em are sayin' it was Miss Lucy and Mr. Haines together, because it was Miss Lucy's shotgun we found in the Canal. But everybody with a lick of sense knows Miss Lucy would be scared to go around at night with a gun on her. And there's still a lot of people are sayin' Marshall Yardley did it, and then killed himself. But Marshall didn't kill himself. I guess last night's about the only night in his life Marshall wouldn't have wanted to die."

Faith's hand in mine trembled, and I pressed it closer to my side, steadying it.

"Marshall didn't shoot himself. Somebody else shot him. And some people are sayin' it was Doctor Yardley himself, because he didn't want his daughter to marry either Mason

Seymour or her own cousin. And there's some are sayin' it was Miss Melusina, because her plans were upset, and she was afraid if Faith didn't marry Mr. Seymour, she'd have to sell Yardley Hall. People think Miss Melusina would sell her own soul to keep Yardley Hall, and after she'd found out her brother had destroyed Mason Seymour's second will, she had to kill her own nephew so he wouldn't marry Faith, so Faith could marry somebody who could save the hall . . ."

Melusina's face had gone the color of the shrivelled inside of a blanched almond skin. Faith shrank closer to my side. I could have slain John Crabtree. He didn't know about Bill, of course, and Bill, his eyes dreadfully unhappy, his lips tight, hunched farther down in his seat, staring at the floor.

"It's pretty generally believed around town that Miss Melusina's the least bit fanatical about Yardley Hall," John Crabtree said slowly. "But if people stopped to think about it, I don't think they'd go as far as holdin' Miss Melusina would go out of her way—even if she decided she was goin' to kill anybody—as to make it look as if Miss Lucy did it."

"Oh, wouldn't she just," I thought. Then I saw the tiny twinkle in John Crabtree's eyes, and I was rather ashamed of myself, all of a sudden.

"The point is, unfortunately, that that's exactly what somebody was tryin' to do. Especially at first. Somebody that knew Miss Lucy had a shotgun and knew, I expect, that Miss Lucy's about as fanatical about Faith as Miss Melusina is about Yardley Hall."

I looked quickly around the room for the old pistol. It was nowhere in sight. So it had been the shotgun, after all. They probably thought by now that I'd put the pistol down the well myself.

"I don't expect they'd figured that a natural like Mr. Haines was goin' to barge in, shout from the housetops that somebody ought to trade Seymour for a yellow dog and shoot it, and then track cockroach powder all over town, and finally just up and say 'It was me all the time.'"

Bill's face darkened.

"Because I figure this had all been planned for some little time," John Crabtree said. "It was precipitated by the sudden announcement of Faith's engagement to Seymour. You see—when Seymour made his second will he left about everything to Yardley Hall. He wrote to his cousin—there's a copy of the letter in the files—tellin' him, not exactly about the will, but that he'd have to cut down his monthly stipend."

Mr. Talbot Seymour's white teeth were set, his eyes fixed on John were bold and insolent.

"You're not forgetting, Mr. Crabtree, that I didn't leave my hotel room after I got to Williamsburg," he said evenly.

"No, and I'm not forgettin' it was your first visit to Williamsburg," John Carter Crabtree said amicably. "—If you don't count the three months you went to William and Mary College before you were flunked out. I guess that was so long ago you'd forgot about it. But that's how you know your way around well enough to go over to your cousin's house in the dark, wasn't it, now? Only you didn't know Miss Faith wasn't goin' to marry Mason. All you knew was if your cousin married, you'd be cut off, both now and when he died."

Mr. Talbot Seymour was the color of old, badly made gravy.

"You didn't know there was a second will, or had been a second will, and that even if Mason Seymour was dead you wouldn't get a dime . . . that's why you took the check for two thousand five hundred dollars that Mason Seymour had written for a faithful servant, wasn't it, Mr. Seymour? Because you couldn't bear to part with that amount, even to a man that had saved your cousin five times that much a year for the ten years he'd been with him?"

George Luton took a step forward, his face white, his eyes shining. "You've got my money!" He almost screamed it.

"You'll get it all right, Mr. Luton," John Crabtree said. "I wouldn't worry, if I were you."

Mr. Talbot Seymour's expression was indescribable.

"But he was already dead when I took it!" he shouted. "I went to see him, to see if I couldn't get some sort of settlement—but he was dead, I tell you—he was dead!"

"I know it," the Commonwealth Attorney said calmly. "He wasn't only dead, he'd been dead some time. Rigor mortis had begun to set in. You had to tear that check to get it out from under his arm. Blood had dried on it, and on the check under it."

Faith beside me trembled violently.

"No, it wasn't you that killed your cousin, Mr. Talbot. And it wasn't Miss Lucy, or Mr. Haines. It wasn't anybody out there on the terrace. It was somebody inside the house, somebody that had another weapon, not Miss Lucy's shotgun, and that threw both of 'em away."

He turned to Melusina Yardley.

"When did you have the well whitewashed last, Miss Melusina?"

# 27

Melusina's hands gripping each other in her lap were as old as time.

"Yesterday morning," she said quietly.

The Commonwealth Attorney's slow voice went on unchanged. "And you did that, Miss Melusina, because you'd seen that brown stain on the well board, and you were afraid . . . that somebody from Yardley Hall . . . ?"

She looked at him for a long instant before her head bent slowly.

"And when did you bring this here"—he pulled the bell-mouthed pistol out from under the table and laid it in front of him—"out of the cellar?"

Her voice was perfectly controlled: "Last week."

"And you took it over, as a present, to Mason Seymour, because you knew he was interested in old guns?"

Melusina closed her eyes and nodded her high-piled white head. The skin around her quivering nostrils was white and opaque as lard.

"The same day he made his will out?" John asked quietly. She nodded again.

"That's the day Mason Seymour signed his death warrant . . . and Marshall's," he said, slowly as water dripping.

"Well, it was very interestin'. At six feet, or thereabouts, the spread of buckshot from this pistol—and it's old but it's in good shape, it could stand bein' fired a few times—looks just like the spread from Miss Lucy's shotgun at twenty feet —or it would have if Captain Callowhill hadn't had a look over things. Mason Seymour wasn't shot from his terrace through the window. He was shot from just across his desk, while he was puttin' his name to a check for a right tolerable amount. The person did it had already fired off a shotgun several times, out in the woods, to get the spread right, and collect a waddin' he could drop on the terrace for us to find. Then this old piece was brought back to be planted at Yardley Hall . . . only it couldn't be dropped in that well, it'd make a splash. So its trigger was balanced on the side of the bucket and lowered carefully, so when the bucket down there was moved again, it would slip off and be lost forever.

"Only it happened Miss Lucy saw somebody at the well, and blood on it next day. And Marshall, seein' Miss Lucy there last night, started investigatin', and that's why he was killed, so this pistol here couldn't be found, and we'd still figure it was Miss Lucy's gun, and that Mason Seymour was shot from twenty feet off, on his terrace, instead of six feet off across his desk—just as the train went by at half-past ten so the noise wouldn't disturb anybody till mornin'."

I looked at Bill Haines. His face was awful. Only Summers Baldwin's arm on his shoulder was keeping him in any kind of control.

"That's why the terrace window was open, so it'd look like the shot came from outside," John Crabtree said. "That's why ten pounds of bright pink cockroach powder was put down from one end of the place to the other—so it would appear nobody inside the house had gone out to shoot Mason Seymour from the terrace.—And nobody had."

His eyes moved slowly around the room.

"Because Mr. Luton here had worked fifteen years for Mason Seymour, as a kind of servant, for a servant's wages, when he wasn't born a servant, knowin' he was down in the will for a big amount if he was still in Seymour's service when he died. And when Seymour was goin' to get married he didn't need Mr. Luton any more . . . and Mr. Luton made up his mind he wouldn't be put off for a check and a fifty dollar a week job. Mr. Luton didn't know either one of two things—one of 'em would have made the killin' useless, and the other unnecessary: he didn't know Seymour'd made a new will, not till he came across the rough draft in the safe, and he didn't know the new will had been burned up. He didn't know, that night at half-past ten, that he was shootin' Seymour a couple of days too late . . ."

There wasn't an instant's quickening of the sleepy drawling pace of the Commonwealth Attorney's slow voice. I stared at him, petrified, as we all did; and then, my heart cold with fright, I turned slowly, like every other person there, to look at the man in the window. George Luton stood there, helpless, white-faced, desperate-eyed, motionless for an instant except that his hands, not deft and discreet any longer, were shaking violently. And for an instant he just stood, his face a perfectly awful mask of horror and guilt, and then turned and tore frantically down the steps, out through the Dutch window. Even by that time I wasn't seeing him any more—I was seeing the suddenly ghastly pale surprise in his face the moment before, when John Crabtree had put the old pistol abruptly on the table, and that hadn't registered then on me, I'd been so appalled at Melusina's face when she looked at it for the first time.

I heard Talbot Seymour say, in a choked voice, "Good God, that's what he said I'd done!"

Sergeant Michael Priddy, standing by the door, hadn't even moved, and I wasn't surprised when I heard those frantic feet on the stone steps stop suddenly, and other feet outside there, and a sudden scuffle, and then silence.

I looked back from the door, my head reeling a little, at the white shocked faces around that room.

"That's why he was so upset about the check bein' gone," the Commonwealth Attorney's slow voice said placidly. "It made character for him—nobody would suspect a person of shootin' somebody just writin' him a check for $2,500.00. And he took the shotgun—he got it when he left that card invitin' you to supper, Miss Lucy; he knew it was there, Joe was cleanin' it over at Seymour's only a month ago—figurin' it would make trouble for anybody but him. Either you, Miss Lucy, or one of the Yardleys. He hadn't figured on Mr. Haines here takin' up the slack instead. Well, he was a bad actor, and I'd guess there's no doubt Seymour'd come to the conclusion he'd better get rid of him before it was too late. If Luton'd known about that second will bein' destroyed . . ."

The Commonwealth Attorney shrugged. Then he looked without enthusiasm at Mr. Talbot Seymour, who had got abruptly to his feet.

"I guess you were just naturally born lucky, Mr. Seymour," he said.

Mr. Talbot Seymour wiped the perspiration from his brow, and managed a smile, but it was not as brilliant as usual. "Then that will still holds," he said. "Boy, oh boy—did you give me a turn for a minute! Come on, Ruth—I need a drink."

Ruth Napier stood still for a moment, then she slipped over to Faith and held out her hand. Faith took it. The dark-haired girl bent forward quickly and kissed her cheek. Then she looked at Melusina and followed Mr. Talbot Seymour out of the room.

Hallie Taswell, still very white-faced, fanning herself with a palm-leaf fan in the window seat, was eyeing the papers in John Crabtree's hand. Then she glanced at her husband across the room talking to Melusina, hesitated, and started toward him. As she came by me I gave her sprigged dimity panier a sharp yank.

"Your letters are at my house," I whispered. "In the lace box up on my table."

She gave a little gasp and caught herself, the blood rushing to her cheeks. "Hugh dear!" she called. "You won't mind if I go on? I've got to be at the Capitol by noon." She picked up her petticoats and scooted out of the room.

It sounds odd, I suppose, and rather casual, the way Luton's cataclysm struck and was gone. It wasn't really casual at all—it was just that every one of us, I was thinking just then, had been possessed by such dreadful fear . . . Doctor Yardley, who thought Melusina had done it; Melusina, who'd thought first it was Marshall and then her brother; Faith who in her heart had feared it was her father; myself terrified for Bill and Faith; Bill for Faith, Talbot Seymour for himself, Hallie Taswell for herself . . . so that each of us was too relieved to the depth of his soul to be more than simply glad it was over.

I got up. My eyes met Melusina's and that same cold extraordinary smile of triumph, so that I had to steady myself against my chair for a moment to keep from collapsing back into it. Faith was gone. Bill, who for all I knew had been welcoming the electric chair as an escape from torment, came over to me.

"You remember Mr. Baldwin, don't you, Miss Lucy?"

Melusina's Great Sacrifice and I shook hands.

"Yes, indeed," I said. "I'm afraid Bill hasn't done much about architecture. I don't think he's even been in the Palace supper room."

Then Melusina came over.

"That awful man," she said. "It's too dreadful . . . I hope it's taught you a terrible lesson, Lucy."

"If it hasn't, nothing ever will," I said, although I'm still not quite sure what she meant.

Doctor Yardley came over to us.

"You'll stay and have a little lunch with us, won't you, Summers?" Melusina said.

I picked up my bag.

"You're staying too, Lucy, aren't you?" Peyton Yardley said.

"No, thanks very much," I said.

Melusina turned. Perhaps it was because her neck was encased in a high boned collar that she had to look a little down her nose to see me.

"Oh, do stay, Lucy. Never mind about your gown. You can freshen up a bit in my room."

I suppose I did look wilted.

"No, thanks," I said, and Bill picked up his hat and took my arm.

"Aren't you staying, Mr. Haines?" Melusina exclaimed.

"No, I'm paying board over at Miss Lucy's, and she'll be making money on me if I miss any more meals," Bill Haines said. "I'll see you later, sir," he added to Summers Baldwin. "Good-by."

In the hall he looked up, hoping, I knew, to see Faith. She wasn't anywhere. Maybe she'd be over this afternoon, I thought to myself. I was miserable too, not seeing her.

Bill and I went down the stairs.

"Why did you do that—not stay, I mean? I didn't mind."

"I don't like that old werewolf," he said. "I don't want any part of her. I wish Luton had polished her off . . . instead of Marshall."

"It's wicked to talk like that."

"I'm sorry."

We walked on across the Court House Green.

"Why did you say you'd shot Mason Seymour?" I asked.

He was silent a moment. Then he said, "When I saw that pistol I thought she'd done it. I saw her in there with something like it in her hand."

"That was the *telephone!*" I cried. It would look like that, from the terrace, and she'd stood there ever so long with it in her hand.

He groaned a little. "Oh, well, I'm just a ruddy fool anyway, I guess."

We passed the Powder Horn.

"Bill, why didn't you tell me you were Summers Baldwin's ward?" I asked. I don't know just what difference it would have made, but I had to upbraid him about something.

He grinned ruefully.

"I guess I wanted you to love me for myself alone. As a matter of fact that's all there is. My dad took his money out of the automobile business and went broke on the Stock Exchange."

He gave an odd mirthless snort. "I guess Miss Melusina's put the K. O. on me, all right."

"You're not going to let Melusina bother you, are you, Bill? What about the Haineses always getting their girl?"

He laughed unhappily.

"I guess I was just bragging. As a matter of fact they all died bachelors."

He gave my arm a little squeeze. "Don't you mind me, Miss Lucy. I always go nuts the end of May."